T0161091

Black and Blue
HEARTS

The Ties That Blind

Darlene Leonard

Carpenter's Son Publishing

Black and Blue Hearts

©2020 by Darlene Leonard

Published by Carpenter's Son Publishing, Franklin, TN.

Edited by Bob Irvin

Cover and Interior Design by Suzanne Lawing

Printed in the United States of America

ISBN: 978-1-952025-15-0

Acknowledgments

Mr. Larry Carpenter, Founder and President of Christian Book Services, Carpenter's Son Publishing, Franklin, TN

> *My gratitude forever for being the visionary who enabled my dream to be fulfilled to reach and heal many hearts!*

The Production Team affiliated with Christian Book Services, Franklin, TN

> *Thank you all for your combined talents and efforts through every phase to bring my book to completion.*

Mr. Bob Irvin, Content Editor / Independent Editor

> *Words cannot describe my appreciation for your kindness, patience, and expertise in bringing the heartfelt message of my manuscript alive!*

Suzanne Lawing, Designer, book cover and layout

> *My appreciation for your wonderful talent and time in creating a valuable book presentation. You have been such a blessing!*

Mr. Aaron Leonard, Marketing Director

> *Much love and gratitude always for your partnership in the programming and development of the beautiful website for my book, your amazing design creativity, and your digital marketing expertise. Above all, my thankfulness for your devoted heart to family. AaronLeonardDevelopment@gmail.com*

Ms. Amber Leonard, Personal Assistant / Travel Companion and Representative

> *Many blessings for graciously opening your home that we may walk this journey together! Your love, kindness, and caring means more to me than you will ever know. I am so thankful for our companionship and your devotion in my senior years. With my love always.*

Ms. Joni Sullivan Baker, Buoyancy Public Relations

> *Many blessings for your outstanding contributions to our project to deliver a lifeline of HOPE to multitudes of hearts! Our team is so grateful for your expertise in launching a book that prayerfully will be an important work.*

Mrs. Amber Bradford Berry

> *I am forever grateful for your kindness, provision, and compassionate spirit. Your passion for wounded hearts is reflected in all you do. Love and thanksgiving from my heart to yours.*

Mr. Vaughn Berry

> *Thank you so much, brother, for your powerful prayers that undergirded me to abide under the Shadow of The Almighty to overcome during the completion of this writing journey. ~ Psalm 91 ~*

Ms. Danalyn Meredith

> *To my heart-to-heart sister in Christ: for your enduring friendship, your encouragement to write this book, and your continual prayers uplifting me through many meltdowns along the way. I lost count of the number of times I sensed your prayers chapter-by-chapter on the road to completion. With love and humble gratitude.*

Dedication

*~ This book is lovingly dedicated
to my courageous grown children and our posterity ~
Every one of you deserves a medal of bravery and honor
for standing victorious against all odds.
You are the greatest overcomers I've ever known.
Each of you now stands tall at the summit of VICTORY.
This legacy is for you.
Heart to heart with all my love, Mama
~ January 2021~*

♥ ♥ ♥

*"No matter how brutally hearts are crushed, mercy does a victory dance as it triumphs over judgment, and kindness shouts above the incessant noise of cruel condemnation, **for love never fails.**"*

Darlene Leonard

One

THE TERRIFYING letter lay open a few menacing inches from Annalee Jackson's pillow, its contents so disturbing that the brutal words played on rewind all night. About 3 AM a strange, raspy voice gurgled at her bedside, spewing distorted sounds into her ear. The muffled utterances became horrifying accusations: "You are worthless and always have been! You can't even be a good mother!" Annalee instinctively reached for her abdomen, barren and tender from a recent four-month miscarriage of a baby she desperately wanted. Scanning the room toward the sickening voice, the night-light illuminated a large, old portrait of her deceased two-year-old son, Lance. His sweet little face was a reminder of the cruel, strategic attack to exploit her suffering with this launch of a fiery dart.

In a quaking whisper, she said, "That's a lie! I am *not* worthless!"

The eerie voice persisted. "Yes you are, and I should know, because I am the Spirit of Worthlessness, and I've been with you from the day you were born!" Annalee carefully turned on her side and slipped out of bed.

She glanced toward her husband, Ned, who slept soundly facing the opposite wall. Recalling his late collapse into bed after the veterans' meeting, he would probably sleep till noon. Trembling, she grasped the letter, slipped on her winter bathrobe, closed the bedroom door, and tiptoed down the hall. She sat by the family room window gazing out at the snowy pine trees.

Is this letter as dreadful as it seemed when it arrived yesterday?

She placed the letter in her lap and slowly reread it. No doubt remained—the chilling words were meant to inflict *everything* they said. Alarmed by the unseen battle, she cried out to the only One who could comfort her.

"Father, help me!" As if on cue, Worthlessness quit speaking. Even after she sensed its departure, she was still keenly aware of the ongoing, raging contempt from the underworld.

For we do not wrestle against flesh and blood, but against principalities, against powers, against the rulers of the darkness of this age, against spiritual hosts of wickedness in the heavenly places (Ephesians 6:12, NKJV).

The letter had to be destroyed because it had birthed an invitation to an unwelcome evil presence.

The stabbing words penned by a family member known her entire life left Annalee's heart crushed through an open door of vulnerability through which the words of a stranger could never have penetrated. Before burning the letter, she reread part of the seething third paragraph one last time:

"How <u>dare</u> you voice your opinion to me about what happened in our family! Have you forgotten? You were <u>never</u>

meant to be born in the first place, so you have no right to speak. Remember: you have no voice in this world _because you are a mistake!_"

The invisible onslaught unleashed an emotional atom bomb that echoed a lifelong mental struggle to find love and a sense of belonging. Still reeling from the letter's impact, she seized it, crunched it tightly, and tossed it into the woodstove. As the morning hours slipped by, she read Psalm 139 and other Scriptures.

For you created my inmost being; you knit me together in my mother's womb. I praise you because I am fearfully and wonderfully made; your works are wonderful, I know that full well. My frame was not hidden from you when I was made in the secret place, when I was woven together in the depths of the earth. Your eyes saw my unformed body; all the days ordained for me were written in your book before one of them came to be. when I awake, I am still with you (Psalm 139:13-16, 18 NIV).

For God has not given us a spirit of fear, but of power and of love and of a sound mind (2 Timothy 1:7, NKJV).

Two

ANNALEE FINISHED setting the table for lunch. She had decorated her and Ned's home with hearts for Valentine's Day. She was placing a red candle on the table when she turned and noticed Ned gazing at her from the doorway. It was reminiscent of the way he beheld her as she walked down the aisle on their wedding day the summer before. They were definitely still newlyweds.

She smiled his way. Ned slowly entered the dining room, slid his arms gently around her waist, and snuggled his head into her neck.

"Morning, babe. More like afternoon, I guess. Thanks for lettin' me sleep in."

"That's OK, hon. Glad you got some extra sleep."

"The meeting ran late. Some vets just got back from deployment. We wanted them to feel welcome."

She was so proud of Ned's contributions to the Veterans League, which sponsored fundraising events for the community, including the Karing For Kids Program that provided gifts and food to underprivileged children and families in their Montana town. The organization also involved assisting local veterans who needed to reestablish their civilian lives after their return stateside. Most suffered with post-traumatic stress disorder (PTSD) and other injuries. Ned wanted to pay it forward by taking time from his own schedule to mentor some of the younger men. He could empathize with them because he also suffered from PTSD's devastating effects.

The thought of PTSD sparked Annalee to ask, "How were your dreams last night?"

He looked down, quickly wiping some tears with the back of his hand. "Well, around sunrise I had more nightmares about the children. But it's all gonna work out, thanks to you."

The rescue of Ned's little children was never far from Annalee's mind. She often told him, "The children are a treasure. Their value means everything. No price is too high to pay."

Children had always been her soft spot, and his children's kidnapping by his ex-wife two years before had left an enormous empty hole in Ned's life. Annalee's administrative position enabled her to retain two attorneys who could help Ned's search. She had connections through her legal and foster care background. The rescue effort had become her full-time job, but it was worth every dime.

A rush of emotion caught Annalee off guard as her mind recalled that morning's unseen battle.

After his embrace, Ned drew back with a look of concern in his blue eyes as he studied her face. "How are you feeling today? Your eyes look red. Have you been crying?"

She nodded silently.

"The baby or that letter?" Like a flash flood, her tears began flowing, and she crumpled into Ned's arms.

"The letter. Oh Ned, the rejection felt so horrible!" Words caught between muffled sobs. "It's as if I'm taking up space and was never meant to be born! I know God loves me. It's just . . . how could anyone write a letter like that to someone they claim to love?"

He shook his head sadly, his military flattop affirming his determination. "I don't understand, but I'm so glad you were born. I'll never reject you!"

"I needed that. It helps to be reminded that I was created for a reason. That I'm not a mistake."

"That's right, sweetie. I think attacks can be the toughest on tenderhearted people."

Annalee looked down. "Thank you for loving me."

"I don't know how I ever made it through life without you. You came to my rescue just in time."

"Just call me your little rescuer." She smiled ruefully. "I'll do whatever I can to help you. We're here for each other. By the way, I burned that letter in the woodstove. It was way too painful."

"I don't blame you. I'm one hundred percent on your side. That was a poison pen letter you had to leave behind. But there are some things you never leave behind. Like we learned in the military, you never leave your partner behind. I'll never leave you, because it's you and me against the world, baby."

Annalee's mind suddenly shifted into a kaleidoscope of mixed messages.

What? How did this switch from the letter to "you and me against the world"?

Annalee began to feel off balance as she tried to analyze what Ned was saying. Yes, the letter was dreadful, but it was only written by one person. She still loved her family and wanted to be part of the lives of the ones who still loved her. She felt as if some part of her family connection was being invisibly torn away. Her mind was swiftly pummeled with questions.

Does Ned think it's just the two of us against everyone else? . . . Is there some kind of "unknown enemy" out there? . . . Does Ned want to separate us from my family?

Maybe it had something to do with what she began telling Ned the other day about her ancestry—the family secrets that happened to her mother and her after she was born. She would have to find time with Ned to finish explaining the history.

But it would have to wait. That wouldn't come today. Too much was going on.

As a bit more time went by, Annalee kept thinking about Ned's statement. *"You and me against the world."* It confused her, but she didn't want to overanalyze it. She wondered: *Maybe that has something to do with "leave and cleave" in our wedding vows?*

Ned led her to the couch and held her.

His masculine scent of musk cologne nuzzled into her long blonde hair as he lowered his voice to that husky baritone she loved. "Honey, you mean everything to me." His loving words whispered into her hair felt like the freshness of spring, breathing life into her wounded soul. He tenderly patted her stomach and whispered, "I'm sorry you've had to take on so much with my anxiety attacks. The battle over Amanda and Justin has really gotten to me, but I'm gonna try to be stronger for you and have faith that we will win the case. And honey, our next baby will be fine. No more miscarriages. Our lives are gonna be so happy, I promise."

Annalee's concerns began melting away with Ned's soothing words. *How wonderful to finally have the love of my life who cares about my heart! I would do anything for this dear man. I can hardly wait to become a forever Mama to his children and give them a life of joy with their father who misses them so much, along with their future baby sibling, who will never be kidnapped from him.*

He cupped her shoulders in his large hands and looked directly into her eyes. "Have I ever told you? You are the finest wife a man could ever want. You really know how to take care of a husband, but do you know what I love most about you? I've never known a woman so gentle and caring—a true Proverbs 31 wife."

Since coming to faith, Annalee had always dreamed of being a Proverbs 31 wife, and with their wedding just seven months earlier, her husband was already reassuring her. She felt greatly honored by his words.

> *"Charm is deceitful and beauty is passing,*
> *but a woman who fears the LORD, she shall be praised"*
> *(Proverbs 31:30, NKJV).*

The man who swept her off her feet during their courtship was still her knight in shining armor during these newlywed months of marriage. Her heart felt so safe in his embrace as she envisioned their future.

"Ned, I've never felt loved the way you love me."

He continued, "You know what else? I've never been fed the way you spoil me with your cooking."

"Is that a hint?" she teased.

He wrapped an arm around her shoulder and guided her into the dining room.

As they chatted over lunch, Annalee's mind returned to the early morning encounter with the Spirit of Worthlessness. She had to tell Ned about it. "Honey, there's something important I need to share with you." He leaned in to give her his undivided attention.

"Something really strange happened this morning that terrified me. It is too awful to handle it alone. I need you to be my spiritual covering with this."

He tipped his head quizzically and reached for her hand. "Sure, hon. Go right ahead."

Three

ANNALEE'S SHOULDERS slumped as tears mingled with words. "I . . . don't know how to tell you."

Ned squeezed her hand. "Whatever it is, we'll get through it together."

The letter's harsh words stung her memory. "You know that part about my birth being a mistake?"

"That was so cruel!" he blurted.

"There's more to it." She trembled, hesitating. "This is bizarre. Please don't think I'm crazy."

Ned's voice rose. "Of course not! It just upsets me that anyone could say such hateful things to you." His tone lowered. "You can tell me whatever you need to."

She stumbled over her words. "This morning while you were sleeping, I had a terrifying experience!"

He drew closer with compassion; Ned read Annalee's non-verbals, that she was wanting to explain every detail of the shocking encounter. After she finished describing the vicious accusations of the enemy, Annalee felt emotionally drained. Ned's eyes flashed with anger.

Ned waited another moment, then spoke. "Thank you for telling me. That letter had to be burned. Honey, we're up against a serious battle, but we're gonna take spiritual authority over it." His voice was adamant. "Nothing like that will ever be allowed to invade our home again! Let's pray right now." He stood and reached to the cupboard for their prayer oil. As they joined hands, Annalee felt a union, as though they were gallant warriors.

As Ned and Annalee released their prayers, a dreadful struggle permeated the air; an obvious tension filled the room. They felt that an invisible enemy had been immediately summoned into their home. Suspended in this unseen realm were stealth opponents in a deadly battle. It had the weight of an enormous conflict. A resounding clash suddenly drew the attention of the combatants, sounds begging description. This was something beyond a mere skirmish—this was mayhem. Never in their previous prayer times together had there been such a sense of the power of Almighty God. It was entirely beyond explanation . . .

♥ ♥ ♥

The battle of invisible entities continued, escalating to a degree unknown to one's normal senses.

Shockwaves intensified as blinding thunderbolts of translucent light penetrated the home in a hallowed, deafening roar. Shards of illumination dashed throughout, engulfing the atmosphere. Ned and Annalee were immersed in electrifying images. What felt like ancient combat saturated every corner, beckoning all who entered—*both* the willing and the unwilling. The spectacular display stunned them both. Their senses were clearly heightened with an awareness of *something* . . . something definitely *felt*.

Gradually, the entire atmosphere began to lower in intensity.

Something was dispelled—and departed.

Someone was the victor.

The turmoil dissolved into tranquility.

Having been saturated in unbelievable power, Ned and Annalee were visibly shaken. They glanced around, uncertain of what had transpired. As peace began to return, they recovered with an awareness that the atmosphere had shifted—and was now radically different.

The intercessory prayer that weekend had unleashed unimaginable power. They felt a partnership with God—something unparalleled in the natural world. Their spirits had discerned invisible, angelic warfare and its supernatural intervention on behalf of Annalee's soul.

They felt stunned!

For He shall give His angels charge over you, To keep you in all your ways (Psalm 91:11, NKJV).

Are not all angels ministering spirits sent to serve those who will inherit salvation? (Hebrews 1:14, NIV)

Again I say to you that if two of you agree on earth concerning anything that they ask, it will be done for them by My Father in heaven. For where two or three are gathered together in My name, I am there in the midst of them (Matthew 18:19, 20, NKJV).

Four

ANNALEE MET Ned at a singles ministry event in early January. He was on staff at a large church in their Northwest Montana town. He was the singles leader while attending Bible college. Annalee was invited by a mutual friend who knew her through her position on staff at another church across town. After the meeting that evening, Ned and Annalee began talking and hit it off. They discussed the Bible and their individual ministry activities.

They saw each other through the winter at group outings— potlucks, snow skiing, and sledding trips. Ned would play his guitar for the group at times. Whenever they met, they shared long conversations about their life experiences. Their heart-to-heart discussions became more meaningful, and this led to a growing relationship.

By spring, Ned and Annalee were beginning to see each other apart from singles' outings. Ned asked her to a five-star restaurant for their first dinner date. She knew it was a financial sacrifice for him.

"I'd love to go to dinner with you, but you don't need to spend that kind of money on me!" Annalee said.

"You are worth it," Ned insisted. Annalee wore her nicest dress and placed spring flowers in her long blonde hair. Ned was the consummate gentleman as he escorted her to their table and seated her gently. After ordering, she excused herself for the restroom. He immediately strode behind her chair and guided her out with a military bow as she exited. On her return to the dining room, Ned rose and remained at attention as Annalee approached the table.

He politely slid her chair for her and said, "You're the loveliest lady in this room."

Annalee smiled; in truth, she was overwhelmed. His impeccable manners, military bearing, and utmost respect in her presence meant more to her than gifts, entertainment, or ambiance. Astounded by his chivalry, Annalee's defenses came tumbling down as she trusted more of her heart to him.

She felt incredibly valued during their courtship, and this was something she had desired her entire life. She had prayed to be an appreciated wife, mother, and homemaker to a godly husband. Ned clearly expressed his desire for the kind of wife he wanted. She was paying close attention to this gentleman who courted her with such honor.

Ned further proved his character and protectiveness during an incident in town one day. A couple of young men suddenly began a loud public argument using foul language on the sidewalk in front of them. Ned positioned himself to protect Annalee. His military stance and demeanor sent a no-nonsense message. He reprimanded the other men: "Stop it! You're using bad language in front of a lady!" After flashing looks of irritation, the men took off. Annalee was stunned at Ned's defense of her honor. Her admiration grew even more.

On a beautiful spring day, Ned invited Annalee to lunch at her favorite Japanese restaurant. As usual, they were sharing experiences and dreams. They even had a lengthy discussion of their previous marriages and children.

Ned had also been developing a great relationship with Annalee's 17-year-old son, Luke. He had taken him to several sporting events and fishing at the river. The companionship of a father figure meant a great deal to Luke, especially given his lifelong battles with learning disabilities, migraines, bullying, all without a committed father. He and his best friend, Marie, had attended special education classes together since childhood. They loved animals and simple pleasures. Luke's favorite hobbies were building military bases for his GI Joes, Legos, and caring for animals. Annalee felt grateful for Ned's kindness to Luke.

One day, Luke confided to his mom, "I really like Ned because he's cool. He's nice to me."

Ned was aware that Luke's birth was nothing short of a miracle. Annalee almost lost him several times during a fragile pregnancy.

A medical mistake during the birth of her first son, Lance, resulted in tragic brain damage and left Annalee with serious internal injuries. She nearly died. Lance passed away just before his third birthday. Annalee was grief-stricken. It was expected she would never carry another baby. After numerous miscarriages, she finally carried Luke full-term. And she dreamed of having more children.

Late in their lunch, Ned leaned toward Annalee as she recounted more details of her testimony.

"What a horrible experience, having your little boy pass away," he said quietly.

"It was devastating, especially since he passed at home," she said. "When I found him, my husband and I went into shock."

Ned stared at the table in stunned silence.

"How did you get through it?"

"It was gut-wrenching." They were both silent for a few moments.

"May I take your hand?" Ned asked gently. Annalee nodded.

Annalee went on with her story. "During the recovery from his loss, I came in contact with other families with disabled or deceased children. It was therapeutic to visit and encourage other bereaved parents to never give up."

Ned's face was a mix of admiration and astonishment. He quietly asked where she found the strength.

"Lance was my inspiration as I searched for answers. I had to find out where my son's soul had gone."

"And that's how you came to faith, right?"

"Yes. My family had no foundation of faith, so we had nowhere to turn for comfort. After a four-year search, I was invited to a church and learned about the Lord for the first time. When I realized Lance is forever safe in the arms of Jesus, it delivered me from the terrible grief, and I've served Him ever since."

"Your testimony is amazing." Ned was quiet again, then asked Annalee if these things motivated her to speak to various groups as she did.

"Yes, it helps seekers looking for truth and encourages others who have experienced terrible loss," she said.

"I don't know what it's like to lose a child to death, but Amanda and Justin have been missing for two years now. It breaks my heart." Tears began to form in Ned's eyes.

"I can't imagine. To me, that almost seems worse, to have them disappear and not know where they are."

"It's been a nightmare. I've driven hundreds of miles following leads to where they might be."

"Have you ever thought of hiring a private investigator?"

"I can't afford one. Their mother, Tina, and her boyfriend are somewhere out on the West Coast, but the welfare agencies can't tell me where they are. They say she's always on the move running from the law."

"How old are the children?"

"In the fall Amanda will turn seven and Justin will be six."

"Aww. What a cute age. I'd love to meet them someday." Annalee felt great compassion for Ned and his children.

"They would love you."

"Well, let's start praying together for them to be found. The Lord knows where they are."

Ned agreed. He had a hopeful look.

Annalee hesitated. "Ned . . . I know Tina did a terrible thing taking them away from you, but I have a question. For your own healing and peace of mind, have you been able to forgive her?"

"Yes. A friend helped me a long time ago, and I forgave her. I just want the children safe with me again."

"I'm glad," Annalee said quietly. "Forgiveness heals the heart and is pleasing to the Lord. Years ago, I needed to forgive the doctor who delivered Lance and injured both of us so badly. It brought me such healing after I forgave him."

"I don't know if I could forgive a doctor for what he did to you and Lance," Ned said. "I guess the Lord helped you do that."

"Without Him, I couldn't have done it. Thankfully, Lance is home safe in Heaven. It took me years to realize it, but now I pray for that doctor to find the Lord, if the man is still living. The doctor's soul is important to God."

"You have an amazing heart."

She looked down. "Thank you. I just never wanted to be a bitter person."

"Annalee, I don't want to be bitter either, but Amanda and Justin are my life. I have to find them." He paused. "I miss them so much."

"You know, with my background in legal work and foster parenting, maybe I could help."

"You would do that for me? You *could*?"

"I'll sure try my best." Ned gave a light squeeze to her hand.

He will wipe every tear from their eyes, and there will be no more death or sorrow or crying or pain. All these things are gone forever (Revelation 21:4, NLT).

♥ ♥ ♥

After lunch, they took a stroll through a beautiful park. Ned began to make it clear he was getting serious about her. He was asking lots of questions and talking about the future.

Annalee paused under a shade tree. "Would my age make a difference?" she quietly asked.

His answer was a swift embrace that became their first hug. "Your age makes no difference to me," he said. "You're a godly woman who would make a great mother for my children."

Annalee felt overwhelmed at his words. In truth, though, she had always looked younger than her age. "I turned 41 this year," she said.

Ned smiled. "I wouldn't have guessed. You are beautiful to me. I've dated girls in their twenties, and I'm not interested. A younger woman wouldn't have the maturity to handle the legal things going on with my life or have the dedication to raise my children if they are found. Besides, I love your heart."

She fought back tears of joy as they hugged.

Annalee found herself thinking, *I'd love to be a mother to Amanda and Justin. Can I make a difference in the lives of this little family?*

Her previous marriage had dissolved after an investigation of his molestation of a 14-year-old girl, later proven true. Twelve years before, he had proposed with expressions of heartfelt love and commitment to her, along with his desire to blend their family with his children who needed a mother. They married when Annalee was 25 and he was a 38-year-old single dad with full custody of his three children, ages 10, 12 and 13. They blended their family with her toddler son, Luke. Annalee loved his children and helped raise them. The children liked her, but deeply longed for their biological mother who rarely visited. Understandably, they wanted a relationship with their mother, so after adulthood they moved 40 miles away to live near her. Afterward, Annalee foster parented for several years. At 37, her 50-year-old husband told her she was no longer young enough for him. She filed legal separation, but he amended it to a divorce, informing her without remorse that he was dating an 18-year-old girl. The betrayal was shattering. She had come to faith during that marriage; in time, it empowered her to forgive. She and Luke began a new journey, but she struggled with longing for family life and the children she helped raise. She was terribly deceived by the emptiness of her own heart.

Annalee had never been treated like a queen, and Ned treated her like royalty. Their marathon conversations seemed to confirm a strong common faith. Ned shared that he was studying for a pastoral position, and they discussed his ministry plans.

As the months passed, Annalee found her heart more and more committed to doing all she could to help Ned and his two children. They talked about creating a family life together. But Annalee was blinded to the fact that her past was not completely healed. She believed empathy was enough to conquer the brokenness she had suffered. Her heart deceived her into believing love could overcome all the legal obstacles Ned was facing. It seemed they could accomplish all of these tasks together. Annalee had no doubts.

She overlooked a critical lesson about the heart.

One day, Ned said the words she had hoped to hear.

"If you will have me," he said, "I can hardly wait to marry you."[1]

Annalee was swept off her feet.[2]

"The heart is deceitful above all things, And desperately wicked; Who can know it? (Jeremiah 17:9, NKJV)

Guard your heart above all else, For it determines the course of your life (Proverbs 4:23, NLT).

Five

IN JULY, Annalee and Ned married at the park where they shared their first hug. With legal expenses ahead, they carefully planned their wedding with the best cost-value in mind. In honor of Fourth of July and Ned's military service, she chose patriotic colors—even an Uncle Sam statue for the park entrance. She designed their invitations and found a lovely gown at a used wedding shop. They bought wedding rings at a used jewelry store. Annalee's mother arranged her flowers and made her veil. Their singles ministry friends decorated. Other church friends donated professional talents—the ceremony administered by Annalee's pastor, music by the praise team, a photographer, videographer, wedding cake baker, and shared potluck reception. Even the weather was unusually mild for the middle of summer. They opted for a "money tree" instead of gifts, and this paid for gas, food, and a simple cabin in the woods.

After a quiet honeymoon, they returned to full-time employment to prepare for their future family. Ned resumed driving a truck for a regional delivery company. His work schedule required him to postpone Bible college, but his veterans' activities continued. Annalee transferred from church secretary to a corporate administrative assistant position which brought her a generous salary increase. Their combined income enabled them to purchase a modest home on a few acres with four bedrooms and spectacular views of Glacier Park and the surrounding area.

Their property included a mobile home for Luke and his new bride, Marie, both 18. They vowed to anchor their very young marriage on trust and companionship, along with an amazing understanding of each other for two people so youthful. Ned and Annalee assured them, "Yours is a marriage made in Heaven!" Annalee taught Marie to balance a checkbook. Both Luke and Marie graduated from Glacier Vista High School with special education diplomas for learning-disabled youth.

Thanksgiving

The day before Thanksgiving, Annalee's kitchen was busy with pumpkin pies, turkey, and trimmings. She patted her stomach happily—a baby was on the way!

The phone rang. "May I speak with Ned Jackson, please?" the caller said after Annalee answered.

"Yes, this is his wife. May I tell him who's calling?"

"Mrs. Jackson, I am Mrs. Davis with Child Services in Oregon. I have information regarding his children."

Annalee nearly dropped the phone.

"Please hold, Mrs. Davis. I'll get him right away." She rushed outdoors where Ned was working. "Honey, Child Services in Oregon is calling about Amanda and Justin!"

Ned dropped his work and sprinted inside. Annalee put the phone on speaker.

"Yes, Ma'am. This is Ned Jackson."

"Mr. Jackson, I'm social worker Nancy Davis with Child Protective Services in Oregon. I'm calling to inform you that the state of Oregon has been awarded temporary custody of your children, Amanda and Justin. They have been placed in care at an emergency shelter home." Tears of joy quickly began filling Ned's eyes.

"That's great!" He flashed a smile at Annalee. "Can we come pick them up for Thanksgiving?"

"Not so fast, Mr. Jackson. It has been over two years since you last saw your children, correct?"

"Yes, but that's because I didn't know where they were. I raised them as a single dad till they were four and five. Then they were kidnapped by Tina, my ex-wife."

"That's unfortunate, but more than seventy-two hours elapsed before our department located your phone number. Our regulations mandate that if a biological relative is not reached within the first seventy-two hours, children in custody become temporary wards of the state. They cannot be released until our ongoing investigation is complete."

"But I'm their father! They know me!" Ned looked Annalee's way, flabbergasted.

"I understand, but these things take time to sort out. Your ex-wife and her boyfriend were apprehended on felony charges. Our department must consider all the facts before a determination can be made."

"But they don't need foster care!" Ned blurted. "We already have a home for them. My wife and I can take off work and make the trip to bring them home."

"I realize your position, Mr. Jackson, but there are procedures." Her tone was formal and reserved.

"Procedures? What else do we need to do?" Ned's irritation was noticeably rising.

Annalee didn't want Ned to blow it with the social worker; she quickly intervened. "Ned, may I speak to Mrs. Davis? I'm familiar with the procedures." He looked stressed as he handed Annalee the phone.

"Hi, Mrs. Davis. This is Annalee Jackson, Ned's wife. We're on speaker phone. I used to be a foster parent, and I'm aware of the seventy-two-hour rule for custodial jurisdiction of a minor. In Oregon, what is the next step required in your investigation process?"

"Mr. Jackson, do you grant permission for me to discuss the details of this case with your wife?"

"Yes, I do. She knows all about this." Ned was obviously still irritated.

"Tina Jackson, the children's mother, will be arraigned on multiple charges after the Thanksgiving holiday. It will probably be a few days before she is coherent enough to appear in court before the judge."

"Based on your comment regarding coherency, is she still in acute withdrawal from the influence of . . . drugs?" Annalee queried.

"Yes, plus another complication," Davis said. "Although she was significantly impaired at the time of arrest, we must investigate some serious allegations she continues to make against your husband."

Ned glared at the phone.

"Parents of some of my former foster children had similar legal disputes," Annalee said.

"Do you still have a foster care license?" Davis asked Annalee.

"Yes, I have two of them—a secular state license and a private Koinonia license. My background includes caring for traumatized children."

"Have you ever met Mr. Jackson's children?"

"Not yet. We were married just under five months ago."

"Since the children don't know you, your licenses may be a big help. That is . . . *if* your husband is awarded custody."

Ned's thoughts were going wild. He couldn't believe this could even be an issue!

"Will a reunification plan be required?" Annalee said.

"Definitely," Davis said.

"Then we will complete the reunification plan for Ned to regain custody of Amanda and Justin. We want to raise them together."

"Understood. I will keep you both informed."

Ned looked suspicious. They had discussed the children, but he had no idea how this process was going to unfold.

"Do you have any more questions for my husband?" Annalee asked.

"Not at this time," Davis said.

"Just a moment, please. Ned, any more questions?" Annalee asked.

He shook his head.

"Thank you for your call, Mrs. Davis. Have a nice Thanksgiving."

"Same to you. I'll be in touch in a few days." As they hung up, Ned was still steaming.

Annalee was quick to speak as soon as the call was ended. "Honey, it's hard to deal with these agencies, but we have to play by their rules."

"I'm their father! I can't believe they're keeping them in foster care instead of letting us bring them home. They don't need foster care!" He rolled his eyes, clearly exasperated.

"I know. Too bad we weren't notified before the seventy-two-hour deadline." Annalee knew these procedures all too well. Given how the events had transpired, she briefly explained what they likely faced ahead. "At least we know where Amanda and Justin are, and that they're safe. We have much to be thankful for this Thanksgiving."

Ned took her hand. "Thanks, hon. That social worker made me so upset. I just don't get their rules."

"I understand, but now that the children are in protective care, we can begin the legal process to rescue them. First step is next week. I need to locate and retain two attorneys—one with jurisdiction here in Montana and another with jurisdiction in Oregon."

"*What?*" Ned looked shocked. "We need *two* lawyers? How can we afford that?"

"Good thing we've been saving up. The children's detainment will make things a lot more expensive, but we'll manage."

Ned was left to just stand there, shaking his head.

"I sure got the right woman in my life." He gave her a warm hug.

Annalee chuckled. "Why don't we talk some more this weekend? I've got a turkey to stuff!"

Commit your way to the LORD,
Trust also in Him,
And He shall bring it to pass
(Psalm 37:5, NKJV).

Six

AFTER THANKSGIVING, Annalee researched custody attorneys in Montana and Oregon. Ned's case required legal defense against Tina's allegations. She contacted a personal friend, an attorney for whom she had worked as a legal secretary. The attorney provided an excellent referral to an organization specializing in defending false allegations.

The coming baby was a comfort. Annalee felt well. She always wanted more children, and three more were on the way! They spent Christmas with Luke and Marie; Annalee's mother, Betsy, and her longtime friend, Mercy; and some other church friends.

Davis, the social worker, sent frequent documents that winter. Ned suffered increased anxiety attacks after the children were transferred into long-term foster care. They were placed in a Koinonia-licensed foster home with a family of faith. Annalee assured Ned, from her training with Koinonia, that the children would have a high standard of care.

Almost nightly, Ned cried and thrashed in his sleep from heartbreaking nightmares trying to rescue his children from dangerous people, raging rivers, or fires. Annalee would wake him to pray with and comfort him.

One day after work, the social worker called to question Ned. Davis's demeanor was always formal, but that day she seemed especially stern. As usual, Annalee put the phone on speaker.

"Mr. Jackson, our investigation unit has continued to interrogate your ex-wife regarding her felony charges. During questioning, she frequently brings up allegations regarding your prior care of the children. She states they were neglected and also exposed to dangerous visitors in your home who put them at severe risk."

"What kind of risk? Who is she talking about?" Ned asked.

"She can't remember, but insists that an immoral individual in your home behaved inappropriately with your children. These allegations are serious enough to consider whether criminal charges should be filed."

"Charges? Against me?!" Ned was coming unglued.

"That could happen, if it is substantiated that you endangered your children by failing to protect them," Davis said.

"But . . . Tina doesn't even remember who! I've never been in trouble with the law. Charges? Jail?"

"Not jail, Mr. Jackson. It all depends on the outcome of an investigation and trial. But past case studies suggest that convictions of that nature have sometimes resulted in sentences of up to twenty years in prison."

The look of shock and fear on Ned's face was palpable.

"Twenty years! Ma'am, I always protected my children, and they were never neglected. People like that never came to our home! My ex-wife didn't take the children out of love for them—she did it to collect welfare money and food stamps. She is lying to you to keep me from getting my children back!"

Davis remained matter-of-fact. "Since we do not know her motives or the facts, we must consider all possible evidence," the social worker said. "Our department has determined we have no choice but to question the children to try to confirm what they may remember."

Annalee gasped, disturbed at the risks of interviewing children so young, confused, and vulnerable.

Ned was quick to jump in. "That could traumatize them! They're only six and seven!"

"Mr. Jackson, we have child psychologists at our disposal trained to interview young children," Davis said. "They use sand and play therapy, drawing, and other age-appropriate techniques to verify the accuracy of their answers."

"But—"

"The decision has already been made, Mr. Jackson. And we are proceeding. You will receive a report."

Ned remained stunned and could only blurt out an "Ohh . . . kay. Will you let us know when there's going to be a court hearing?"

"Yes, we will. Goodbye." Suddenly: dial tone.

Ned's face took on the look of utter defeat.

"How could Tina do this to the children? She knows it isn't true! I'll never forgive her for this!"

Annalee knew it was her job to remain calm. "This is not over, hon."

Ned suddenly whirled on her and snapped. "Yes it is! I'm facing twenty years! Can't you see that?"

Annalee felt her stomach churning. Never had Ned raised his voice to her. And yet, she didn't blame him. He was completely stressed. And she knew that, if somehow Ned was sentenced to prison, she didn't yet have stepparent adoption to raise the children herself. She began envisioning legal strategies, document preparation—and huge legal fees.

Annalee quickly recalled the Bible verse that a soft answer turns away wrath, so she spoke softly to Ned. "You will be exonerated. I'm awaiting a return call from the legal organization I told you about. This issue does complicate matters, but we will overcome and get the children back."

Ned hung his head. "I was wrong for snapping at you, hon. You're only trying to help me."

And then Ned did something he'd never done before. He clung to her like a needy child.

> *I will contend with him who contends with you,*
> *and I will save your children (Isaiah 49:25, NKJV).*

Mid-January

One weekend Ned approached Annalee with a serious look. "Honey, I need to talk to you about something. Do you have time?"

"Sure, I'll take time." She sat beside him. "Oh, did I tell you? I can feel the baby kicking now! The doctor says I'm almost at four months."

"You're already starting to show. You and the baby look beautiful!" He stroked her stomach lightly.

Annalee felt special and encouraged Ned to share what was on his heart.

Ned looked down and his face grew troubled. He started out nervously. "I need to tell you—you know the false accusations Tina has been saying about me? She's still trying to get to me, to punish me."

"Help me understand. What do you mean?" Annalee took Ned's hand.

"The way she treated me was always bad. I mean, really bad. It started soon after our marriage. This is embarrassing for a guy to talk about. For a long time I didn't understand what it was, but . . . when I was married to Tina, I was abused as a husband, physically and mentally. She's repeating it now in a different way."

Ned went on to bare his soul, and past, to Annalee. He explained that, in the first three years they were married, he was in active duty and the couple lived in base housing. "Before she arrived on base, as a surprise, I bought a houseful of new furniture and a car for her. I thought she would enjoy caring for our home and making friends with other wives on base—potlucks, patriotic events, things like that. She hardly needed to cook because I mostly ate at the dining facility. But when I got off duty, the house was a mess." She also smoked inside, which was against base policy, Ned explained, and the military did random inspections of housing. "She got mad and started hollering about not having to follow rules," he said.

Things just got worse. "Our first Christmas, I made the mistake of surprising her with a puppy to keep her company. One night after I got home, she and a bunch of soldiers were at the house drinking. The little puppy stumbled around and they were all laughing at her. Turned out they had given her quite a bit of alcohol. Tina was out of her head and screaming at her for getting sick on the floor and making a mess.

"First thing, I ordered everyone out of the house and started cleaning up the vomit. I cleaned up the puppy, gave her some water, and carried her to her bed. She fell asleep. Thank God, the puppy didn't die. Tina was so drunk. She was staggering in my way, furious at me for ending her party. I led her to the bedroom, and she collapsed on the bed." In short time, Ned said, he found the puppy a new home. He went on to describe a cycle of abuse and wild living by Tina.

"After three years, I had been hospitalized several times for injuries, then had a mental breakdown and was diagnosed with PTSD. After the breakdown, I knew I couldn't qualify for Officer Candidate School, which had been my dream. So I just requested a discharge. The military granted me an honorable discharge based on humanitarian reasons."

A short time later, Ned moved he and Tina back to Montana to be closer to her family, thinking this would make her happier.

"We had a couple of pretty good years, so I thought we could make it. I was too young to understand that Tina never wanted to settle down. I really wanted a family, and Tina finally said it was OK. Amanda came along first, then Justin a year later. I was thrilled to be a father, but after they were born, she showed no natural motherly affection for them. It came out that Tina never wanted to be a mother. She really never wanted the children.

"I found out she was partying while I was at work, and that she was even drinking and doing a few drugs when she was expecting them." Fortunately, he said, the children showed no signs of birth defects from that use.

Ned described how the children were neglected and, he suspected, Tina was having multiple affairs.

"When I got home, Tina would scream about the babies crying all day and how she didn't want to take care of them. She would hit me with anything in sight. One weekend I tried to get her to help me clean the house. She got so angry she clobbered me over the head with an iron skillet. I must have had a concussion because my head hurt for days. I was way too embarrassed to tell the police my wife was beating me. And I kept it hidden because I felt such shame."

With Amanda just fifteen months and Justin just three months, Tina left with another man.

Ned found a Christian daycare for the children, continued working, and lived as a single dad caring for them for some time. Four years later came their kidnapping.

"Tina turned up all of a sudden asking to visit the children," Ned shared. "She and her boyfriend had been nomads living in Arizona somewhere. I should never have let her see them.

"A few weeks went by, then she found out where we went to church. One Sunday, I checked them into the children's church room and went to the main service. Back then, parents didn't have to show an ID to pick up the children. So after service was over, I went to pick them up and they were gone! The children's pastor said their mother had picked them up. That's how she kidnapped Amanda and Justin—from Sunday school. She just disappeared out of town with her boyfriend."

Seven

HEARTBREAKING REPORTS were mailed from Child Protective Services. When the children were placed into care, they were severely malnourished. It turned out their mother had sold her food stamps for cash and drugs, so the neglected children were so hungry they climbed into trash dumpsters behind fast food restaurants in search of food. In two years they started more than thirty schools in thirty different counties on the West Coast. When their neglect became obvious to teachers, Tina was called in and questioned. The next day they were gone. They lived in campers, slum motels, and vans in dreadful conditions with drug dealers and other dangerous people.

Annalee knew from experience what most foster children had previously endured. She didn't want to imagine what Amanda and Justin had been through the previous two years. Only God knew everything that happened.

Ned shared memories of their time with him and their childlike innocence until the ages of five and four. He assumed everything would be the same. He spoke with great anticipation of a possible reunion with the children.

Annalee warned him. "Honey, I wish I could tell you the children will be undefiled, but according to the social worker's reports, they've been through trauma we can't even imagine. You would be shocked at the stories of what my former foster children experienced. Trust me, these reports we are getting are only the tip of the iceberg. I need to prepare you. They have been traumatized, and we will need to give them *lots* of TLC."

After reaching the legal organization recommended by her friend, Annalee located two attorneys who specialized in defending cases like Ned's. Attorney Steven Owen had jurisdiction in Oregon where the children resided; the other, Glen Morris, had jurisdiction in Montana, where Ned and Annalee resided. She negotiated with both attorneys, who kindly agreed to monthly installment payments. Her entire salary went to attorney fees—thousands of dollars—but she was certain it was worth it. Ned's salary covered living expenses. She was extremely careful with their budget and, in fact, began setting aside funds for legal fees soon after their wedding. Since Annalee was accustomed to money management, Ned asked her to handle the checkbook and make sure the monthly bills were paid.

On a deeper level, Annalee and Ned were very concerned about the children's vulnerability to the investigation process and their being able to recall details of life with their father two years earlier. How could the children be expected to answer questions realistically at their young ages, especially considering the horrific two years with their mother?

One day a new investigation report arrived in the mail with more grueling details of what the children had been through. "I will *never* forgive her for putting the children through this!" Ned shouted. He began pacing the living room like a lion, and his anxiety was unsettling to Annalee. "I feel so helpless. I can't do anything for them—except wait to see if I'm gonna spend twenty years in prison!" He glanced at Annalee, who remained quiet. He eyed their Bible on the coffee table. "And pray."

"I couldn't agree more. We do need to pray—and forgive," Annalee offered softly.

"*Forgive?* How can you expect me to forgive what she's done to them? Putting them in harm's way around all those men? Now I know why I've been having those nightmares!"

Annalee calmly reached for the Bible and thumbed to one of her favorite Scriptures.

"My mind is being torn apart," Ned went on, anxiety-struck. "The kidnapping was bad enough, but now this!" Suddenly he calmed, just a bit, and focused on Annalee. "It just hit me. How did you ever forgive that doctor for tearing you up and damaging Lance's brain?"

"It wasn't easy, but I was . . . stuck."

"Stuck?"

"Yes, stuck. In a place of torment in my soul—just like you said. Torn apart from the inside out. I realized I could never move forward until—" She paused.

"Until what?" Now Ned's attention was riveted on her.

"Until I could forgive him—and everyone else who has ever wronged me in my life. After coming to faith, I realized forgiving him was the only way the Lord could forgive *me* for everything I've done wrong in my own life. He gave me peace and healed my mind. Hon, everyone is looking for peace. But peace can only be found in the Prince of Peace, who helps us forgive others unconditionally. Make sense?"

"Yes, I learned that in Bible college. I do need to forgive." It seemed as though a window had opened to Ned's soul.

"Jesus explained why people end up being tormented. Do you want me to read it?" Annalee asked.

"Sure, go ahead. I can't handle the torment anymore."

"Here are some Scriptures that really helped me forgive the doctor." Annalee began reading.

"Then his master, after he had called him, said to him, 'You wicked servant! I forgave you all that debt because you begged me. Should you not also have had compassion on your fellow servant, just as I had pity on you?' And his master was angry, and delivered him to the torturers until he should pay all that was due to him. So My heavenly Father also will do to you if each of you, from his heart, does not forgive his brother his trespasses" (NKJV).

"That's from Matthew 18:32-35," Annalee said. "This one is from the same chapter, verses 21 and 22."

Then Peter came to Him and said, "Lord, how often shall my brother sin against me, and I forgive him? Up to seven times?" Jesus said to him, "I do not say to you, up to seven times, but up to seventy times seven" (NKJV).

"Here is another good verse from the Book of Matthew."

"But I say to you, love your enemies, bless those who curse you, do good to those who hate you, and pray for those who spitefully use you and persecute you"
(Matthew 5:44, NKJV).

She flipped to Luke. "I love this translation from the Berean Study Bible. The wording shows the incredible forgiveness Jesus had for those who tormented him while He hung on the Cross suffering for our sins."

Then Jesus said, "Father, forgive them, for they do not know what they are doing." And they divided up His garments by casting lots. The people stood watching, and the rulers sneered at Him, saying, "He saved others; let Him save Himself if He is the Christ of God, the Chosen One" (Luke 23:34, 35, BSB).

"I need help to forgive Tina," Ned said. "Let's read them again."

Annalee did.

"Do you want to pray to release and forgive Tina now?" Annalee asked quietly.

"Yes, I do. Would you pray for me, sweetie?"

Annalee prayed with everything she had that Ned be able to forgive Tina from his heart. She prayed his repentance would have an impact on the decisions of the investigation team, Child Protective Services of Oregon, and the legal system on his behalf. She prayed for supernatural wisdom for their two attorneys to prepare Ned's case successfully, to be guided by the Holy Spirit for his defense. She prayed that Ned's humble heart would change the situation to allow him to be set free of all criminal charges. As she prayed, Ned took her hand and bowed his head. After a pause, he began to pray.

"Father in Heaven, I repent for holding a grudge against Tina and ask you to forgive me for the bitterness I felt toward her. Lord, I do forgive her, and we pray for her salvation and ask you to deliver her out of that drug life. Please heal the children from all bad memories and keep them safe always."

Ned soon closed his prayer in Jesus' name. It all seemed such a victory to Annalee.

Eight

IT HAD BEEN a very busy month. Ned worked full-time plus overtime and attended his veterans' meetings. Annalee also worked full-time. After work she spent a great deal of her time preparing records and letters for Child Protective Services.

She requested numerous character reference letters from family and friends on Ned's behalf. She faxed the reference letters to both attorneys and CPS Oregon along with copies of her foster care licenses to prove her experience in caring for traumatized children.

Ned's reunification program had to be completed in the event he was exonerated and regained custody. Annalee and Ned had no idea what the outcome or time frame might be, so they decided to complete the required program as soon as possible. Together they began attending Ned's reunification classes, which ironically were taken at the same time the Oregon custody investigation was taking place. Their classes were twice a week from 7 to 9 PM—the reunification plan class and the parenting class. They found the classes very informative. They learned state childcare regulations and new research on child development. Though Annalee had parented for more than two decades, she loved advanced education.

♥ ♥ ♥

Luke and Marie stopped by one evening as Ned and Annalee were leaving for class.

When Luke asked where they were going, Annalee reminded them of the parenting class.

"Oh, that's right. You're gonna go learn how to be a mom after you already raised me, all the foster kids, and three other kids!" teased Luke with a wide grin. He and Marie burst out laughing. Life had been so serious lately that laughter was great medicine. Ned and Annalee soon joined in. Marie had known Annalee since her childhood, as her "second mom," so the parenting classes had become a family joke.

After class, Ned and Annalee often stopped for pie and coffee to relax and discuss what they learned. That evening Ned offered the same.

"Thanks, but not tonight," Annalee said. "I'm not feeling very well."

"What's the matter?" Ned looked concerned.

"I started cramping in class, but we needed to finish. I'll go right to bed when we get home."

"Shouldn't I take you to the hospital, hon?"

"Oh, I'll be OK. I just need to get off my feet," Annalee said.

"If you're sure. I'll take you right away if you change your mind."

As they were entering their home, Annalee collapsed against the doorway. Ned caught her as she faltered.

"Are you sure you don't want me to take you to the ER? You look a little pale."

"This happened a few times with Luke," Annalee, an extremely tired expression on her face, said. "I've just been worn out lately. Can you help me get into bed?"

Ned braced her with his strong arms and guided her to the bedroom. He helped her change and climb into bed.

"Be sure and wake me up if you need me, OK?"

"I'm sure little one and I will be fine. I'll catch up on my rest this weekend."

Ned hesitated, thinking. "Maybe you should take a couple days off work."

"Aw, that's sweet. But we can't afford it. We need every dime."

"Have I told you lately I love you? Valentine's Day is soon. We're gonna do something special."

She smiled sleepily. "I love you too."

Ned turned off the lights as Annalee rolled over seeking sleep.

"Oh . . . it hurts so bad!" Annalee cried aloud in the stillness of the night. "Lord, don't let the baby die!"

Ned awoke with a start and flipped on the light to find Annalee doubled over, crying out in pain with a pool of blood under her.

"Oh, dear God!" He reached for the phone on the nightstand, dialed 911, and tenderly held her until the ambulance arrived.

The sirens wailing in the darkness got louder as the ambulance pulled onto their property. Ned hurried to the door and the paramedics raced to the bedroom. One look told the story.

As they gently began transferring Annalee onto the gurney, Luke and Marie rushed into the house and ran down the hall.

They saw the bed. "Oh, Mama! What's wrong with you and the baby?" Luke cried out.

"It feels like labor!" Crying inconsolably, Annalee pleaded with the paramedics. "Please save my baby!"

Luke and Marie leaned over the gurney and hugged her. "We love you, Mama!" Everyone was visibly emotional.

"We promise we'll take good care of your mom," one of the paramedics said. "We're taking her straight to the hospital."

Ned held Annalee's hand as she was wheeled out. "May I ride with her in the ambulance?"

"Yes, sir. That's fine."

"Dad, we're gonna follow you and Mom."

"Ok, son. See you at the ER," Ned shouted over a shoulder as he climbed in the ambulance.

The emergency vehicle dashed across town, sirens blaring and lights flashing.

After being wheeled in, the doctors asked the family to remain in the waiting room while they examined Annalee. In about thirty minutes, a doctor walked across the waiting area to the three of them.

"Mr. Jackson, your wife is going to be fine," he said. Ned and the family looked relieved. "But I'm sorry to have to tell you . . . your baby didn't make it."

Ned struggled to hold back tears. "I'm so glad my wife is OK. What happened to the baby?"

"Your wife had a traumatic miscarriage at sixteen weeks. It was already too late when she arrived here. We've run some tests and examined the baby. It was a little boy. We need to admit your wife for a D and C and keep her overnight for observation. The nurse is bringing you a surgical consent form."

"Our baby brother died?" Marie quietly moaned. She and Luke began to weep as they held each other.

The doctor looked at them with kind eyes. Ned leaned over and gave them a quick hug, then asked, "Doctor, what is a D and C?"

"It is called a dilation and curettage, a simple surgical procedure. After a miscarriage in the second trimester, the uterus still contains tissues from pregnancy. We need to clean out those remaining tissues to prevent infection or heavy bleeding."

"How is she doing right now?" Ned asked.

"At the moment she's pretty upset, so the anesthesiologist is with her right now preparing to put her to sleep for the procedure."

"When can we see her?"

"You can visit her after she is in her room. The procedure only takes about fifteen minutes, then she'll go to Recovery. The nurses will keep you posted. Her records indicate she has tolerated general anesthesia without nausea in the past. She will be drowsy afterward, which should help her relax the rest of the night. I will talk with you later and let you know how everything went, Mr. Jackson."

Ned quietly thanked the doctor.

Marie and Luke were still crying. Ned wrapped his arms around them. "Your mama's a strong woman. We will all help her, and God is gonna bless you with another baby brother or sister." Ned was trying to hold back his own tears.

He was heartbroken, but Ned knew he needed to be strong to support Annalee. He prayed for wisdom to know how to comfort her when she woke the next day.

When Ned entered her room later that night, Annalee was sound asleep. He looked with sadness at her flat stomach as she lay on her back. The doctor entered soon after and told Ned the surgery went well, that she should make a complete recovery. Ned thanked the doctor for his kindness and care. Annalee meant everything to him.

Ned wanted to protect her during recovery, but he also knew his wife. She would want to try again for a baby as soon as she felt healed enough. Ned confided in the doctor, and he suggested they wait at least several weeks.

Nine

NED DOZED IN the chair by Annalee's bed. In the morning he awakened to muffled sobs. Annalee's hands covered her sunken abdomen. He leaned over and wrapped his arms around her.

"Why?" she cried.

Ned spoke soft words, and the morning was spent consoling each other in shared grief, but mostly in silence.

Luke and Marie arrived later with a bouquet of flowers in a vase with the words "You Are My Sunshine." There were gentle hugs. "Mama, you're the best!" Luke said with tears in his eyes. He was such a sensitive young man, easily touched by emotion. "We're so sorry we lost our little brother."

"You're the only mom I have now, and if I have anything to say about it, you're gonna get through this," Marie said, sheer determination in her voice. She had a way of being firm yet loving. Marie was a strong girl who had been through a lot, so she always spoke with words of powerful encouragement.

"By the way, Mercy is on her way over," Marie said. "We wanted to call her last night, but Dad said it was too late." That surprised Annalee. She thought Ned would have remembered that she and Mercy had an agreement. For over twenty years they always showed up for each other during any emergency—24/7, rain or shine, day or night. Had Ned forgotten?

"Thanks for letting her know," Annalee said, smiling at her grown children. She winked at Marie with a special kind of mother's love. If anyone could plant a stick of dynamite under Annalee to get her back on her feet, it was Marie. She also smiled at Luke, her tenderhearted son. He was one of those rare men not afraid to show emotion, and Luke was quickly given to tears when he heard a humanitarian story about people or animals in danger or in need of rescue. Marie, on the other hand, would place her hands on her hips and say, "We gotta do somethin' about that!" Luke and Marie would often stop to assist homeless people or stranded motorists. They were even known to stop to encourage and pray for people arguing in public. (That could be risky!) They shared a mutual understanding of life's hardships that gave them unique insight. They rescued dogs and cats, so their house was a zoo. Various difficulties came with the territory. Marie had grown up with seizures and learning disabilities[3] from childhood injuries. Luke was born with delayed brain syndrome[4] and painful migraines. They were learning to navigate life on their own terms as young adults. The outside world might not understand, but their family did.

"Mama, Grandma asked us to pick her up later so she can visit you at home today," Luke said.

"Thanks, you two."

❤ ❤ ❤

A bit later, Mercy walked in. "Hi, family. Marie called me this morning. I would have been here last night if I had known." She handed Annalee an envelope with a hug. "Dear one, there are no words." Her middle-age face was strained with concern. Mercy had exceptional gifts for inspiration, wisdom, and maturity. The envelope contained a personalized creation beautifully illustrated with a condolence poem penned in calligraphy.

"Mercy, it's beautiful!" Annalee said. "Did you write this?"

"Yes, it was inspired." Mercy was always humble when she said things like this. "It came to me this morning after Marie called."

"Aww, your friendship means everything." Annalee admired her friend's strength and creativity.

"Likewise, dear one," Mercy said. "That's why we've resonated all these years." She turned her attention to Ned. "I'm so sorry for the loss of your little one. I know your budget is tight with the legal expenses, especially since Annalee needs time off now. Are you returning to work tomorrow?"

Ned nodded.

"Ned, I'm happy to rearrange my writing schedule to look after her. That way you can concentrate at work knowing she is in good hands." Ned's eyes shifted to his wife with an odd look of hesitation, then darted back to Mercy.

"Well, uh . . . sure. Thanks, Mercy," he said. He looked strangely uncomfortable.

"Glad to assist. It is a joy to help the only family I have. I need to run, but please keep me posted."

A short time later the doctor came in. "Good morning, everyone." He gently touched Annalee's shoulder. "How is our patient this morning?" She tried to answer, but suddenly her words choked on still more tears.

"May I have a moment to examine your mom?" he asked Marie and Luke, who then stepped out.

After a short exam, the doctor said, "Mrs. Jackson, I'm releasing you to go home with a prescription for a mild sedative at bedtime. It will help you sleep during recovery. I recommend lots of rest for a few days, and no lifting for several weeks."

Annalee softly gave her thanks as the doctor patted her hand.

"Thanks so much, Doctor," Ned said. The two men shook hands, and the doctor once again expressed his sorrow for their loss.

Recovery

ANNALEE WAS released about noon. Upon arriving home, Ned helped her to the bedroom. Emotionally exhausted, they fell asleep holding each other. Later in the afternoon they slowly made their way down the hall and heard the front door open. "Dad? Mom? You awake?"

Ned guided Annalee to the sofa, laid out a towel, and placed a pillow behind her back. Luke and Marie stepped inside with her mother, Betsy.

"Anybody hungry? I cooked supper." Betsy was an excellent cook. Luke and Marie carried in the food while Betsy headed to the sofa. She draped her arms around her daughter. They began to share warm mother-daughter conversation. Betsy was normally opinionated and strong-willed, but that day her aged eyes looked red and tearful with compassion.

"Honey, I love you. I'm so sorry you lost the baby."

Annalee felt great comfort from her mother's love, resting her head on her shoulder for a moment the same way she had as a child. Betsy cupped both her hands around her daughter's hands. Annalee studied the wrinkled hands and felt an outpouring of protective love for her aging mother. In that moment, she needed to talk.

"Do you remember me telling you I could feel the baby's tiny feet kicking?" Annalee said quietly.

"I do. That was such a good sign. At four months, we all thought you were far enough along to make it full-term this time. I don't know what a miscarriage is like. It must be devastating."

"Devastating is the right word," Annalee said. "Losing Lance was dreadful—the worst I've ever been through—but this is a different kind of heartbreak. Miscarriage feels like . . . " Annalee struggled for the words. "Like death invading my own body to attack my baby. I couldn't even save him. Yesterday, he was alive inside me. Today, he is gone."

Tears rolled down both women's cheeks.

"My little boy and I never had a chance to meet," Annalee said quietly. "One of my greatest comforts is knowing that someday in Heaven I will hold him in my arms and hold each of my other babies too. More healing will come this time by adding another name to my list."

"List? What do you mean?" Betsy asked.

"Haven't I told you? It gives me comfort to give each of my babies in Heaven a name, so I have a list on the wall in the master bedroom."

"I never knew that. Why did you start that list?"

"Well, years ago, after Lance's birth and his passing, when I started having miscarriages, the grief after each miscarriage was so heart-wrenching I was looking for a way to heal and find closure. So I began choosing a name for each baby, and it helped me say goodbye to that baby and begin the process of moving forward in life."

"That's understandable. What about all the miscarriages you had in the first few weeks before you knew if they were boys or girls?"

"I was given the idea to create a list of names for both boys and girls. I asked the Lord to assign the names to the right babies. Only He knows for whom they were chosen."

"What an idea! I never thought of that before. Lance has many siblings in Heaven."

"Yes he does, Mama. Thank you for your encouragement. I want to try for another baby when I'm strong enough."

"Remember, you need to give yourself plenty of time to recover," Betsy said gently. "Don't rush it. I still believe God has a plan for another grandbaby to join Amanda and Justin and the family."

Take delight in the LORD, and he will give you your heart's desires (Psalm 37:4, NLT).

The LORD lifts up those who are weighed down (Psalm 146:8, NLT).

Then call on me when you are in trouble, and I will rescue you (Psalm 50:15, NLT).

Ten

LUKE DROVE Grandma Betsy home after supper, and the entire family collapsed into bed early. Ned gently, slowly helped Annalee with all preparations for bed. She took her sedative and fell into a deep sleep. It had been a long, exhausting day.

❤ ❤ ❤

Mercy arrived next morning as Ned was leaving for work. He hugged his wife and said a quick goodbye.

As the door closed, Mercy said, "Morning, dear. Looks like you got some sleep." She gave her friend a gentle hug.

"I did. It helped a lot. Thanks for coming over."

"I wouldn't have it any other way." With a grin and a flourish, she proudly held up a grocery bag. "You're going to love today's lunch and dinner entrées! Jell-O, bananas, applesauce, and cinnamon tea. Yum!" Mercy had a way of painting a silver lining on the darkest cloud, and she could do so without anything even resembling a paintbrush in her hand.

Annalee chuckled a little. It felt like she hadn't laughed in many days. She loved her friend's delightful sense of humor.

"How about some scrambled eggs for breakfast? Soft foods are easy on the tummy."

"Sounds good. I was able to handle Mama's mashed potatoes last night, and some Jell-O for dessert."

Before long the two women were chatting on the sofa holding breakfast trays. When they were both single, they met for lunch twice a week. Since Annalee's wedding their lunch dates had become only occasional ones, so they had lots of catching up to do. Mercy always enjoyed Luke's joke about "taking classes to be a mom." Mercy updated her friend on such things as an oil painting she was finishing and the progress of her latest Christian novel.

With over twenty years of friendship, the two women understood each other. For years they had shared joys, holidays, tears, and emergencies. Both possessed an unusual degree of empathy and sought unique ways to bring healing to others. Mercy used her creativity to inspire people. Her artwork, novels, and poetry were outstanding. Annalee's empathy predominantly involved her mission to heal wounded hearts, raise children, and assist others through her administrative gifts. Annalee's favorite hobby was researching the meanings of friends' names and creating posters to inspire them to fulfill their destinies and purposes associated with those names.

Mercy was working hard to think of other topics to keep the conversation light and carefree. She knew Annalee needed a break from all the recent pressures in life.

"Oh, by the way, have I told you about the research I recently discovered?" Mercy said with excitement. "It is related to that unique type of empathy we each feel toward people, animals, and creation. I've always wondered why our responses to life are so intense. Now I better understand why we connect so well."

"Really?"

"Yes. The term is called highly sensitive people,[5] otherwise known as HSPs."[6]

Annalee was fascinated and wanted to learn more.

"It only involves about 15 to 20 percent of the population," Mercy said. "It isn't a disorder, but it is uncommon enough to be misunderstood by the majority of people—especially with the kind of world we live in."

"That's understandable. I would love to learn more about it," Annalee said.

"Quite a bit of research is being done, and there are definite characteristics," Mercy said. "Most of the traits fit both our personalities. For example, HSPs are hypersensitive when they encounter suffering or harshness."

Annalee thought for a moment. "Do they try to avoid violent movies or become emotional around conflict?"

"From what I've learned so far, those are some of the traits," Mercy said.

Annalee wondered if HSPs were more introspective and prone to retreat during difficult times.

"You got it!" Mercy said.

"My goodness! Maybe HSP has something to do with that vow I made as a child," Annalee said.

"I have a feeling you're right."

"You know, I never understood why that vow has haunted me all my life. Will you let me know if you learn more information about highly sensitive people?"

"Sure. I'll keep looking," Mercy quietly said.

The vow to which Annalee referred was something few people, other than Mercy, knew about.

♥ ♥ ♥

Annalee had always appreciated Mercy's friendship. She was a loyal, honest, and compassionate friend.

Mercy definitely lived up to her name. She was such an encourager, and she gave wisdom and love way beyond the callings of most. Her life, an uncomplicated one, was devoted to her faith. Her prayer life gave her peace, simplicity, and discernment, an overflowing spring from which she always provided wise counsel.

As a writer and artist whose earthly journey had eluded finding a soul mate, Mercy's life was a mix of solitude and simplicity undergirded by solid faith. An only child whose parents were deceased, her middle-age years had settled into a fairly predictable routine—with the exception of "providential assignments." Those were times when others, facing deep crises, intersected with her world. Often, the crises had involved her best friend on earth, Annalee, who Mercy knew as a "tenderhearted rescuer" whose family had become her own.

Eleven

The Vow

AT THE AGE OF nine, Annalee had made a childhood vow—one she felt compelled to maintain forever.

She was restricted from athletic activities under written orders from her doctor due to medical issues. That made her very unpopular with her young classmates in school. They could not understand why she couldn't join in. After being viciously bullied on the playground one day, she stood on the sidelines in tears and, for a nine-year-old, began to think very deeply.

I know how it feels to have hurt feelings. How many other kids feel like I do?

She was not raised in a churchgoing family and had no knowledge of the Bible, but she felt that God somehow understood her life's toughest moments, so she frequently talked to Him in private, even from her earliest memories. From the time she could print, her mother taught her to write thank you notes on stationery whenever she received a gift. She was taught that it was proper to use a salutation at the beginning and a complimentary closing at the end. Annalee didn't know the "proper" way to pray, so, based on her upbringing, she always spoke to God through the same etiquette.

As Annalee stood on the playground that day at the tender age of nine, she made this vow:

> *Dear God, I never want to be anybody's enemy.*
> *Help me be perfect so I don't make anyone mad at me.*
> *I promise I will never hurt anyone's feelings my whole life.*
> *Please help me be kind and loving to everyone forever.*
> *Thank you, God.*

In her young mind, this vow was unbreakable. One she had to live up to for life.

Little did Annalee realize that, no matter how hard she tried, her childhood vow was impossible to keep, especially in a complex world that has ways of inflicting unrelenting pain on its inhabitants. Somehow, she thought she could be perfect if she simply prayed. She would not find out until much later in life that there is only one perfect Person who has ever lived.

And yet, that vow continued to live on in her memory for decades . . .

Twelve

OVER THE NEXT few days, Annalee continued to regain strength as she progressed in her recovery. A significant emotional turning point came when she was able to choose a name for her little boy and add it to her list: Jonathan David. Choosing his name helped give her another step toward closure. While Ned was at work each day, she and Mercy shared mutual encouragement, prayer, and renewed hope.

One morning Annalee and Ned woke to a beautiful fresh snowfall. The pristine landscape was a fresh reminder of God's faithfulness to cover life's disappointments and recreate nature's beauty as white as snow. Ned had a different reaction, however, as he reached the front entry and began to tug on his snow boots. "Oh man, it's gonna be fun driving a truck in *this* today."

Ned's job moved forward, and he got a raise from his employer. Annalee and Ned were grateful for the financial relief, especially with her time off work. Every day, Mercy faithfully took care of Annalee and even prepared supper for the three of them each evening; it was ready when Ned returned from work. Ned expressed cursory thanks for her efforts each night, but he remained strangely distant from Mercy during their conversations. Things felt awkward. The glances between Annalee and Mercy indicated they were both aware of this, but they chose not to discuss it. Annalee thought it might have something to do with Ned's recovery from the loss of the baby, or perhaps his mind was preoccupied with the pending legal matters.

The mail was stacking up, but Annalee decided to take a break from business for a few days and leave the mail alone. After she made the decision, she mentioned it to Mercy. Her friend agreed this was a perfect time for mental recovery along with her physical recuperation. Annalee thought Ned would agree since she had been working so hard for months. She raised the issue one evening over supper.

That evening, after Mercy left to go home, Ned asked a question. "Does Mercy try to give you marriage or legal advice?"

Annalee was surprised because that topic had never come up before. "Mercy and I talk about many different subjects, but we never breach each other's boundaries, and she doesn't interfere in our private lives," she told Ned.

"It just seems like the two of you are pretty tight."

"Well, we've known each other over twenty years. She has been a dear friend through thick and thin."

"But with our marriage, we need to make sure we never let anyone come between us," Ned said.

"I would never let that happen," Annalee agreed. "We're supportive of each other, that's all."

"I just want to make sure no one ever ends up being an outside influence." He seemed annoyed.

"Honey, of course you are number one in my life, but Mercy is not an outsider. She has been part of the family for over two decades. Remember we discussed that when we were engaged? She has no family but us."

"Yeah, she is like family. But what is most important is you and me."

"Of course."

Ned persisted. "But you take her advice, don't you?"

"On some matters, yes. She is a woman of great wisdom and maturity who has been an inspiration and a faithful friend. Is that a problem for some reason?"

Ned suddenly pulled back from the deep discussion. "No. I guess I just have a lot on my mind, especially with everything going on."

"Are you concerned about the legal case or finances? Is that it?"

"Yes, I wonder how we're gonna keep up with the lawyers with you being off work and all."

"Honey, no worries. Our family doctor has confirmed that my recovery is going well, remember? I already contacted both our attorneys and explained our situation. They were very sympathetic and decided to defer two weeks of payments while I'm off. They even agreed to continue working on your case in the interim."

"Well, that's a relief. Sometimes I forget I married a lady who takes care of everything."

"Thank you. I'm returning to work next week too. You have nothing to worry about, especially with Mercy. She is a devoted friend—not just to me and the kids. She has adopted you too." Annalee grinned as she said the last part.

"Aw, sweetie, I'm sorry. So much has gone wrong in my life, I just get carried away. Thanks for tryin' to keep me calm."

Thirteen

ON FRIDAY morning Mercy didn't arrive until after Ned had left for work. She entered with her usual contagious smile and greeting.

"Hey, girlfriend," Annalee said. "Coffee is ready. Want a cup?"

"Love it. Great to see you getting stronger every day," Mercy said, laying down her things.

They sat at the kitchen table. "Do you feel well enough to handle the house from now on?" Mercy asked.

"Yes. I've even felt well enough to start decorating the house for Valentine's Day. Remember when you took me to the doctor the other day and he said I'm healing up well? His office called and said my lab work came back. I'm no longer anemic! He released me to return to work on Monday."

Mercy shared her excitement. "Are you up for fixing supper for yourself and Ned tonight?"

"Sure, I can handle that." She noticed an awkward look on Mercy's face. "Are you OK?"

"Annalee, I need to be honest." Mercy paused a beat. "I don't want to impose on your household. Have I offended Ned?"

"Not at all! You haven't done anything but be a huge help to us since the miscarriage."

"He just seems uncomfortable around me, and I wondered if I need to ask his forgiveness for anything I've done—maybe something I'm unaware of?"

"I think Ned is still adjusting to our marriage and the fact that you and I had a preexisting friendship long before he and I fell in love. He's also preoccupied with all the legal matters and expenses."

Mercy looked unsure. "Dear one, if you discover there is anything that needs to be resolved on my account, please let me know. I would want to make it right."

"Of course. But I'm not aware of anything. We will always be BFFs!" They chuckled.

But in truth Annalee herself was still a bit baffled by Ned's confusing conversation the night before. Why hadn't he allowed Marie and Luke to call Mercy the night she was admitted to the hospital? Did he feel threatened by their friendship or the fact Mercy was a spiritual mentor in her life? There was no logical reason for Ned to feel a contradiction of loyalties.

Was Ned trying to isolate Annalee from her longtime friend? Was Ned paranoid?

And this question, even, entered her mind: did his military involvement cause Ned to be more suspicious than he needed to be?

Her mind began racing with a myriad of things Ned had shared in different conversations.

She knew he had been severely abused as a child. He said he had been in "covert operations" in the military and had post-traumatic stress disorder. He said it would be more than thirty years before he could share anything about his secret military assignments. The truth was, Annalee didn't even want to know—she figured that, as a highly sensitive person, her mind probably couldn't handle such things. She would much rather focus on matters of the heart. So, each day, Annalee chose to meditate on basic truths.

I must keep the vows we shared on behalf of each other's children at our wedding.

He loves me and loves his children. I want to "rescue the perishing"—love and care for the orphans.

It would be wrong not to do good when I have the knowledge to do so.[7]

The Lord gave me these skills to prepare me "for such a time as this."[8]

❤ ❤ ❤

The next day Ned was in a great mood. He approached Annalee to say, "Sweetheart, Valentine's Day is getting close. Are you feeling well enough to go out tonight for an early Valentine's dinner?"

"Can we afford it since I missed time off work?"

Ned just smiled. "Honey, I promised, so I saved up money before everything happened. Will you be my Valentine?"

"Yes, I'd love that!" Annalee giggled.

"Well then, why don't we get dressed up for a night out on the town?"

Just as it was during their courtship, Ned took Annalee to an elegant restaurant. He treated her like a china doll, delicately escorting her in and out of the car and then into the restaurant. Just as before their wedding, he executed a military bow when she stood to leave the room and when she returned. Her mind was once again captivated as she recalled the military hero she fell for.

How could she have doubted him? Ned was indeed her knight in shining armor. She felt sure of it.

The previous night's conversation evaporated from her mind.

♥ ♥ ♥

Annalee was warmly greeted by her colleagues when she returned to work the following week. She was surprised to see her desk decorated with fresh flowers, balloons, and get well cards. She felt overwhelmed. Throughout the day, various co-workers stopped by her desk to make sure she was feeling OK. She was encouraged and happy to be back.

During lunch break, a few of the women presented her with a colorful envelope, soliciting a promise that she not open it until after work. When she reached her car that afternoon, she sat in the driver's seat and opened it privately. She pulled out a large condolence card signed by everyone in her department. Some had written personalized notes of sympathy, hope, and encouragement. Most amazing of all was an enclosed money collection taken on her behalf. Annalee was stunned to see the amount collected was nearly equal to the two weeks' salary she lost while being away. She was extremely grateful for the wonderful people she worked with.

♥ ♥ ♥

When she reached home, Ned hadn't yet arrived. She picked up the phone and called Mercy. She shared the incredible kindness of her colleagues and her wonderful Valentine's date with Ned.

"I'm so happy for you! The Lord is taking such wonderful care of the two of you," Mercy said excitedly.

"Ned is pulling in the driveway right now, so I need to go." Annalee couldn't wait to show her husband.

"You both have a great night, dear one."

Ned walked in the door and set down his lunch bag as he removed his snow boots. Annalee couldn't wait to show him, so she met him in the entryway. "Look what I received at work today! Just about enough to cover the time I missed off work!" She showed Ned the card and money.

"Honey, that is awesome!" he said. "That was so nice of your coworkers."

All seemed well on the home front.

Fourteen

ANNALEE FINISHED her thank you letter then started into the mail that had piled up during her recovery. A custody hearing notice had arrived from Child Protective Services in Oregon; the hearing was scheduled for a Monday during the last week of February. Ned and Annalee were required to appear in court.

Time was of the essence.

During the interview process with her new company, Annalee had anticipated the possibility that occasional future travel might be required on behalf of the children, so she briefly discussed the issue with management. The company was comprised primarily of managers with families, people who would empathize with the critical need to facilitate the children's rescue. She was extremely grateful management considered her business qualifications sufficient to justify such a request. They had been so gracious during her two weeks' leave of absence for the miscarriage as well.

The following morning, Annalee met with her department head and arranged time off for the custody hearing.

She began the arduous process of making arrangements for the meeting. Ned's credit had been ruined by his divorce and lost income incurred during periodic searches for the children. Fortunately, Annalee had credit cards and an airline travel card, so she called her airline to arrange flights to Oregon. But the high cost of airline tickets within the two-week window proved prohibitive. She knew of a special airline program that provided a discount for emergencies or bereavement flights. She spoke to the director of the designated department and explained the issue, requesting a discount. After faxing some information, he granted the discount.

She notified both attorneys' offices and arranged to be represented in court by Mr. Owen, their Oregon attorney. Additional legal fees and court costs would be a reality. Last, she called the children's social worker to request a meeting with Justin and Amanda during their trip to Oregon. Thankfully, that request was granted also. She was excited to finally be able to meet the children in person. Ned was relieved and grateful that he would be able to see his children again as well.

Ned and Annalee remained busy with all the arrangements needed for the visit. The days went by with a blur.

That was the case with one exception: the infamous day of Annalee's encounter with the Spirit of Worthlessness the following weekend.

❤ ❤ ❤

On the night before Valentine's Day, Annalee waited for Ned to fall asleep before placing a Valentine card on his nightstand. It read: "For My Beloved Husband With My Love" and had a romantic poem handwritten inside the card. Next to the card she laid a small chocolate heart. She also had created a framed name poster using Ned's first and middle name.

She awakened the next morning to Ned caressing her hair as he knelt at her bedside with tears in his handsome blue eyes. His first words were, "Happy Valentine's Day, sweetheart. Thank you so much. I have never, ever received a Valentine card from my wife! What did I ever do to deserve you?" Annalee smiled. She thought all wives bought cards and wrote affectionate notes to their husbands on special holidays. Ned helped her sit up by setting a large pillow behind her back. "I have something for you." She smiled softly. He presented her with a large heart full of chocolates and a card that read "For My Wife With My Love Forever." In the next moment she found herself cuddling a musical teddy bear playing a tune and clutching a red heart. She knew these gifts had been a financial sacrifice for Ned.

"Wow, honey, you've outdone yourself! Looks like I should have splurged on you!" Annalee grinned.

"No need, sweetie. You are rescuing my family. Everything you're doing means so much. You are my dream come true." Ned reached for his guitar and strummed her a love song.

Annalee simply cried. This romantic expression of caring was new for her. Gifts had never been her focus, but she was grateful for Ned's generosity. Her love language (from the well-known Gary Chapman book, *The Five Love Languages*[9]) was words of affirmation, so communication, encouragement, and verbal reassurance meant everything to her.

This first Valentine's Day was memorable. The remainder of February seemed to fly by as they prepared for their trip.

❤ ❤ ❤

They landed in Portland on a Saturday morning, rented a car, and glimpsed some magnificent views of Mount Hood as they headed through the beautiful Cascades toward a small mountain town where the children lived with their foster family. Ned and Annalee's anticipation and excitement were beyond words.

As they drove, they discussed the children and what to expect. Annalee had her dream of caring for these little ones, and Ned shed tears more than once as he anticipated seeing his long-lost children.

Having been a foster parent, she was aware of obvious behavioral signs that typically present themselves in children who have endured trauma. But she was determined. She and Ned had completed the last of Ned's reunification and parenting classes during her miscarriage recovery. She also used that time to read up on the latest research on childhood trauma. If she was blessed with the opportunity to become Amanda and Justin's new mother, Annalee told herself, she wanted to be completely prepared. She told Ned of past experiences she had with traumatized children. They agreed it was imperative they be completely united to create a beautiful new beginning for the children if the court granted them custody. Annalee wanted nothing more than to show unconditional love and security for these two precious children.

Arriving in the lovely wooded town of Pinebluff[10], they found the address and pulled into the driveway. They sat for a few minutes to pray and gather their thoughts. Annalee spoke first. "Ned, remember last November when I had that unusual experience walking down the driveway to the mailbox? My heart was burdened for the children, and I pleaded with the Lord to not allow them to remain in a terrible situation for years since He is the only One who knew where they were.

I asked Him out loud, 'If we are the ones destined to raise them, will you please restore them to us before they become teenagers, while they're still young enough for us to give them healing and a wonderful childhood?' I'll never forget that day when I came back and told you about that prayer. Isn't it incredible how we found out about them just two weeks later, the day before Thanksgiving?"

"Yes, I remember that, hon. It was an amazing miracle."

"We both know the Lord answered that prayer. This is such an important day. Will you please pray for our visit with the children? We want them to feel secure with us. You probably know this already, but this visit is important to your investigation and reunification."

"Well, I do know we wouldn't even be here if it wasn't for you," Ned said.

"I'm thankful for all the help we've had, including my attorney friend who got us in touch with these attorneys. The Lord rescued the children from the awful situation they were in." Annalee paused. "Our purpose this weekend goes way beyond the visit. The children have their own social worker, and she will ask the foster parents how well our visit goes."

"Wow." Ned took a deep breath. "There's a lot more to this than I thought."

"That's understandable," Annalee quietly said.

"I can hardly wait to see them, so why don't we pray now?" Ned said. He took her hand and began the prayer of a caring, desperate father. When finished, they took a few more deep breaths, gathered the presents they had brought for the children, and made their way to the front door.

The foster parents, Mel and Monica, welcomed them with kindness and hospitality. The home seemed warm and comforting. After more than two years of being apart, Amanda and Justin were reintroduced to their father. They were a little shy at first, but within minutes they plopped on the sofa on either side of their dad. Ned fought back tears as he held them in his arms once again. He began calling them by the nicknames they had been raised with in their earlier years: Sissy Bear and Brother Bear. (Ned was Papa Bear.) Their eyes lit up as they recalled those names of endearment. That seemed to help break the ice. Soon, they were chatting like typical six- and seven-year-olds. They would repeat the nicknames a few times during that weekend.

Amanda and Justin were delightful children who strongly resembled their dad, and it was such a relief to see that they had regained weight in the three months since their rescue. At first, Annalee would sit with more room between her and Ned and the children. Before long, however, Amanda and Justin were reaching for her, inviting her to scoot down to be next to all of them. Annalee was thrilled and allowed herself to entertain thoughts of being a mom to these two.

A short time later, Amanda and Justin suddenly jumped off the sofa. Each grabbed Ned and Annalee by a hand and began leading them down a hallway. "You wanna see our rooms?" Ned and Annalee looked back at Mel and Monica to confirm their permission. The foster parents waved them on with nods and smiles.

"We would love to see your rooms!" Annalee said. The children skipped along as they headed down the hallway.

The first stop was made by Justin. "Here is my room! Me and my foster brother share it together," he said proudly, leaping onto his bed. He didn't seem able to contain his excitement. Annalee wondered if he had ADHD[11]; she had dealt with this condition before. "Here is my Christmas toys that me and my foster brother play with," Justin said, moving around the room. "It's lotsa fun!"

"That's awesome! Did you receive the Christmas presents we sent you and Sissy in the mail?" Ned asked.

"Ya mean that big box? That came from *you*?" Justin's eyes grew wide. Ned and Annalee nodded and grinned.

"Gee, thanks!" Justin said.

"We really liked the nice presents. Thank you," Amanda said quite politely, and with a smile.

Justin wanted to show them everything in his room, item by item. He described each toy and game, along with some new clothing bought by Mel and Monica. Annalee was impressed that these foster parents cared enough to make sure they had a new wardrobe and nice Christmas. It reminded her of how she had provided for her foster children in past years.

Amanda patiently waited for her little brother to finish. She looked as if she was evaluating the situation. She was a sweet, friendly child with a cooperative nature and tender smile. She had playful moments but was more subdued than her brother. She seemed to mix in much more of a sensitive side. She continued to hold Annalee's hand. Annalee's dream was to comfort this little girl who had been through so much. She periodically would glance over and detect a faraway, distant look on Amanda's young face. Was she preoccupied or thinking of something beyond the moment? Annalee made a mental note to look into the results of the child psychologist's interview with Amanda to see what this precious little girl divulged.

Could Amanda be trying to forget something? Annalee wondered. *A memory she didn't know how to articulate? Secrets?*

Fifteen

ALL IN ALL, it was turning into a wonderful visit. After a few more minutes Ned said, "How about we see Sissy Bear's room?"

"Oh yeah! Sissy, let's go!" Justin hollered as he dashed into the hallway ahead of everyone.

Amanda led them to the room she shared with her foster sister and happily showed off her Christmas presents. She spoke softly. Although her brother was only one year younger, Amanda's demeanor visibly revealed their birth order. Documentation clearly showed that for the last two years Amanda had lacked the chance to simply enjoy being a little girl. As the elder of the two, she had assumed a false position of responsibility as Justin's "caregiver" during the dangerous time with their biological mother; it was clear that both children lacked adult care and security. Amanda seemed mature and reserved for the tender age of seven, and she was protective of Justin. However, at the same time this little girl seemed to recognize that their improved environment now included being properly cared for by responsible adults. She seemed to be grasping that she no longer needed to be Justin's sole "caregiver." She deserved, and needed, a joyful, carefree childhood with peace in her young heart.

Ned and Annalee were permitted to take the children out for lunch. Ned drove, and as they climbed into the car, the children said, "Annalee, can you sit back here with us?"

"That would be fun!" she said. Realizing they both needed attention, she sat between them. From her past experience with foster children, she was surprised by their apparent level of trust and affection during this first meeting with her, but she also recognized they had been starved for proper affection for a long time.

"What do you like best about your new school?" she asked the children.

"We like our new friends," Justin said with excitement. "And we love the snow." This little boy was quite literally squirming for attention.

Amanda was more reserved, of course, but she also welcomed affection. Amanda laid her head on Annalee's shoulder, which surprised Annalee. She asked, "Sissy, do you have any hobbies that you like?"

"Well, I like different things," she said timidly. "I draw sometimes." They talked about snow sledding, building snowmen, board games, and children's TV shows. Annalee worked hard to make the two children feel comfortable, but she also allowed them to take the lead. They sat quite close on either side of her, so she wrapped an arm around each of them, and they loosened up even more, including some giggling.

Ned pulled into a fast food restaurant, and the children wanted the normal fare of hamburgers and fries, and they got milkshakes as well. After eating the children wanted to play on the indoor slides. Ned joined them, but Annalee's abdomen was still physically tender; she enjoyed watching and laughing with them from the sidelines. For Ned's part, he had never expected to see his children again, let alone safe and sound. Annalee hoped this experience would help him overcome the nightmares he had suffered from for so long.

After a couple of hours they were due back at the house, so they headed to the car. The children asked if Annalee would sit between them once again. Ned smiled as he observed his children warming greatly to his wife. By now they were chatting and laughing, and in time each of them laid a head on her shoulder.

After they reached the house, Mel and Monica asked the children to play in their rooms so the adults could visit. With the living room quiet, they discussed the CPS reports.

It was lengthy, and all four shared what they knew of the children's history in the last two-plus years. Mel and Monica had read many of the same reports as those sent to Ned and Annalee. Due to the CPS reports of the children's neglect, starvation, and exposure to drugs and criminal activity, Annalee shared how she had prepared herself to observe behavioral signs which might be similar to her previous foster children. Given the environment from which the children had been rescued, she suspected they had probably been subjected to lewd conduct as well.

However, when Annalee would question the social worker regarding her suspicions, the response was usually shifted to Tina's allegations against Ned and his supposed failure to protect the children. At one point, around December, one of the social workers even intimated that if Ned was not granted custody, Tina's boyfriend could be considered an appropriate custodial "father figure" for the children. This was because he "appeared to have a positive fatherly relationship with the children," according to her observation. Given the lifestyle he and Tina had exposed the children to, Ned and Annalee were horrified at the thought. Mel and Monica agreed. "That would have been a terrible idea," Mel said.

Ned and Annalee explained that during their phone calls with CPS, both of them insisted that Tina's boyfriend be investigated as well. Ned and Annalee didn't know it, but CPS had begun actively investigating the boyfriend around November after his arrest. It was discovered he had a criminal record prior to the felony charges he and Tina were now facing.

Mel and Monica shared information that the children's social worker had provided in the course of their experiences with the children. They were careful to disclose only what they were permitted to share.

Ned opened up with Mel and Monica about the kidnapping of the children, his grief during their two-year absence, and his lengthy search for them. Ned and Annalee shared their desire to provide a future for the children, and Annalee shared a bit more about her background in legal work and foster care.

Ned and Annalee updated the foster parents on the custody hearing and their completion of the reunification plan and parenting classes. They shared about their home life with Luke and Marie and the family joke about Annalee "learning how to be a parent." Mel and Monica chuckled at that one. Ned and Annalee described their property and plans to begin preparing the children's rooms in the event the court ultimately granted them custody. And they expressed their gratitude for everything Mel and Monica were doing.

Monica suddenly changed gears. "Have you both received some . . . uh, news regarding Tina's boyfriend—the man she's been living with for several years?"

Annalee said she had received an envelope, but in the rush to catch their flight she'd packed it away and not yet opened it.

"That's probably it," Mel said. Monica paused, then spoke again. "We just found out that her boyfriend died of a drug overdose. He was only in his thirties. It happened after they started investigating him."

"Oh no!" Annalee gasped. "Do you think he was trying to escape the investigation?"

"That's what we wondered," Mel said. "It's the timing . . . "

"Do you know if CPS found out any details from him about the children?" Ned asked.

"We have not been told," Monica said. "Authorities were still questioning him."

"A life of partying and drugs never ends well, especially for the innocent children caught in the middle," Annalee said. "I saw it plenty of times as a foster parent."

"It's all very suspicious," Ned said.

"If we're granted custody, I'll be on the alert to see if the children mention him," Annalee said. "They're so young, but if something bad happened involving him, I'm sure their feelings will be revealed in time."

"Thanks for letting us know," Ned said. "The children mean everything to us."

"Of course," Monica said. She welcomed them to visit the next day following church. Ned and Annalee expressed their thanks.

After hugs for all, including the children, Ned and Annalee headed to the hotel and opened the CPS letter. It was indeed official notification of Tina's boyfriend's death.

Was this accidental? During investigation it added to the questions.

Whatever caused it, Annalee had even greater concern for little Amanda and Justin.

"It would be better to be thrown into the sea with a millstone hung around your neck than to cause one of these little ones to fall into sin." — Jesus (Luke 17:2, NLT).

Then Jesus called for the children and said to the disciples, "Let the children come to me. Don't stop them! For the Kingdom of God belongs to those who are like these children" (Luke 18:16, NLT).

Sixteen

THE FOLLOWING morning Ned and Annalee caught up on some much needed sleep. At 1 PM they joined the family for lunch and another delightful visit with Amanda and Justin along with their foster brother and foster sister, who were of similar ages. There was a great deal of activity and excitement as the children donned snowsuits to go sledding with the parents cheering them on. Later, back in the house, they shared hot chocolate, popcorn, and laughter as the four children danced to some of their favorite children's tunes on CD. It was a wonderful day.

After the busy afternoon, Mel and Monica asked the children to play in their rooms while the adults had more conversation in the living room. They discussed emotional behaviors shown by Amanda and Justin.

"We know you're flying back out tomorrow after court, so we want to update you in person," Mel said. "We hope we can be helpful so you both can be prepared."

"Thank you. We were hoping to have a chance to go over those issues," Annalee said.

Ned looked concerned. "Are the kids doing OK?"

"Considering the reports of what they've been through, they seem to be doing surprisingly well," Monica said. "After three months with us, we've had plenty of time to observe behaviors at home and school."

"First of all, you're probably aware that they're both behind in their educations," Mel said.

"The social worker said something about that," Ned said.

"Not surprising, either, considering their environment for over two years," Annalee said. "According to our records, they were enrolled in at least thirty schools in different counties all over the West Coast, not to mention what probably went on with the people they were exposed to at home with bio mom."

"Exactly right," Monica said. "So our local school designed IEPs for them. That seems to be helping."

Ned asked for clarification.

"Oh, honey, it's that program we talked about after we met—the learning disability program at school that helped Luke," Annalee said. "The individualized education plan is designed for students who need extra help to overcome learning difficulties."[12]

Ned said he remembered, but then quickly added, "But both the children seem very smart."

"You're right," Monica said. "Both children are very bright. They just got behind."

"It has nothing to do with their intelligence," Mel added.

"I'm hoping as they catch up," Annalee said, "Amanda and Justin will learn compensation skills. It's a great replacement skill that also works with LD. Luke and Marie sometimes come up with amazing ideas the average person would never think of. I sure wouldn't!" She laughed. "Totally apart from learning challenges. When Luke was growing up, the neurologist said he mentally processed with the other side of his brain—a type of compensation. When Luke was seven, he was frustrated because he couldn't remember the four-digit code to his bike lock, so he found some tools and took out all the tumblers. I found my little seven-year-old had reassembled the lock with the four digits of his birthday to remember his code. I was shocked!"

"That's amazing!" Monica said, shaking her head.

"Isn't it, though?" Annalee said. "That example gives me so much hope for Amanda and Justin in moving forward. Who knows? They could grow up and use compensation to overcome bad memories to become entrepreneurs or invent new business methods. Their possibilities are endless. They'll be overcomers!"

Ned asked of any other important news regarding Amanda and Justin.

"You should be aware that Justin has been having behavioral difficulties in school," Monica said. "As you've probably noticed, he is extremely active. In school he loves to be the class clown, the center of attention. That interferes with his concentration and focus."

"We did notice that," Annalee said. "Has ADHD been considered?"

"Yes, his therapists have discussed it," Monica said. "But they've hesitated to prescribe anything yet."

"I personally think he's just an active little boy looking for a father figure he can trust," Mel said.

"Well, I'm sure looking forward to being in his life as his father again," Ned said.

Annalee patted Ned on the hand. "And you'll be a wonderful father too, honey."

"Justin is a very loving, kind little boy," Mel said. "I enjoy teaching him how to build things."

"He is such a love bug," Monica added. "The main thing you need to know right now is that he needs lots of supervision to keep him out of harm's way."

"I've had experience with ADHD children," Annalee said. "It goes with the territory." She paused. "What can you tell us about Amanda?"

"Amanda is more mysterious," Monica said. "With her, I think there is a lot beneath the surface."

"So do I. Do you sometimes notice a faraway look in her eyes?" Annalee asked. "As though she is thinking of something beyond the moment?"

"Yes, we've noticed that, and so have her teachers," Monica said. "She seems to daydream a lot, and that interferes with concentration and learning. We think she is preoccupied with worries in her little mind."

"Do you ever have the impression her mind is locked up in a little box all alone with memories, struggling to process experiences, perhaps troubling things she is too young to even articulate?" Annalee asked.

"I believe that describes it exactly," Monica said. "Something only a mother would understand."

"I've noticed that too," Mel said. "But didn't know how to pinpoint it."

"Do you think she is sad?" Ned asked Mel and Monica.

"We think so, but she covers it well," Monica said. "She keeps her feelings to herself."

"As her dad, I want to help her recover so she can trust again," Ned said. "Little girls need a dad to love them."

A recognition came to Annalee: Ned was saying all the right things. She thought he had an understanding of what the children needed.

"How is she doing in school?" Ned asked.

"Her teachers report that she is well-behaved in class," Mel said. "Her main difficulty is daydreaming, and she seems to have frequent stomachaches in the mornings, as if she wants to avoid school."

"The stomach issues are probably emotional," Annalee said. "They haven't been bullied, have they?"

"Not that we know of," Monica said. "But her shyness may be connected with circumstances they were rescued from."

"I think you're right," Ned said. "I've missed my little ones so much. What we really want is to give them a wonderful life to help them heal and have a new beginning."

"We have the same goals, honey," Annalee said.

Annalee looked back to the others and changed gears. "If everything goes well in court tomorrow, I'll talk to our local Christian school when we get back. They have an individualized program that will help both of them. It will put them in a more protected environment than a large school and give them a lower teacher-to-student ratio. It's worth the money."

"Sounds like you are both on the right track," Mel said. "Amanda and Justin need lots of love and care. Monica and I would like to share one more important thing with you." He turned to Monica, and she nodded. "Honey, why don't you explain?"

"Well, we just want you both to know that, above all, we pray that Ned receives custody as their biological father," Monica said. "And Annalee, we can tell that you love children and want to do everything you can to help them as their new mother. We want to let you know that we've fallen in love with Amanda and Justin. But, just in case . . . if anything goes wrong with the custody hearing and you don't win the case, we would love to adopt both children or become their guardians. And, of course, you would be welcome to visit them anytime."

"That is so kind of you," Annalee said.

"Yes, thanks so much for caring," Ned said.

"It's comforting to know the children have a backup plan just in case," Annalee said. "We are both very grateful for everything you are doing." She paused. "We appreciate your hospitality, and we'll be in touch after the hearing tomorrow."

By this time the children were bounding back into the living room, begging the adults to follow them into the bedroom to show off their joint creation—a Lego castle creation complete with a mote, knights, and miniature horses.

After admiring their work, everyone exchanged hugs and Ned and Annalee bid the children goodbye. Both children asked when they would be back. They understood Ned and Annalee had flown on a plane, but they didn't comprehend the distance needed to make their visit. Ned and Annalee promised they would stay in touch by phone. The weekend had been such a beautiful experience. It gave them so much hope for the next day's hearing.

♥ ♥ ♥

The custody hearing began promptly at 9 AM. Both sides presented their respective arguments. Ned and Annalee's Oregon attorney, Steven Owen, was very professional, organized, and well-prepared for Ned's defense. His legal practice specialized in juvenile custody hearings with a specific expertise against false allegations. The strength of his presentation clearly negated Tina's allegations and proved them undeniably false. His knowledge of the pertinent case law was a huge strength.

All this was confirmed by the judge's final decision that day. Ned was exonerated of all allegations, and any threat or fear of prison was suddenly gone. Words could not describe Ned and Annalee's immense relief as they left the courtroom that day. They were so grateful for their attorney's skill and work; every dime paid him was now worth it. Annalee presented attorney Owen with another payment tucked in an elegant thank you card. Deep in heart, she remembered the prayer of Hannah in the Book of 1 Samuel.

When finished with their attorney, Ned and Annalee found a phone and started making calls to family and friends— Marie, Luke, Mercy, and Annalee's mother, Betsy. Everyone was thrilled. They were also able to reach Ned's aging parents at their assisted living home in the Midwest. They also were heartened by the news.

The last call was to Mel and Monica before leaving for the airport. "Oh, we are so thrilled for you both!" Monica said. "It looks like the two of you are destined to raise Amanda and Justin. When your next custody hearing is scheduled, we'll plan another visit. Keep us posted."

"We sure will," Annalee said. "We're so grateful for your friendship. Thanks for loving our children."

For this child [these children] I prayed, and the LORD
has granted me my petition which I asked of Him
(1 Samuel 1:27, NKJV). —Hannah's Prayer

Seventeen

AFTER RETURNING home Annalee and Ned were confident the children would be joining them—they just didn't know how long the process would take. Owen, the attorney advised them there would be at least one more custody hearing in the coming months. Annalee continued to work on letters and documents.

The reunification plan required proof of completion of their classes, incomes, and photos of their home and fully furnished bedrooms for each child. They were also required to send photos and certificate of title to prove ownership of a vehicle large enough to safely accommodate the family. They found a used Suburban in good condition, a baby car seat, and enough room for times when Luke, Marie, and Annalee's mother could all join them.

They had permission to stay in touch with Amanda and Justin by phone, so Annalee and Ned had conversations with them often. It was time to begin decorating their bedrooms. Annalee had to find out their favorite colors without giving away her secret. One evening she called to ask if the children could "use your imaginations" to tell her their favorite colors.

She tried to make a game of this to dodge their questions, and after a few minutes she had the answers she needed.

Amanda's favorite colors were pink and blue—"but mostly pink," she said.

Justin's answer wasn't at all surprising.

"Oh, I like bright colors. Bright red and white and bright blue!" he said with excitement.

"Ah, patriotic colors! Awesome. Just like your daddy. You remember he was a military man?"

"Yeah, I'm so proud of my daddy!" Justin said. Annalee smiled at the thought of the father-son relationship they would have and how Justin would admire his father as he grew up.

She and Ned worked together to find children's furniture and fresh coats of paint, and soon the rooms were good as new. Annalee began imagining the looks on their faces when they would walk into their newly decorated rooms. For Ned and Annalee, all this wasn't work but instead a great deal of fun.

Amanda's room was decorated with a beautiful four-poster bed with a lace canopy. Her furniture was pink and white with a matching dresser, vanity table, and seat. Annalee found a lovely pink lace comforter with touches of blue. Justin's room was done in primary colors: red, royal blue, and white.

Annalee found bargains at thrift stores to decorate their rooms, and Betsy sewed each of the children beautiful bed pillows to match. Annalee painted personalized letters spelling "Amanda" and "Justin" on each of their walls.

Ned was thrilled with her work and gave Annalee lots of praise. And hardly a day went by without Ned saying he loved her or thought she was beautiful. Annalee felt confident she had married the right man, one who knew how to love and raise a family. She envisioned she and the children presenting Ned with "Father of the Year" cards on Father's Day. She pictured grill-outs and the children laughing and running through sprinklers in the yard.

One day in May Ned cozied up behind Annalee while she was working at her desk and asked how their financial and bill situation looked.

"All is well," she said. "The house payment and other bills are paid, and both attorneys received their checks this month. There's enough to finish grocery shopping." She spoke of stocking up extra goods, and said, "Our cabinets, fridge, and freezer will be stocked before winter comes. If the children arrive before Christmas, we'll have plenty of baking goods and they can help make cookies, pies, and banana bread. I'm very excited by all of this!"

A deep look of love filled Ned's eyes. "I never dreamed my children would know a life like this. I love you so much. You're going to be a great mama to them. And thanks for managing our bills so carefully."

"Well, we couldn't do it without teamwork. You work just as hard as I do." Annalee smiled. "But you need to know something." She paused. "Something is coming up in the future that just might put a little crunch in our budget."

She had his attention. Annalee couldn't suppress a grin. "Well, you know how much I love my coffee in the mornings? For some strange reason, the smell makes me feel nauseous now."

She thought Ned was going to leap across the living room. He wasn't one to smile a lot, but in that moment he split a grin wide enough to drive his truck through.

"A baby? Really? Are you sure?"

"Well, my calendar is off too." Annalee laughed.

"Aww, honey!" He took her hands in his and gently twirled her in a pirouette around the living room. "When will our baby be due?"

"If my estimate is correct, little one will arrive between Christmas and New Year."

"What a celebration! Baby Bear!" Ned laughed. "How can we be blessed any more than we are at this moment? We can start calling ourselves the J-Team—for the Jacksons."

"The J-Team. I like that. With three little bears in the household!" Annalee giggled at the thought.

"Can I take you out for a little dinner celebration?"

"As long as it's a bargain place," she said with a laugh.

Ned reached in his pocket. "I've got a little cash on hand. We'll be OK. You deserve a treat, Little Mama."

"Before I formed you in the womb I knew you, before you were born I set you apart" (Jeremiah 1:5, NIV).

I praise you because I am fearfully and wonderfully made; your works are wonderful, I know that full well (Psalm 139:14, NIV).

Being confident of this very thing, that He who has begun a good work in you will complete it until the day of Jesus Christ (Philippians 1:6, NKJV).

Eighteen

THROUGHOUT THE spring, Ned and Annalee worked to finalize everything required by Oregon CPS. By the end of May, they had completed both the children's bedrooms, so they forwarded all the required photos and documentation to their social worker in Oregon. Annalee was feeling well and only experiencing minimal morning sickness. They received updates from Mel and Monica regarding the children's progress and kept in touch with Amanda and Justin by phone several times a week.

In June they received documentation from CPS Oregon advising them of another custody hearing on a Monday in two weeks. After contacting Owen's office in Oregon, Annalee once again arranged time off work and contacted the airline, which approved another generous flight discount. Ned and Annalee also contacted Mel and Monica to schedule a visit with the children the weekend before the hearing.

When they landed in Portland they took the same beautiful route through the Cascades into Pinebluff.

When they pulled in the driveway, Amanda and Justin came running from the house, jumping around the rental car and waiting for Ned and Annalee to step out.

"Good to see ya!" Justin hollered with excitement.

Even normally reserved Amanda had a huge smile on her face. "Mel and Monica said you guys were comin' to see us!"

"Did ya come on the big plane again?" Justin asked.

"We sure did!" Ned said.

"It's great to see you two!" Annalee said, reaching down to give warm hugs.

Ned and Annalee chuckled at being greeted with such cheerful enthusiasm. What a joy to realize that regardless of their life experiences, these small children had retained the ability to give and receive affection. They seemed amazingly intact. Ned knelt and gathered both the children as they ran into his arms. Tears of joy were flowing once again. Every time Ned was with the children, he didn't seem to skip a beat as a sincere, devoted father.

"Happy summer, you two!" Annalee said. "We love you both so much!"

The children practically knocked her over with their next round of enthusiastic hugs. Annalee wasn't showing yet, so she discreetly guarded her stomach as she returned their embraces. She felt so grateful that these precious little ones were already feeling comfortable with her!

Both children bounced from foot to foot watching their dad as he reached into the car's back seat to retrieve presents. The children had good memories. On the previous trip, Ned and Annalee had come with presents for all four of the children—Amanda and Justin as well as Mel and Monica's little boy and girl.

Since it was summer, this time they brought toys for the family swimming pool. The children's eyes lit up as they saw beach balls, inner tubes, and colorful pool rafts being lifted from the backseat. Ned and Annalee had even stopped at a gas station on the way to air up all the pool toys.

It was an exciting reunion inside the house.

"Mel and Monica, can we go swimming with our new pool toys?" Justin asked.

"Pleeeeeeze?" squealed all the children in unison.

The kids dashed into their rooms to put on new swimsuits. The foster parents explained that they had enrolled Amanda and Justin in swimming classes for the summer to keep them safe in the pool. The children were excited to show off their new swimming abilities.

Monica brought out sweet tea and lemonade, and they ordered pizza. The adults enjoyed watching the children swim and play with their new toys. Ned and Annalee were impressed at the emotional progress the children had made in just the four months since their last visit. The security of a family atmosphere was doing them a great deal of good. Their weight was becoming stable for their height and ages. No matter how long the custody process might take, it was a relief to know the children were in good hands in a loving home.

As they watched on the nearby patio, Mel and Monica updated Ned and Annalee on the children's progress through the end of the school year. The school IEP program had been a positive experience for both; their reports were encouraging. Amanda's daydreaming was having less of an impact on her concentration. Justin was still vying to be the center of attention, but his teachers were doing their best to keep him safe and divert his attention with alternative learning methods. The children's therapists had been unable to determine exactly what they had been exposed to, but their behavior during play therapy sessions and some of the answers they gave revealed they had been exposed to child endangerment and probable defilement. It had been determined that their biological mother would probably never be able to regain parental rights due to criminal charges and her unwillingness to complete a rehabilitation program. Sadly, she and her boyfriend had been arrested on felony charges for sales, possession, and distribution of illegal controlled substances.

Ned and Annalee enjoyed the day greatly, hugged their wet young ones wrapped in towels, and headed to the hotel for a night's rest.

All evening at the hotel, Ned couldn't stop talking about his plans and dreams as he looked forward to their life together as a family. He continued to express his deep love for Amanda and Justin. Annalee felt as though she had been placed on a rescue mission for these two beautiful children. She sincerely believed she had been "assigned" by God to ensure Amanda and Justin had a new beginning, one filled with a sense of purpose and destiny and surrounded by unconditional love. Annalee often thought about the Book of Esther, believing she was on assignment for the children "for such a time as this."[13]

The following day the two families enjoyed Sunday afternoon together. Annalee shared the good news that Amanda and Justin would have a baby brother or sister come winter. All agreed this was best kept a secret until after the children were reunited with Ned and Annalee permanently. Mel and Monica were so happy for them—this was to be one more blessing for the completion of their family.

The next morning they met with attorney Owen just before the custody hearing. Due to the circumstances involving the biological mother, he believed Ned would soon be appointed custodial parent. He was confident the case was drawing near its close. He again argued compellingly for Ned in court.

Annalee had provided supporting documents and photos to both the Oregon and Montana attorneys proving she and Ned had met all the requirements of Ned's reunification plan. Owen presented documents and photos as exhibits to the judge proving that the family had a sizeable home, proof of income, the children's bedrooms completed, the family Suburban purchased, as well as Annalee's certifications proving her foster care experience. In addition, Mel and Monica submitted positive reviews on behalf of Ned and Annalee's visits with the children. Mr. Owen presented the court with a Show-Cause Order in support of Ned becoming Amanda and Justin's permanent custodial parent.

The social workers had more supporting reports. The biological mother had been offered a rehabilitation program fully funded by the state; however, she had left the program without permission during its first week. She had invalidated her parental reunification plan and was sent back into custody. The judge carefully reviewed the facts from both sides, indicated he would take everything into consideration, and told all parties they would be notified of the court's determination soon. Court was dismissed.

Afterward, Owen told Ned and Annalee that he was confident the outcome would be found in their favor and said he would contact them as soon as he received the Show-Cause Order and the state's custodial release of the children.

Greatly relieved, Ned and Annalee called Mel and Monica and their family before heading to the airport.

But thus says the LORD: "Even the captives of the mighty shall be taken away, And the prey of the terrible be delivered; For I will contend with him who contends with you, And I will save your children" (Isaiah 49:25, NKJV).

casting down arguments and every high thing that exalts itself against the knowledge of God, bringing every thought into captivity to the obedience of Christ, and being ready to punish all disobedience when your obedience is fulfilled (2 Corinthians 10:5, 6, NKJV).

Nineteen

WHEN THE Fourth of July arrived, Ned took Annalee to dinner to celebrate their first anniversary. They reminisced on their first year of marriage, recalling how much had been accomplished in just one year. Two innocent children whose whereabouts were unknown had been located, amazingly, after which a major battle was undertaken on their behalf. After a grueling and labor-intensive legal battle, they were now on the verge of victory. Annalee frequently prayed for Amanda and Justin's restoration and healing from the memories of the perilous lifestyle from which they had been rescued. The long but worthwhile legal journey prompted Annalee to ponder the vulnerability of children in general and the origin of her own birth and early childhood in particular.

Meanwhile, she was almost four months along, and this pregnancy seemed much more stable than the one before. It appeared this baby was coming along just fine. Her doctors were keeping a close eye on her because of her age and the recent miscarriage, but thus far she was doing well and under excellent care.

As Annalee began to draw near the four-month time frame during which she previously miscarried, she would at times think back to the unwelcome visitor—"Worthlessness"—that she had tried to forget. Those emotions were sparked by the letter from the relative and the mental battle she had endured since childhood. There were times Annalee's aging mother Betsy would vent as she shared remembrances of intense family abuse she experienced for giving birth to Annalee out of wedlock years before. Betsy's long-term memory was strong, intact, and carried decades of remembrances. After venting, Betsy would often reach for Annalee's hand and reassure her she was thankful her daughter had been born. Annalee attributed those vulnerable moments to her mother Betsy's fragile state of mind and age.

Annalee thought of the time angelic forces had intervened on her behalf when Ned prayed for her. She knew they were real and powerful! When she felt vulnerable, she confided in Ned. He would say that they needed to set aside time so he could understand her ancestry. They had been so busy that it had been postponed, he said, for too long.

One hot weekend in late July, Ned and Luke worked for hours chopping and stacking cordwood to prepare for winter. Montana summers are short, but long daylight hours prevail for outdoor work in what is often referred to as The Last Frontier of the Lower 48. Due to its far north proximity, the midsummer sun doesn't set until about 10:30 PM.

Ned had stepped in from working outdoors. After a shower, he entered the dining room. Annalee had spent most of the day cleaning house and had supper ready. After they finished eating, Ned took her hand. "Remember all those heart-to-heart talks we had when we were engaged?" he asked.

Annalee smiled. "How could I forget? We could talk for hours on end and never run out of conversation."

"We've both been through a lot in life," Ned said. "We understand each other's hearts. No wonder we fell in love."

Annalee nodded, remembering those marathon talks during their courtship. It always seemed as if they were making up for lost time. After they had a seat on the living room sofa, Ned drew a much more serious tone. "Honey, you've spent the last year helping me with my family. Tonight, would you like to tell me more about your childhood? Remember you told me there were some important things about your mama and your birth? It had to do with that evil visit you had back in February."

"This would be a good time," Annalee answered quietly. "I'm so close to the four-month mark that it's a reminder of that awful visit condemning me and saying that I couldn't even be a good mother. Ned, I want to be a good mother to Amanda and Justin and to our new baby."

"I already know you're gonna do fine, hon," Ned said.

Annalee got quiet for just a moment before going on. "The scars of my heart are invisible. The last thing I ever wanted was to disappoint or hurt others, but I feel as if I've failed to live up to my own expectations. Remember that childhood vow at age nine? It was to never hurt anyone my entire life—and it was impossible to live up to. The world we live in is fragile, and broken hearts need to be understood. People need to be valued for who they are. My mission is caring for others. On one hand, it is rewarding. But on the other, have I taken it too far? Maybe I'm still trying to live up to that vow.

"I want to live my life for the right reasons." Annalee paused. "And sometimes it feels that I've become a rescuer for the wrong reasons. Does that make sense?"

"I'm trying to understand," Ned said.

"For example, foster parenting is a noble cause, and I'm grateful for people like Mel and Monica and the work they are doing for Amanda and Justin. They're doing it for all the right reasons. I sincerely want to parent Amanda and Justin from a position of strength—not weakness."

Annalee took a deep breath. "In the past, I didn't realize the brokenness from childhood which led to devastating relationships. In order to feel validated, I felt compelled to rescue. I love children and teenagers, and I've helped care for many of them, but life's callings should be lived for the right reasons according to why we were created."

"Honey, you are doing everything for all the right reasons—out of your love for them," Ned said. "You don't need to question your motives. I promise you: we have a beautiful life ahead of us."

Now it was Ned's turn to pause. "But there is more on your mind, isn't there?"

"Well, yes. In the process of trying to survive life on the home front and rescuing children, I failed to comprehend the emotional pain experienced by Mama Betsy in her earlier life, especially her sacrifices for me. That was the last thing I would ever want to do! She and I both suffered brokenness, but in different ways."

"So you didn't realize this was happening?" Ned asked.

"Not at the time. I didn't realize till much later how greatly she needed empathy for her own suffering."

"So it started when you were young?"

"Yes, in the beginning. I married my first love in my senior year of high school. There were things I couldn't face: first as a child, then as a teenager—personal battles. Marriage seemed like a way to escape those battles—but it wasn't. He was unable to show love and protect a wife, and I was too young to under-stand how to respond to domestic violence. Neither one of us were raised with an understanding of faith, so we had no point of reference to know how to receive healing and restoration."

"I understand. Honey, when did this feeling of unworthi-ness begin? And can you tell me more about your mom? She seems to have a lot of pain beneath that strong will of hers."

"She does," Annalee said. "She has really opened up in her senior years. Her pain began in childhood, continued in teen and young adult years, and escalated after I was born. It con-tinued from there. I must have internalized it; from my earli-est memories, I never felt worthy." Annalee stopped to think more deeply.

"Recent research has shown that infants absorb their en-vironment, even before birth," she said. "So that feeling prob-ably originated in utero, absorbing the rhythm of my young mother's broken heart. She had a great deal of naiveté after a one-time romantic encounter with a long-term friend left her abandoned."

"So your biological dad left your mom in the lurch?"

"Yes, he did. Mama was terrified and afraid to tell anyone. In those days, not many babies were born out of wedlock. Mama doesn't like to talk about him, so I don't know very much."

"And she was living with your grandma, right?"

"Yes, she was helping support Grandma and her three younger siblings. Mama was a very gifted artist from child-hood, but after me, she couldn't complete her lifelong dream of graduating as a fashion designer from the art academy. After Mama got older and told me about it, I felt so badly for her. But she says she is thankful for the help and heart-to-heart talks in her old age—even glad she didn't end up being a Hollywood designer."

"She has done so much beautiful artwork in her life," Ned said.

"Yes she has. Her art has touched many lives."

"So no one explained anything to her about the pregnancy?"

"From what she told me, she kept me a secret as long as she could. You see, back in 1950s America matters like this were not openly discussed—at least not in Mama's family. She didn't know she was carrying a child until she felt me moving within her. Imagine: she wasn't clear how it happened! Then she was terrified.

"This is how naive she was: two years earlier, at age 22, she rode several buses to work and the art academy. She and another young lady, a coworker, had a chance to share the rent on a two-bedroom apartment near their work and the academy. So Mama went home and talked to Grandma, who responded, 'I know why you want your own apartment—so you can entertain men!' Mama answered, 'But how could I do that? I don't even know how to sing and dance!' That's because Mama thought 'entertaining men' was like those dance musicals from the fifties. Isn't that a hoot? Mama doubled over laughing when she told me about it recently. We both cracked up. I'm serious! That's how innocent she was. It was a different world back then."

"Oh my goodness!" Ned laughed. "A different world for sure. So your mom was almost 24 when you were born and still living at home with your grandma, right?"

"That's right. She sure didn't get that apartment!" Annalee laughed.

"So what happened with you? She didn't tell anyone?"

"Only my biological father . . . after she figured out he was the reason. And when Mama told him, he said he wanted nothing to do with a baby and disappeared."

"Oh wow." Ned got quiet. "She must have felt so alone."

"Exactly. She was left vulnerable and unprepared, and back then there were no crisis pregnancy centers like there are now to help young mothers. Mama had weight issues, so she wore loose clothing, but that could not prevent the inevitable day she went into labor and the secret was revealed."

Ned paused, then turned to a new idea.

"So what do you think happened in your mind as a growing baby?" he asked.

"Well, I think the shocking realization of my mother's confusion and loneliness grew side by side along with me, and alongside her fear of the unknown. She had no idea what to expect. Perhaps I absorbed the intensity of the ensuing months of isolation as Mama attempted to conceal the baby growing inside her."

"What happened after you were born?" Ned asked quietly.

"Mama said there were *long* family meetings reminding my young mother of her 'unforgivable transgression.' She said things intensified with screams hurled at Mama for bringing home an unwanted child outside the bonds of marriage. As an infant, I'm sure I absorbed some of Mama's guilt as a constant reminder that the family's good name had been ruined. You see, I was a little person caught in the midst of what they called Mama's 'mistake'—after I was born, she became the black sheep of the family. Mama was an innocent young lady who really didn't understand the facts of life. She said my conception was a one-time encounter."

"And then the accusations kept coming?" Ned asked.

"Apparently, yes. From what I understand, the extended family looked down on her."

"Wasn't there some kind of an accident with you when you were little—that scar on your forehead?"

"Actually, that wasn't an accident," Annalee said. "According to Mama, that happened at age two with the thud of hitting the bottom of a long staircase after being shoved down the stairs by an aunt who left the family decades ago. I guess she thought she was doing everyone a favor by trying to get rid of the family mistake."

"Oh no." Ned just shook his head.

"Thank God my angels really worked overtime that day," Annalee said with a small laugh. "I forgave that lady long ago. She's probably no longer in this world, so I sure hope she asked the Lord for forgiveness afterward. Not for my sake, but for hers."

"I still don't get it," Ned said. "What happened to your mom was not the unpardonable sin!"

"You're right, but I was born in a different era of America. In the 1950s, a young woman in a 'family way' was usually shipped off to a distant relative for a year, and the baby was adopted out. After returning home, a 'lengthy visit' or an 'educational journey' served as a decent-sounding excuse for her long absence. If no suspicion was aroused, people were none the wiser. These explanations sufficed to preserve the family name."

"Seems like your mom suffered so much judgment," Ned said.

"Yes. Mama went through a lot. In fact, the doctor who delivered me offered to adopt me. But Mama was determined not to give me up no matter what, bless her heart!"

"She was a brave woman in her time," Ned said quietly.

"Yes she was. She sacrificed a lot for me," Annalee said. "Only in her elderly years have I come to fully understand how much she went through. I want to do everything I can to take care of her."

"I agree," Ned said. "We need to do our best to help her. Now it makes more sense spiritually why you've faced this lifelong battle. Honey, I want you to know you have nothing to fear." His voice spoke with the spiritual authority and sincerity of a man in love.

Annalee had no reason to doubt his word.

"Talking through this has been a big help," she said. "Thank you for caring, hon." She felt a sense of serenity, and security, to have a man at her side determined to stand up for her. She was thankful he cared enough to dig deeper into her life history.

"From infancy on, there were those around me who never planned for me to inhabit this world, much less have a voice in it," Annalee said. "That was the meaning of that letter."

"Now I understand how 'Worthlessness' gained an early foothold in your life," Ned said.

The godly may trip seven times, but they will get up again. But one disaster is enough to overthrow the wicked (Proverbs 24:16, NLT).

Twenty

ON A DAY IN early September, Ned and Annalee were sitting in their sun porch looking at the pine trees while enjoying lemonade. The sun was shining brightly, and the reflection of the porch glass caught Ned's left hand. Annalee had noticed this before, but never mentioned it.

"Hon, how did you get that scar on your left hand?" she asked.

"Haven't I ever told you about that?"

"I guess not. But I did notice it in our wedding pictures. After they were developed, it showed up on that photo of our left hands wearing our wedding rings."

"Yeah, the sun really reflected that scar," Ned said, glancing again at the scar. "Are you sure you want to know?"

"Well, when you put it that way, I probably should," Annalee said with a small smile.

"To be honest, that happened when I was four years old trying to defend my mom," Ned began. "Dad tried to shoot her one day out on the farm, so I ran and stood in front of her. Dad was so drunk he missed the shot. So he smashed a beer bottle and threw it at her. When I held up my hand to keep it from hitting my mom, the broken glass slit my hand open. Dad was so furious at me for standing in Mom's way that he told me I was no longer his son. He never stopped beating me, so I finally left home at 13 and stayed with friends while I finished high school and went into the military." Ned's voice was stressed, and his face darkened.

Annalee nodded compassionately, realizing how horrendous Ned's childhood must have been.

She took his hand and kissed the scar. "It's amazing you had the courage to stand up to him as a four-year-old, Ned. You know, your dad wasn't a well man, and it sounds like your mama was too terrified to do anything about it. People say terrible things under the influence of alcohol."

"That's true," he said. "I got some terrible beatings as a kid, and I later found out that my dad was treated the same way by his dad the generation before. Dad was never in his right mind after a missile grazed his head onboard a ship in World War II. He brought the war zone home to Mom and I."

"Generational bondages, right?"

"That's right. When Dad drank, Mom and I were the scapegoats."

"Has he expressed being proud of you now as an adult? I'm sure he has done a lot of thinking now that he's elderly and he and your mom are in their final retirement years."

Ned nodded. "One day after I grew up, my dad and I had a serious talk, and he told me he thought I had grown up to be a man who truly understood him. He was thankful I still visited him no matter what happened."

"That must have meant so much to you. Were you able to forgive him for your childhood?"

"I finally did. It was easier after I became a believer."

"I'm so thankful to hear that. It must have brought you a lot of healing."

"Yes. It did. Thanks for encouraging me. I don't have to stay in that painful place."

"You're right. You don't, and now you have a new opportunity to leave the past behind and build a brand-new future with your own family. You have so much love in your heart for your children. You don't have to repeat the mistakes of the past."

"You have no idea how much that means to me," Ned said as he reached for her hand.

An angry person starts fights; a hot-tempered person commits all kinds of sin (Proverbs 29:22, NLT).

Twenty-One

SUMMER PASSED quickly in Montana as Ned and Annalee continued working and paying the attorneys. Periodically they received notifications from Oregon with reports from the social worker as well as updated treatment summaries from the therapists working with the children.

They stayed in regular contact with Amanda and Justin and received progress reports from Mel and Monica. In August Amanda and Justin returned to school in Oregon with a new IEP designed for each of them. Ned and Annalee were encouraged to hear how well the children had done during the summer.

In early September Ned and Annalee received a phone call from Mr. Morris, their Montana attorney, with good news. He explained that he had a conference call with Mr. Owen, their Oregon attorney, and it appeared Oregon was getting ready to release custody of the children from the state. Mr. Morris suggested Ned and Annalee remain on standby in case they needed to fly to Oregon for one final hearing.

About a week later, the same attorney sent them a letter stating that, based on the judge's final decision, Oregon was preparing to officially relinquish custody of both children to Ned and Annalee. He followed up with CPS Oregon as well as the attorney in Oregon and discovered that the state of Oregon was even planning to pay for the return flights of Ned, Amanda, and Justin from Portland to Montana in early October.

Ned and Annalee were thrilled with the news. They called Mel and Monica to see if they had received the same information and found out they had. Mel and Monica congratulated Ned and Annalee on their upcoming permanent family reunion in Montana. All four adults agreed it would be best to hold the news and then surprise the children on the day of departure. Annalee placed a call to the airlines to request a discounted one-way ticket for Ned to Portland. As they prepared for the children's arrival, Ned and Annalee visited Glacier Vista Christian School in Glacier Vista, Montana[14] to enroll the children for the coming year. They brought a copy of the children's previous school records from Oregon and met with a special education teacher to set up individualized programs.

It wasn't long until they received the official Show-Cause Order, signed by the Oregon judge, granting permanent parental custody to Ned effective Thursday, October 2. Ned flew out on Wednesday, October 1 with documents in hand. He also brought along a special thank you card for Mel and Monica for everything they had done for the children in the previous ten months. Ned called Annalee from their Oregon home to say Mel and Monica were hosting a farewell party for the children. Mel and Monica had bought them new luggage, so they were bringing their new school clothes as well as their wardrobes purchased in previous months. It was quite a farewell party, with tears of goodbye from the foster parents and foster siblings who had grown to love Amanda and Justin. Everyone promised to stay in touch.

♥ ♥ ♥

Their flight to Montana was scheduled for Friday morning, October 3. The children had never flown on a plane before, so this was an exciting adventure with their dad. Ned had lots of stories to tell them on the plane. They had never seen the magnificent mountains of Montana from the air. It had been so long in their young lives that they didn't remember details of the majestic creatures native to the area such as moose, mountain lions, or grizzly bears. Ned told them stories of how the bears love to pick huckleberries from the bushes and pluck fish from the rivers. The children were amazed and talked about these things for several days. They promised to go huckleberry picking the following summer and make huckleberry jam and huckleberry ice cream.

Annalee, Betsy, and Mercy all worked together to make homemade lasagna, garlic bread, tossed salad, and a chocolate cake. Luke and Marie decorated the house with balloons and streamers and a large welcome home banner hanging across the dining room. There were balloons attached to the pine trees in the yard, and pink, blue, red, and royal blue streamers attached to the front door.

Luke and Marie had saved a paycheck and bought brand-new bicycles for Amanda and Justin. The bicycles were waiting on the back porch for a surprise after supper.

It was truly a red-letter day!

The Suburban had been parked in the local airport, so Ned was able to bring the children home while Annalee and the family finished preparing the house and meal. Late that afternoon, the Suburban pulled into the driveway. Ned made his way to the house with the children gathered in his arms and Annalee met them at the door. There were tears of joy all around.

Amanda and Justin were home.

The entire family was gathered and shouted "Welcome home!" as the children pranced into the house to hugs and greetings. They first ran up to Annalee, who was now six months along. They were accustomed to seeing her slender, so they looked a little surprised. (Ned and Annalee had planned to have a short meeting with them after supper to tell them about their new little brother, who would be arriving in three months or less.) As Annalee made introductions, the children hopped from Grandma Betsy to Aunt Mercy, then wrapped their arms around Luke and Marie, who welcomed their new little brother and sister. The children were so excited they didn't know what to do first.

As Ned brought in their luggage, Annalee gave them a grand tour of the house. Last, each was taken to their lovely new rooms. The children were absolutely stunned. Justin, of course, ran to his bed and executed a huge bounce to indoctrinate his new sleeping place. Amanda looked around at her white lace canopy bed, something she had never experienced before. She was overwhelmed at having a little girl's bedroom all her own.

They gathered in the dining room and said a prayer of thanks over a hard-won victory. Then they enjoyed their first supper at home together followed by the special cake for dessert. The children chattered about their experience on the plane and the excitement of looking down on the clouds. They talked about seeing the mountains from the air and how beautiful they were.

Afterward, Luke and Marie showed them their new bicycles on the back patio—a pink one for Amanda and bright red for Justin. The children were overwhelmed with excitement. They wanted to ride the bikes immediately. Ned and Annalee let them have a short amount of time with the bicycles riding around the property, and then the bikes were brought into the garage for the night.

It was an evening to remember like no other. It was a family reunion that Ned thought he would never experience. He found himself vacillating between tears of joy and laughter.

After the children came in for the night, Ned and Annalee called them to the sofa and said they needed to have a short talk. They were noticing Annalee's big tummy, but they didn't seem to realize what it meant. Annalee put her arms around the children and said, "How would you like to have a baby brother?"

The children began jumping up and down and laughing with joy. "A baby brother? That will be so cool!"

"Well, right after Christmas, we will be bringing home your brand-new baby brother. He is growing here right now," Annalee said as she patted her stomach. Little Amanda reached over and gently rubbed the area. "Baby brother is in there?"

"Yes, he sure is! And he can hardly wait to come out and meet you two!" Annalee chuckled.

Both the children were delighted. They asked lots of questions about the baby's name, if he could sleep with them, what he would eat, and many other funny questions that small children ask. The conversation was loads of fun for all of them.

Amanda said, "We have to be real careful about your tummy, don't we, Annalee? Cuz baby brother is in there, right?

That's why you're so fat?" Amanda's little face suddenly turned red and looked a bit embarrassed. "Oops, I didn't mean—"

Annalee burst into laughter and wrapped her in a hug.

"It's OK, honey. Yes, my tummy is kind of fat right now, isn't it?" She giggled. "You're right. We have to be very careful with babies in the tummy, and after they're born, because they are very little and need lots of care. But both of you are going to be a wonderful big sister and big brother."

The night ended with more questions and excitement about the new family member on the way. Ned reached for his guitar and strummed some simple songs as the family sang along.

Before the children knew it, it was time to spend the first night in their brand-new rooms. Ned and Annalee tucked them into bed, said their prayers, and thanked the Lord for these precious children who had now become their own.

Children are a gift from the LORD;
they are a reward from him (Psalm 127:3, NLT).

The LORD is my shepherd; I shall not want. He makes me
to lie down in green pastures; He leads me beside the still
waters. He restores my soul; He leads me in the paths of
righteousness For His name's sake (Psalm 23:1-3, NKJV).

"He will feed His flock like a shepherd; He will gather the
lambs with His arm, And carry them in His bosom, and
gently lead those who are with young"
(Isaiah 40:11, NKJV).

Twenty-Two

THE FOLLOWING morning the children slept in. Ned headed to the kitchen to fire up the pancake skillet. When the children got up, they were busy exploring the house. As Annalee stepped from the bedroom, the children came racing down the hall to give her hugs.

"Good morning, Annalee!" Amanda squealed.

"And good morning, baby brother!" Justin giggled.

"Yeah, that's right," Amanda said. "We can't forget baby brother."

Both took their little hands and gently placed them on Annalee's stomach.

"Good morning, you two!" Annalee said. "Would you like to sit down with me on the sofa?"

Justin was excited to do so, and he quickly shared the news of his dad in the kitchen making pancakes.

"That's his favorite breakfast to make on weekends," Annalee said. "You like pancakes?"

"Yeah, we love 'em!" Amanda said. "Do you have blueberry syrup?"

"No, but we might have huckleberry syrup from last summer. Huckleberries grow wild around here."

"Yum!" both children seemed to squeal at the same time.

The three made their way down the hall and into the kitchen. Ned and Annalee exchanged a hug, and he wrapped an arm around her as he flipped a pancake.

Annalee poured her coffee and sat on the sofa, the children on either side of her. Suddenly, she felt the kicking of little feet. "Would you two like to feel your baby brother kicking?" she asked.

"Yes! Yes!" they said excitedly.

"OK, here's how we do it. We have to be real gentle." First, she took Amanda's hand and placed it on one side, then Justin's hand and placed it on the other.

"Now, be real patient and keep your hand in that spot very gentle. Then baby brother will feel it, and he will move his little foot or his little hand right under yours. It will feel like a thump underneath your hand."

Patience paid off. In a few minutes, there were a few thumps, and the children were ecstatic. "He's moving! He's trying to play with us!" Amanda said, a huge smile on her face.

"He likes us!" Justin said as he began bouncing on the sofa.

"He sure does, and he knows you're his brother and sister, but we have to be careful around my tummy, honey," Annalee said. "We need to be careful not to bounce him around, because baby brother is in a big water bubble."

Justin's eyes grew as wide as saucers. "He's in a water bubble? Ya mean like a water balloon?"

"Sort of like that." Annalee laughed.

"Ya mean he's growing inside the water?" Amanda asked. "How does he breathe in there?" she said, her inquisitive little mind trying to figure this out.

"It's a special way that God makes babies grow inside a mama's tummy. The bubble keeps baby safe and warm. Somehow, God makes it so brother can breathe in there until he is ready to be born."

"Wow!" Justin said.

"Is that how we grew when we were little babies—inside a water bubble?" Amanda asked.

"Yes, honey, that is the same way God made you and Justin too," Annalee said.

"Well, it's a cool thing that you're gonna give us a new baby brother!" Justin said.

Amanda suddenly looked deep in thought.

"Annalee, is it OK if we call you mama?" she asked.

"Yes, I wanna do that too," Justin said. "Cuz you're our new mama, and you're mama to our baby brother too."

Annalee and Ned had both agreed that it would be up to the children how they wanted to address her. Their surprising question made her heart leap for joy.

Annalee was amazed and thrilled they had asked her this so quickly. "Yes, of course. I would love for you to call me mama," she said while trying to hide tears forming in her eyes. "And I'm going to call you my daughter Amanda and my son Justin. You two are my children forever!"

She turned and saw Ned's smiling face from the kitchen. It was a special moment for all of them.

After breakfast, Annalee accompanied Amanda into her bedroom and helped her unpack. She had bought Amanda new hangers, so they hung up many of her clothes and placed the rest in her dresser.

"Amanda, did you learn how to make your own bed at Mel and Monica's?"

"Oh yes," Amanda said. "Monica showed us how to make our beds, and we did it every day. You wanna see how I can make my bed?"

"Yes, that would be great!" Annalee said.

Amanda made her bed while she talked about how much she loved its canopy look, and that she had never seen anything like it. She was a very grateful little girl. Of course, Amanda left plenty of wrinkles under the comforter, but Annalee showed her how to straighten them. Annalee then showed her how to put her dirty clothes in her hamper for laundry day. She asked Amanda to get dressed for the day and headed to Justin's room to help him.

She found Justin having a great time using his bed as a trampoline bouncing between the mattress and window curtains. She chuckled at the look on his face when he realized he'd been spotted! He stopped immediately and had a sheepish look on his little face.

"Now Justin, we don't behave that way, do we?" Annalee asked.

"No, Mama. I promise I won't do that again," Justin said with as much sincerity as a six-year-old can muster.

"OK. We want to take good care of our nice new bedroom, don't we?"

Justin hung his head. "Yes, ma'am." Annalee then gave him a hug and snuggled him into her arms.

Annalee similarly spent time helping Justin unload his luggage, organize his clothing, and put his suitcases in his closet. He said Monica had taught him how to make his bed, so Annalee waited to see how it would turn out. He tried his best, but Annalee knew that learning this task would take time and patience; he was only six, she reminded herself. She also showed him how to use his hamper for dirty laundry. He proudly showed her that he had put his dirty blue jeans in his hamper the night before when he changed into his pajamas. Annalee finished her time with him, giving him more love and a few more instructions for the day.

The children wanted to see what their dad was doing outdoors and ride their bikes around the property. Ned and Annalee spent some time reminding them about the wildlife that lived in Glacier Park. Although it was miles away, there was still an occasional bear or moose that "doesn't read 'no trespassing' signs very well," Ned said with a smile. The children smiled as though they mostly understood the joke. Sightings were rare, Ned said, but he warned them that if they saw wildlife in the distance, they should head into the house immediately. Wildlife came with the territory here, he said. All Montana parents tried to be diligent about warning their children.

Ned and Annalee greatly enjoyed this Saturday while developing a new routine of a busier schedule with the children.

Sunday morning, the family had breakfast and left for church. Luke and Marie took Grandma Betsy. Annalee introduced the children to the Sunday school teachers and a few of the other children. They seemed to enjoy their time in Sunday school. They came home with some Bible verses and drawings they had made of harvest vegetables, squash, and pumpkins. Those were their first creations to be hung on the refrigerator.

Sunday flew by. Before they knew it, it was Monday morning, time to get ready for their new school. The fall season here was quite a bit colder than Oregon. The Montana autumn chill was already in the air, so Annalee helped them with their fall clothing and lightweight coats.

Ned headed to work in his truck and Annalee drove the children in the Suburban. When they arrived at Glacier Vista Christian School they were introduced to their teachers. Amanda's teacher was Mr. Michael Austin, and Justin's teacher Mrs. Kiara Adams. It was a small school, one in which it was easy to make new friends. Annalee had filled out a permission slip for Mercy, Luke, or Marie to pick up the children whenever necessary.

After handling the children's transition at school, Annalee headed to work. She was still working full time to pay off both attorneys, and her entire salary had been dedicated to paying the attorneys for almost a year. The good news was their balances were nearly paid in full.

Mercy had offered to pick up the children from school and take care of them until Annalee got home from work. Annalee worked about fifteen minutes from home. It seemed everything in this day was going smoothly—until Annalee pulled into Mercy's driveway. Mercy stepped onto the front porch.

"I need to speak to you privately before you take the children home," Mercy said. They stayed on the porch while the children watched TV inside. "When I picked up the children from school, Justin's teacher, Mrs. Adams, asked to have a word with me. She said she had a hard time managing Justin today. She said he's a very happy, friendly child, but he wants to be the center of attention, the class clown. Apparently his behavior caused several disruptions in class today. Finally she had to have the school principal take him to the office to have a talk with him."

"Uh-oh," Annalee said. "His foster parents in Oregon said there were similar behaviors at his school there. I just didn't think it would begin here so quickly."

"Well dear, Mrs. Adams understands the children have been through trauma," Mercy said. "She is willing to work with Justin. She just wants you to be aware of what happened. She thinks the principal made an impression on Justin today, and she's hoping it will help set things straight for class tomorrow."

"Well, thank you so much for helping me with the children and letting me know. I'll have a talk with Justin at home. By the way, did he behave OK for you?"

"Yes, he did just fine. Very happy, although he's extremely active, I must say," Mercy said with a laugh.

"That's consistent with what Mel and Monica told us in Oregon as well. They said at home and at school they always had to keep a close eye on him to make sure he's safe and out of harm's way."

"Sounds like you have your hands full, girlfriend," Mercy chuckled.

"No joke," Annalee said with a smile. "But I've been through this rodeo before with foster care. The difference is these little ones are now my own. I'm dedicated to them for life, but I want to make it legal with a stepparent adoption."

"Well, if anyone can do this, you can," Mercy said, giving her friend a hug.

You will keep him in perfect peace, Whose mind is stayed on You, Because he trusts in You (Isaiah 26:3, NKJV).

Twenty-Three

AFTER ARRIVING home Annalee called Mrs. Adams and asked her to explain what happened in class. The teacher was very sympathetic. She said Justin was a friendly and loving child. He had greeted her that morning with a hug and an apple for her desk. (He must have grabbed it from the fruit bowl in the kitchen.) Unfortunately, he also acted out with passive resistance—difficulty with obedience, focusing, and staying on task. During class time, he sprang from his seat several times and frolicked around the room, diverting the attention of other children, Adams said. The other first-graders began giggling and cheering him on, and this just encouraged him. After she returned him to his seat, Adams told Annalee, he repeatedly interrupted her lessons with verbal outbursts of childish jokes, opinions, and unnatural laughter. By afternoon the class was behind schedule because of the multiple disruptions, she said, so she had no choice but to take Justin to Michael Cormack, the school principal.

Annalee was familiar with many of these behaviors. Mrs. Adams and Annalee agreed that Justin may be working to cover up negative memories with childish comedy, demanding center stage to create a facade of self-importance. Adams expressed her desire to do everything possible to help Justin adjust to his new life. She recommended a parent-teacher conference as soon as possible to develop a revised individualized program similar to the Oregon IEP. Annalee apologized once more, and the two scheduled a time later in the week for the conference.

Amanda only had one simple page of homework, so she headed to her bedroom desk. Annalee used that time to sit down with Justin for a private talk. How to explain focus to a six-year-old first-grader with a history of trauma? Annalee drew on everything in her arsenal regarding communication with young children. She first reassured Justin that he was loved and not in trouble. He was shifting in his seat looking distractedly around the room, so Annalee called on a technique she had learned years before. She took both her index fingers and pointed them from her eyes to his.

"Are you looking at me now?" she said.

"Oh yes, Mama. I see you!" Justin chuckled.

"Good!" Then Annalee cupped her ears, smiling. "Your ears are your 'catchers.' Got your 'catchers' on?"

"I got my catchers on!" Justin laughed hugely. He was enjoying the game.

"Good! We're going to talk about something super important."

"OK, Mama. I got my catchers on." He cupped his hands around his ears. Truly, Annalee thought to herself, he looked adorable.

She knew he had been deprived of motherly love and proper attention, so she tried to explain things with as much love as she could. She began with explaining the difference between right and wrong kinds of attention. Whenever Justin got sidetracked, as he invariably would, she would repeat, "We need to put our catchers back on," and cupped her ears, then pointed to his eyes again. Justin would refocus. It was labor-intensive, but that became their signal to focus from then on.

Step by step, Annalee carefully taught that disrupting class was the *wrong* kind of attention, and that laughing and kindness with friends during free time was the *right* kind of attention. She tried to explain right timing versus wrong timing— work time versus play time. Then she explained the right kind of attention in class so Justin could learn, and the wrong kind of attention, such as interrupting Mrs. Adams.

Justin looked up at her innocently with his beautiful blue eyes. He nodded his head, saying, "Yes, Mama. I want to do good." Annalee didn't know how much he had actually retained from their talk, but she believed he was sincere.

After a few minutes, Annalee decided this was as much as Justin could handle for now. Since he had no homework, she held him close and told him she loved him, then released him to go play while she started supper.

After Ned got home, she briefly explained what happened and told him of their scheduled parent-teacher conference later in the week.

"What? His *first* day of school?" Ned said, looking stressed.

"Remember Mel and Monica dealt with issues in Oregon? Justin's mind is scrambled from things we don't even know about. When he feels more secure with us as his permanent parents, it will help him adjust."

"It's just . . . he wasn't this out of control in a class when he was younger," Ned said. "He didn't have these problems when he was three and four years old in Sunday school."

"True, but he hadn't gone through trauma and malnutrition when he was younger either," Annalee said.

"Ned, these children have been neglected, unloved, and only God knows what else. We need wisdom and patience."

"You're right, hon. I've missed them and love them so much. Thank you for bringing them back to me."

"Loving and raising them is our mission together," Annalee said with a smile, returning to her dinner preparations.

♥ ♥ ♥

They finished supper, baths, pajamas, and bedtime prayers. On weeknights everyone went to bed early.

About 1 o'clock in the morning, Annalee was in the bathroom when she heard a strange noise. She stepped into the hallway and realized the noise was from Justin's room. She stepped by his doorway and saw him crouched down doing something with the wall receptacle. There was a slight burning smell! She walked in and flipped on his light. Justin jumped back, surprised anyone was awake.

"Justin, what are you doing?" she said, instantly alarmed at how much danger he was in.

"I couldn't sleep, so I'm fixin' the wires on my nightlight," he said. "I'm really good at stuff like that."

Annalee bent down to discover the nightlight unplugged, the wall socket cover plate removed, and a kitchen knife next to it. Two different colored wires hung loosely from inside the receptacle box. The vinyl covering was torn away from the ends and appeared singed from the exposed metal inside. That accounted for the smell.

"Justin, are you OK? Did you get shocked by that wire?" Annalee said, horrified.

"Ya mean zapped?" Justin said. "Yeah, a little bit. Then I thought I better put it back together."

"Oh, Justin! You could have electrocuted yourself!"

"What's that? Ya mean like 'z-z-z z-z-z-z-z'?" Justin twitched and jerked his arms in a distorted wiggle.

"Yes, son." Annalee had dealt with ADHD before—but never children who awakened at night and dismantled electrical outlets! Her little boy's dangerous childish curiosity was an entirely different ballgame.

There was no way she was going to leave him alone in his room for the rest of the night, so she took his hand and led him out, flipped on the hall light, headed to the power box, found the breaker to his bedroom, and switched it to off. She grabbed a flashlight and then switched on the kitchen light.

"Son, sit down here and let me take a look at your hands."

"Oh, I'm OK. I just got zapped a little, but it didn't burn me or nuthin'," he said innocently, oblivious to the dangers of handling live wires. Annalee thanked God she had awakened.

After checking his hands thoroughly, she examined his eyes. His pupils looked normal.

"Oh, hi Daddy," Justin said. She turned and saw Ned in the doorway.

"What's going on?" Ned said, rubbing his eyes.

"Honey, I'll explain in a minute. Here's a flashlight. I need you to go into Justin's room and check the wires behind where his nightlight was. They've been . . ." she paused. "Uh, pulled from behind the socket plate. I'm concerned about a smell coming from the wires. The power is shut off to his room." She went to the toolbox to find electrical tape and handed the tape to Ned.

"Thanks. I'll wrap the ends of the wires while you hold the flashlight. That should be OK for the night," Ned said.

Ned finished the job in a few minutes. They stepped back into the kitchen.

"Justin, what happened?" Ned asked.

"Well, Daddy, I couldn't sleep, so I wanted to fix my night-light." Ned looked down at the kitchen knife, then over at Annalee. They were both wide awake now, and very concerned.

"Justin, don't ever touch electric wires again—they're dangerous! You could have electrocuted yourself!" Ned looked very distressed.

"That's what Mama said. Sorry I woke you guys up."

"I'm very glad you woke us up," Annalee said. She sensed he still had no idea of the danger.

Annalee headed to the garage to find a blowup mattress and air pump.

"Justin, you're going to sleep with Daddy and Mama tonight in our room," she said.

"Good idea," said Ned. He looked disturbed, annoyed.

Ned blew up the air mattress while Annalee grabbed blankets, then put Justin to bed in their bedroom, closing the door. Now they fully understood what Mel and Monica meant when they said they "needed to keep Justin safe out of harm's way." Annalee made a mental note to call them for more details.

The next morning, before work, Annalee made a call to a neighbor who was an electrician. She asked if he knew of a way to install protective devices on every receptacle and switch in Justin's bedroom that would guarantee the little boy couldn't gain access to the wires. The electrician said he could devise something, so Mercy let him in the house to do the project that day.

That morning Annalee left a few minutes early to drop the children off at school. After delivering them to their classes, she stopped by the school office to warn them of Justin's propensity for "fixing electrical wiring." The school secretary looked aghast.

"Will you please make a note in his records and warn his teacher and principal so he will never be left in a room unattended?" The secretary said she would. Satisfied she had taken precaution, Annalee left for work.

Just before lunch, Annalee got a call at her desk. It was Mr. Cormack, the principal. He had Justin in his office and asked Annalee if she would have a word with him over the phone. Apparently Justin had decided to climb on his desk and perform a little dance to entertain the children during class time, laughing all the while. Terrified he would be injured or land on another child, Mrs. Adams commanded him down, but Justin was determined to finish his routine atop the desk before he suddenly sprang from it. He banged his knee and bruised it, but was otherwise OK, the school nurse had reported. After a very difficult morning attempting to maintain control, Adams called on Principal Cormack again.

Annalee got on the phone with Justin and had another talk with him. This time she was a little more stern. She couldn't afford to take more time off work—she was finishing paying off both attorneys. Afterward, she reassured the principal that she and Ned would both be attending their upcoming parent-teacher conference. She said she was also getting ready to make a call to the family physician.

Annalee next reached the family doctor's office and said she needed an excellent pediatrician, and she was referred to one with great recommendations. She immediately called and made an appointment.

"Come to me, all you who are weary and burdened, and I will give you rest. Take my yoke upon you and learn from me, for I am gentle and humble in heart, and you will find rest for your souls. For my yoke is easy and my burden is light." —Jesus (Matthew 11:28-30, NIV).

"I have told you these things, so that in me you may have peace. In this world you will have trouble. But take heart! I have overcome the world." —Jesus (John 16:33, NIV).

Twenty-Four

"WHAT! HE GOT in trouble *again*?" On hearing the news, Ned was alarmed. They were in the kitchen as Annalee cooked supper. She immediately regretted telling him. She reasoned Ned was just too tired to handle this news right now.

"Hon, remember in Oregon we talked about the possibility of hyperactive disorder? I set an appointment for a pediatrician to evaluate him—not only for ADHD, but for other possible medical issues."

"But this is only the second day of school!" Ned's voice was rising by the minute. "And now we're losing sleep at night!" He was practically barking. Annalee was surprised by this reaction, which seemed over-the-top. She had noticed previous times he had been annoyed—even upset—but never to this degree.

"Look, we're both exhausted right now," Annalee said, seeking to calm him. "Sorry I brought it up. We can discuss his schooling another time. How about we finish supper and get to bed around 8:30?"

"You're right. We just need some rest. We didn't get much sleep after the night-light incident."

"True—except for Justin. He conked out on the air mattress." Annalee couldn't help but chuckle a bit. "Oh, by the way, he can sleep in his room again tonight. You know our neighbor, Tony, the electrician? I called him this morning and explained what happened. He made it a priority to get the job done today. He reconnected those wires and modified all of Justin's outlets with heavy-duty steel cover plates. He can't get those things off now." Annalee handed the electrician's bill to Ned. "Tony made sure the modifications will prevent Justin from being able to do that again."

Ned glanced at the bill.

"Thanks. You did good. But what if he wakes up and decides to roam the house while we're asleep and mess around with plugs in other rooms? He could burn the house down!" Ned was irritated, grumpy.

Annalee stopped to reflect. She knew parenting is a 24/7 job with ups and downs requiring loads of patience, especially with traumatized children. She thought Ned clearly understood this before he was awarded custody.

"Ned, he's just a little boy!"

"But he thinks he knows what he's doing. That's scary!"

She began trying anything she could think of to calm Ned. "I really don't think that's going to happen. We need to take things one day at a time, don't you agree?"

Ned's eyes looked as if a light bulb had gone off. He seemed to realize he had been heading to an extreme. "I'm sorry. We're both tired. I need to calm down."

"Thank you. I know this isn't easy, but he can't help it. We have to be patient."

"You're right, hon."

"This weekend, how about we call Mel and Monica for more details on Justin? Maybe it will help."

"Good idea. Let's do that."

"OK. Will you keep an eye on the food? It will take about forty-five minutes. I'm checking on the children."

Amanda was in her room drawing a picture with her new coloring pens and tablet. "Look, Mama. I'm makin' a pretty picture of punkins for our Thanksgiving party at school."

She showed Annalee. "Good job, honey. Keep up the good work!" This sweet child had moments of coming out of her shell.

Then Annalee wondered: *Where is Justin?* He wasn't in his room. She held her breath, deciding not to call his name out. Ned was already too stressed. In the bathroom, she discovered Justin precariously perched on the bathtub ledge in his slippery socks playing Tarzan with the shower curtain rod! It was about to break free. He was facing her.

"Justin, don't move!" He froze. She shut the door immediately, quietly as she could.

"Stay still. I can't lift you, son."

"Oh yeah, cuz of baby brother," Justin said innocently.

"Yes. We need to get you down safe. Stay still." She placed her hands around his waist to stabilize him. She pointed. "Now slowly scoot to the right—this way—to the shower wall." He did. She touched his right hand. "Now lay this hand against the tiles." She leaned in toward him and bent forward. "Now we're taking this hand . . ." She reached for his left hand and placed it on her right shoulder. He was frightened enough to obey without question. "Don't jump into my arms. Just lean on my shoulder while you step down. Now, Justin. Step down slow—one foot at a time."

Annalee breathed a huge sigh of relief as he climbed down safely.

She quickly decided not to tell Ned about this one. The outcome seemed too uncertain.

"OK, stay put." Annalee paused. "Justin, look at me—both eyes. Got your catchers on?" She cupped her ears with her hands, fighting back tears.

"Yes, Mama, got my catchers on." His beautiful blue eyes were looking at her with big question marks.

She opened the door and called out to Ned.

"Honey, I'll be back soon. Would you please finish up the food?" She heard an "OK" from Ned in the kitchen.

"Justin." As she gathered him in her arms, tears of relief flowed and she began praying for him.

"Mama, what's the matter?"

"Son, you could have gotten hurt really bad. I need to show you something." She took his hands and patted them against the porcelain tub. "Do you feel how hard that tub is?"

"Uh huh." She showed him the porcelain sink and ceramic tiles on the floor.

"Do you know what would happen if you fell and hit your head against that tub or sink or floor?"

"Um, I guess it would hurt," he muttered.

"Yes, son. It would hurt real bad, and it could hurt your brain."

"Oh, I wouldn't like that. It would prob'ly gimme a bad headache, wouldn't it?"

"Yes, honey, it would be an awful headache. It could also break your arm or your leg. We would have to take you to the hospital."

"Ooooo, I wouldn't like that. The doctor would have to gimme a shot or somethin', huh?"

"Well, yes. And probably much more than that."

"I'd have a real bad headache like the one I had when I was with my other mom."

Annalee blinked, then asked, "What do you mean?"

"When she got really mad at me and knocked me over on the porch. I fell down the stairs outside and hit my head real hard. It hurt so bad and I was seeing stars and everything. And then I fell asleep."

"Oh, Justin!" Her tears were starting up again. "What kind of stairs were they?"

"They're white, like they make sidewalks out of. You know, the kind you can draw on with chalk."

Concrete! Dear God, he must have gotten a concussion that day!

"Justin, what happened then?"

"I dunno. I fell asleep for a looong time, and then I woke up and my head hurt real bad and my eyes were kinda funny."

"You had trouble seeing with your eyes?"

"Yeah, I could not see good with my eyes, and I kept fallin' over. And I got real dizzy."

"Honey, did your other mom take you to the hospital?"

"Nah. She didn't wanna do that."

"What did she do for you?"

"Well, I told her my head hurt real bad, so she gave me somethin'. Then I got real sleepy again so she told me to go lay down somewhere."

Annalee felt sick to her stomach. Now his behavior was making more sense. Justin had received an untreated concussion. He must have been only four or five at the time since he celebrated his sixth birthday with Mel and Monica.

Annalee realized she had to do something about Justin's risky behavior and the danger he was putting himself in.

"Son, put your catchers on."

"OK, Mama. Got my catchers on." He nodded his little head and cupped his ears.

"Will you promise me you won't climb up on the bathtub again? I don't want you to fall and hurt your brain and get another bad headache. Your brain helps you learn, and walk and talk."

"Really?"

"Yes. Really. So you promise me you won't climb on the bathtub or your desk at school anymore? Or anything else?"

"OK, Mama. I promise."

"Pinky swear?"

"Pinky swear," he said, curling his pinky finger around hers.

Annalee had a lot to discuss with the pediatrician.

♥ ♥ ♥

Thankfully, everyone caught up on their sleep that night. The next evening after work, Annalee decided to catch up on laundry. She grabbed both hampers from the children's rooms and headed to the laundry room. As she was sorting the clothes into the washing machine, she found pieces of garlic bread and chocolate cake stuffed into the rolled-up cuffs of Justin's jeans. She remembered these were the jeans he wore the first night he arrived from Oregon.

Poor little guy! she thought to herself. He wasn't sure there would be enough food for him, so he was stashing it—just in case. Their welcoming meal of lasagna, garlic bread, salad, and chocolate cake wasn't enough to assure little Justin that he and Amanda would always be fed.

What would it be like to be a child living for more than two years in a situation where the only thing in the cupboard was a bag of sugar?

What would it be like to be four and five years old walking unsupervised on roadways to look for Dumpsters behind fast-food restaurants searching for half-eaten hamburgers? God's angels must have been watching over those two precious children to keep them from being kidnapped or worse! Bless their hearts.

Annalee took a deep breath as all this washed over her.

Her heart broke and tears welled in her eyes as she held the jeans up and scraped the remnants of food into the trash can. She carefully checked all the remaining clothes from both children but found no other evidence of stashed food.

Justin and Amanda were outside riding their bicycles as Ned worked in the yard, so Annalee checked Justin's room to see if he had stashed any other food. Sure enough, underneath his bed were a couple of brown bananas, breakfast muffins, dry cereal, and several other food items. The unwrapped food was already drawing ants, so she grabbed a broom, removed everything from under the bed, vacuumed the carpeting, and sprayed disinfectant. Justin walked in just in time to see her finishing vacuuming.

"Mama, what are you doing?" he asked. He then saw the kitchen trash can with the food thrown inside. He turned red-faced and looked embarrassed. She took both his hands in hers and asked him to sit on the bed.

"Mama, I didn't mean to steal the food," he began, glancing unsteadily at the trash can.

"Son, everything is OK," she said. "Honey, you are not in trouble over the food."

"Really? My other mom used to get real mad if she caught us takin' food if we stayed somewhere that had a kitchen. And she didn't like it if me and Amanda looked for food when we stayed in a van or camper."

Justin's face brightened. "But me and Amanda got really good at findin' food behind the hamburger stands or the taco places. People told us we were really good Dumpster divers!" He said this with an innocent pride. "Sometimes we would find lotsa good stuff, like almost a whole hamburger or almost a whole burrito or a buncha fries. Then we were full and we could go to sleep."

Annalee felt like she was about to lose it emotionally, but she tried not to show it in front of Justin.

"Son, you will never have to Dumpster dive for food again." She took his hand and led him to the kitchen. "Let's go take a look inside our pantry, OK?"

"OK!"

"I want you to see how much food we have for the family." She opened the pantry door.

"Wow! That's a lotta food!" he said. "I never seen that much food!"

She opened every cupboard door that had food stocked in it, then opened the refrigerator. After that, she took Justin's hand and led him to the garage. She opened the freezer and showed him their frozen food supply. Then she showed him the cold storage that was kept in the garage, such as potatoes, winter vegetables, and canned goods. He looked astounded.

"Justin, our family has plenty of food, and we will always have plenty of food to feed you and Amanda and the whole family."

"Even baby brother?" Justin asked innocently.

"Yes, baby brother will always have plenty of food too," Annalee said, smiling. They stepped back into the house. "Let's sit down at the kitchen table." As they sat, she went on. "Justin, the kitchen is where we keep our food. We have breakfast, lunch, and supper, and on school days you will always have your lunch at school." She paused a moment.

"Son, you do not have to pack food in your jeans or under your bed."

Justin looked down sheepishly.

"You are not in trouble at all. You just didn't know if we would have enough food for you and Amanda all the time, right?" He nodded as if he still wasn't sure whether he was in trouble. She thought of an idea that she hoped would lighten things up. "Let's put on our jackets and step out to the front yard."

"OK!"

As they stepped out, Annalee pointed to a very large tree in the front yard. Squirrels scampered throughout the tree, dodging in and out of their dens. "Justin, you see how those squirrels run around collecting nuts for the winter? Do you see how their cheeks are so big and fat? That's because their cheeks are full of nuts."

"Where do they take 'em?" Justin asked.

"They take all those nuts back to the holes in the tree where they sleep at night. That's how they feed their babies. All good mommies and daddies feed their babies. So Daddy and I go to work, then we buy our food at the store, and we bring it home to feed our little ones just like the squirrels collect the nuts and feed their babies."

Justin's eyes looked as if his mind had just comprehended something huge. "Now I get it!"

"Awesome! But the squirrels don't need kitchens or refrigerators, do they?"

Justin began laughing uproariously, as only a six-year-old boy could do. They laughed about squirrels, nuts, and food. After a big hug, they walked back to the house. The lesson had been learned, and Annalee never found food stashed in Justin's jeans or his room again.

I was young and now I am old, yet I have never
seen the righteous forsaken or their children begging bread
(Psalm 37:25, NIV).

Rescue those being led away to death; hold back those
staggering toward slaughter (Proverbs 24:11, NIV).

"See that you do not despise one of these little ones. For I
tell you that their angels in heaven always see the face of my
Father in heaven" —Jesus (Matthew 18:10, NIV)

Twenty-Five

"HI, MRS. Adams. This is Mrs. Jackson calling about our parent-teacher conference on Friday."

"Hi, Mrs. Jackson. We're visiting often enough to be on a first-name basis. You may call me Kiara."

"Thank you, Kiara, for all you are doing. Feel free to call me Annalee. We're getting to know each other. I'm sure your experiences with Justin so far have challenged much of your training in special education."

"Well, I must admit, your little guy is definitely directing me back to my textbooks." She laughed.

"Same for me—hearkening back to my foster care days," Annalee said with her own chuckle. "He's a horse of a different color. He invents more dangerous behaviors than any child I've cared for my entire life!"

"I'm in total agreement with you," his teacher said.

"Kiara, do you have a school psychologist on staff?"

"We do have a Christian child psychologist with a private practice in town, Dr. James Barry. He is not on staff at the school, but he offers his services on a consultation basis for our students."

"Do you think you could arrange for him to attend our conference for Justin this week?" Annalee asked. "We have insurance, and I believe it's critical to have a child psychologist on board. We'll retain him privately as well."

"I'll give him a call. Anything that you want me to discuss with him when I call?"

"Yes. Last night I found out something significant. Justin apparently sustained an untreated concussion with extended loss of consciousness between age four and five when he was living with his bio-mom. It may help explain some of the behaviors we've been seeing at school, home, and church."

"Oh my goodness!" Kiara gasped. "I'm so sorry. I'll be sure to mention that to Dr. Barry and see if he can make it."

"Thank you so much. You have my office number if you need me. Otherwise, we'll see you Friday."

That evening, Annalee had no choice but to tell Ned what Justin had told her. She hoped it would help him have greater patience in dealing with Justin's issues. But when she told him about it, he launched into a furious tirade against Justin's mother, Tina. It brought his anger over the kidnapping and mistreatment to the surface once more.

A few more skirmishes occurred with Justin that week. School and children's church were doing their best to accommodate their little son. But home was another matter altogether. Ned's increasing verbal agitation behind closed doors intensified as Justin's incidents escalated across multiple fronts.

On Friday the parent-teacher conference at Glacier Vista School was a group effort on behalf of a little boy who desperately needed help. Kiara Adams, Principal Cormack, Dr. Barry, and Ned and Annalee were all in attendance. Everyone contributed to the revision of an individualized educational program for Justin.

Dr. Barry agreed that Justin's description of the event in his young life sounded like an untreated concussion and said the loss of consciousness over an extended time would have intensified its effects. He surmised that the impact with the concrete on Justin's young brain may have impaired the frontal lobe—an area of the brain critical to decision-making. If so, that could cause his behavior to misfire moment by moment and would explain the irrational, impulse-driven actions. Dr. Barry recommended a neurologist and suggested a full consultation with neurological tests. He also offered to begin private therapy with Justin and collaborate with both the neurologist and pediatrician to put together a psychological and medical profile for him.

The doctor's input was crucial to the creation of a customized education program. Annalee was so grateful that Dr. Barry could attend and would be involved moving forward. Fortunately, the expense was covered by a Child Victim Insurance Program used for crimes committed against children in the U.S. It was complex, but Annalee carried specific insurance cards for both children that provided 100 percent guaranteed payment to all medical providers.

As the meeting wrapped up, Mrs. Adams said she would put the new program for Justin in place immediately. With the holidays coming up, school festivities would help, she believed. Dr. Barry scheduled Justin and Amanda's separate intake appointments so therapy could begin.

♥ ♥ ♥

Annalee stepped inside Mercy's house to pick up the children while Ned waited in the Suburban. Mercy's eyes were red and swollen as if she had been crying. Amanda and Justin scampered toward Annalee with big hugs, but she noticed Justin was limping. "Son, are you hurt?" He pulled up his pant leg to reveal a badly scraped knee which had been cleaned and bandaged. She helped the children out to the Suburban and told Ned she would get a ride home from Mercy. Annalee quietly whispered in Ned's ear, "Be sure to keep a close eye on Justin."

"Will do, hon," Ned said. "Why don't we order pizza tonight for supper?"

She agreed that was a great idea and waved a big goodbye as the family drove off.

She stepped back inside to see Mercy wiping tears from her eyes.

"Mercy, what in the world is going on?" She wrapped her arms around her friend.

"My dear, now I understand what you mean about little Justin. How do you keep your sanity?"

"It's one day at a time, just like the old Christy Lane song," Annalee said. "What happened?"

"Well, I thought both the children were still in the living room. That's where they were when I turned on the Gospel Kids DVD. I set up the drawing table with their coloring books and pens and told them I would be in the kitchen if they needed me. I had baked some cookies, so I was taking cookie trays out of the oven. It was only a few minutes." She paused and drew a breath.

"All of a sudden, I heard screaming from the back deck! 'Help! A bear is gonna eat me!' I grabbed the pepper spray and took off as fast as I could. The dining room slider was open, so I ran out to find Justin with his leg caught in the wooden baluster of the deck railing. For some reason, he had rolled up his pant legs and tried to climb over, then saw the bear and fell back onto the deck with his leg caught. He scraped up his knee pretty bad. Thank God it wasn't a Grizz, just a black bear eating off my huckleberry bushes out back. She wasn't even paying attention to Justin. I guess he's never seen a bear in the wild before."

"Oh, hon. I'm so sorry! That must have frightened the wits out of you!"

"Yes, it did. You know how high that deck is—about fifteen feet above my patio. If he would have fallen the other way, I don't know if he would have survived it . . ." She shook her head and the tears began again. "I only took my eyes off him for a few minutes!"

"Dear friend, it's not your fault. This type of thing happens all the time with Justin. That's why we had the school meeting."

"Dear God! All the time? How do you keep that child in one piece?"

Those words seemed to tickle Annalee's funny bone; maybe they both needed something lighthearted at that point. "That's a good way to put it," Annalee said. "I guess that's the challenge: let's try to keep Justin in one piece until he grows up!" She began chuckling, then it became a belly laugh—quite a sight with the size of her belly at that moment. Then it became contagious. Before they knew it, they were both doubled with laughter. It felt great! Annalee caught herself wishing she and Ned laughed more. It was invigorating.

"You know what the Good Book says? Laughter is good like a medicine. I think we both got a big dose," Mercy giggled.

"Well, did this adventure end up with you giving Justin the bear talk? You know, every Montana kid knows the difference between a Grizzly and a black or brown bear," Annalee chuckled.

"Honestly, I was too shook up to think of it. My mind was focused on making sure he was OK and cleaning up his knee," Mercy said.

"No problem. We'll cover that another time. Just remember: no guilt, no shame. You did the best you could. You kept him in one piece." Then the laughter began again. It was so rare in her home that, for Annalee, it felt therapeutic.

♥ ♥ ♥

That weekend Annalee made a call to Mel and Monica to ask them any more details about Justin they could offer.

"Hi, Annalee. It's so good to hear from you," Monica said. "How is everything going?"

"To be honest, it's never a dull moment with Justin. That's one of the reasons I'm calling."

"Oh my," Monica said. "We will be happy to help in any way we can."

"Thanks so much. First, though, how is your family doing?"

"We're all doing well. We're praying about taking in another foster child."

"We wish you the best going forward. Any child is blessed to have you for their foster family. We're so grateful you were there for Amanda and Justin."

"That's wonderful to hear. It's a difficult calling, but definitely worth it."

Annalee decided she had better begin the discussion about Justin.

"Remember the comments you made about keeping him out of harm's way?" Annalee asked. "I wondered what you encountered at home, and what his teachers reported with his classroom behavior in Oregon."

Mel was on the line also. "We had to keep Justin safe from harm because of dangers when he was unsupervised," he said. "I stepped into the garage one day just in time to catch him trying to fire up my power drill so he could drill into an electric socket." Mel seemed to catch himself. "Oh, I'm sorry. I forgot to tell you about that!"

Annalee was glad Ned wasn't involved with the call at this point; he was spending time with the kids to allow her to focus on the conversation. If he asked her about it, she told herself, she would only share bits and pieces.

"It's OK. It's hard to keep track of all his escapades," Annalee laughed. "We had a similar experience. Justin tried to 'fix' the wires in his night-light socket with a kitchen knife in the middle of the night."

"Oh no! Was he hurt?" Monica asked.

"No, thank God. I was up in the night and heard sounds in Justin's room, so I discovered him. The next day our electrician installed heavy-duty modifications on all outlets in his room."

"We're so glad he didn't electrocute himself!" Monica said.

"Any other risky behaviors at your house?" Annalee said.

"Well, one day in the winter all the children were outside sledding on a hill in our yard, and Justin went off by himself," Monica said. "He found a long, thick rope in the garage, dragged it out, and threw it over a large pine branch. He was trying to play Tarzan by swinging from the rope to swing into the pond on our property, but the pond is way too far from the pine tree! So he missed the pond by a long shot. We had a couple feet of soft new snow on the ground at the time, which softened his fall. Better anyway. The pond would have caused hypothermia. The other kids heard him yelling after he fell. Thank God, he wasn't hurt."

"Wow, I'm so glad he was OK. Justin's teacher here in Montana is having an interesting time trying to keep his class under control. You know, the whole class clown thing?"

"Understood. As you know, at school out here he climbed on tables to entertain the class."

"Same here, but yesterday we had a parent-teacher conference with school staff and a child psychologist, and they are implementing a revised plan. I've scheduled an evaluation with a pediatrician and a neurologist."

"Good idea. Maybe they can suggest a protocol for helping with focus and staying on task."

"By the way, did you ever hear about Justin suffering a prior concussion?" Annalee asked.

"No! When did he suffer a concussion?"

"It happened with bio-mom, about age four or five. Poor little guy hit his head on concrete so badly he lost consciousness for a time . . . well, we don't really know how long. He was never medically treated, but he clearly remembered details and the side effects he suffered. The child psychologist believes it accounts for the lack of impulse control that causes the dangerous behaviors. He referred Justin to a neurologist for tests."

"We are sorry to hear that, but glad he's getting help," Mel said. "We had no idea."

"That's understandable. We wouldn't have known either if Justin hadn't told me by accident after a Tarzan stunt in the bathroom. Oh, one more thing: did he ever wake up in the middle of the night and roam around the house or get into anything?"

"We did have a couple of incidents when he woke up in the night, but our son was in the same room," Monica said. "He came and woke us up when Justin started making noise by pulling out toys to play. We put Justin back to bed. After that, we began waking him up about an hour earlier each morning so he would be extra tired at night. We also eliminated drinks after about 5 PM. That helped with his bladder at night."

"Those are some great tips," Annalee said. "Thanks. We will keep you posted. And happy Thanksgiving."

They had a very cordial ending to what seemed, to Annalee, a most productive talk.

A merry heart does good, like medicine, But a broken spirit dries the bones (Proverbs 17:22, NKJV.)

But Jesus said, "Let the little children come to Me, and do not forbid them; for of such is the kingdom of heaven" (Matthew 19:14, NKJV).

Religion that God our Father accepts as pure and faultless is this: to look after orphans and widows in their distress and to keep oneself from being polluted by the world (James 1:27, NIV).

Twenty-Six

AS FALL went on, Ned worked more overtime. Annalee finally paid off both attorneys, and this was a huge relief. She reduced her work hours since she was only weeks away from birth and needed afternoons to make the rounds with Justin's medical appointments and her frequent visits with Principal Cormack.

The neurologist had completed several types of EEGs and other neurological tests, and these confirmed that Justin had sustained a mild closed-head injury from a past event. His pediatrician, neurologist, and child psychologist collaborated and suggested a referral to a Christian child psychiatrist, Dr. Palmer. They all came together to create a coordinated specialty care team along with his school staff for a personal treatment plan.

Annalee started Justin with Dr. Palmer for therapy. Annalee sensed a good connection with her and found the doctor a tremendous resource in providing guidance. There came a point when Dr. Palmer requested an appointment with Annalee for a serious discussion about Justin's behaviors.

"Mrs. Jackson, I have evaluated the results of our care team, and our unanimous findings conclude that we're dealing with several diagnoses," Dr. Palmer said. "There is ADHD—attention deficit hyperactive disorder; NOS Psychosis—nonspecific; and Passive Resistance, sometimes known as passive aggression. Both children also suffer with Complex PTSD, but there is hope for victims of trauma. With time and trust they can recover. With children, they need dedicated caregivers committed to helping them grow up over the long term with unconditional love."[15]

Annalee took all this in, then responded. "Dr. Palmer, I want to help Justin and Amanda heal and recover. It was worth the long legal battle. You said they need dedication, and that's what I'm determined to give them—a mother's love and a wonderful childhood. Thanks for explaining everything about passive resistance. Some of my foster children used to apologize, promise to obey, then repeat the same misbehavior within days or even hours! I know he is young, but Justin's pattern is the same. He repeats disobedient behaviors at home, school, and church.

"All the adults in charge explain in detail why something is dangerous or disruptive, but he turns right around and repeats it again. He seems so sincere when he is caught. He looks up at me with those beautiful blue eyes in total humility, makes promises, and then reoffends before you can blink an eye. Why would a child choose time-outs and losing recess multiple times a week? Could he have a short-term memory deficit from the concussion, blocking him from remembering things he just did?"

"No, Mrs. Jackson, short-term memory loss is not the issue here," Dr. Palmer answered. "There is strong evidence in Justin's neurological findings to suggest that he has a strong, resistant will. This is symptomatic of passive resistant behavior. Justin is downright determined to do things his own way. He makes conscious decisions. It is difficult to recognize this behavior because he does not respond in ways that appear defiant or rebellious. When confronted, he acts sincerely unaware, or apologetic, while using avoidance to keep from doing what he is refusing to do. That is classic passive resistant behavior—again, sometimes known as passive aggressive. In other words, the behavior is outwardly passive, but inwardly resistant. This complicates managing his behavior and keeping him safe."

"No wonder! Thank you for explaining the complexity of this," Annalee said. "I thought I understood it before, but you've helped me comprehend so much more. No wonder it has been so difficult trying to extinguish these negative behaviors. Doctor, there have even been times I've asked Justin why he did something he knew was wrong, and he replied, 'Just because I wanted to.' So that is how the strong will works?"

"Exactly. You have just described the way that behavior works, Mrs. Jackson. It makes no sense for Justin to repeat suffering consequences, but it is the nature of passive resistance. It is frustrating both for the child and the parent. I'm going to prescribe medications to help manage symptoms and keep him safe."

Dr. Palmer looked up from writing to ask, "Shall we schedule Justin for a therapy visit next week?"

Annalee agreed more visits were needed. She wanted Dr. Palmer in their corner. Annalee scheduled Justin for consultation with her on a weekly basis. The psychiatrist prescribed three different medications for ADHD, passive resistance, and psychosis to help manage his behavior to increase focus, reduce impulsivity, and, hopefully, keep him safe.

On her way home, Annalee thought of other things she could do to aid this process. She bought a collection of children's Gospel DVDs and some family movies, and beginning that night she taught the children some simple verses.

She was greatly hoping all these steps would help bring Justin and Amanda comfort and healing.

Train up a child in the way he should go, And when he is old he will not depart from it (Proverbs 22:6, NKJV).

"Peace I leave with you, My peace I give to you; not as the world gives do I give to you. Let not your heart be troubled, neither let it be afraid." — Jesus, the giver of this gift (John 14:27, NKJV).

Twenty-Seven

IN THE FALL, Amanda and Justin turned eight and seven. Their first Thanksgiving together as a family was approaching.

Annalee decorated early for the holidays, knowing she would be busy with their newborn son by Christmas. The family was excited for baby brother's arrival.

She was lending a hand in the kitchen for Thanksgiving, but Ned, Betsy, Mercy, Luke, and Marie were doing most of the work. Amanda was delighted to be helping to the best of her ability.

"Can you believe last Thanksgiving we got that call from the social worker about the children, and this Thanksgiving they're with us! Isn't it amazing?" Annalee said excitedly to the group.

All but one person gave whoops or hollers.

At that moment, Justin dashed through the kitchen in his socked feet and slid, crashing down on his side.

"Oooooh, that hurts!" he moaned.

"Yep, just *amazing*," Ned said sarcastically as he glanced over with the look of annoyance he usually displayed whenever Justin got himself in a difficult spot. These looks were becoming increasingly more judgmental. Annalee hadn't mentioned them to Mercy, but for those who caught on, the tension around Ned was getting quite thick.

"Son, are you OK?" Annalee asked. She immediately went over to help him up.

"He'll be OK. He'll probably bang himself up another twenty times before the day is over," Ned said, his tone not a pleasant one.

Mercy was close enough to hear this, so Ned's comment did not escape her. She noticed that, thankfully, Justin didn't seem to hear his dad's remark, but that Amanda did. Mercy had been observing lately that Annalee seemed more reserved, as if she wanted to avoid getting herself or the children in trouble with Ned. It was evident she was carrying a great deal of weight from all this.

"I'll be all right, Mama," Justin said. "You can't bend over cuz of baby brother, huh?"

"Sorry, son. I can't."

Justin slowly tried to get up off the floor. "I'll be OK," he said. He looked toward his father, who did not turn his way to help him.

Mercy went over and helped him up while casting a concerned look Annalee's way. Obviously, things were not going well. Annalee was actively planning ways to avoid things going wrong.

Annalee said, "This weekend, I'm taking you and Sissy to the store to buy you some house slippers to wear inside. They have non-skid bottoms. I want you to always wear them in the house, understand?"

"OK. Great! Can I get dinosaur slippers?" Justin asked.

Amused, Annalee smiled at him. "Of course! You sure you're all right, son?"

"Yeah, I'm fine now, Mama." Justin scampered off holding his hip.

♥ ♥ ♥

The first Thanksgiving with the children was memorable in many ways. Annalee continued to hope for the best. The week after Thanksgiving the children got their new slippers. Annalee hoped they would prevent future mishaps around the house.

The Christmas season was now upon them as the family prepared for baby brother's arrival.

♥ ♥ ♥

School resumed the week after Thanksgiving as well as the children's pediatric and therapy appointments. Annalee was nearing her maternity leave in December, so Ned was working more overtime. His schedule did not permit him to attend therapy appointments, but there were multiple times during the school year that both Annalee and Ned were required to attend meetings regarding Justin landing in the principal's office. Annalee had started abbreviating the children's therapy reports to minimize the stress Ned was already under.

One morning the first week of December, Annalee received a mid-morning phone call from Kiara Adams.

"Annalee, I'm sorry to bother you at work, but something very serious happened with Justin this morning. An aide is covering my class so I can call you personally."

"Oh, Kiara, I'm so sorry! What is going on?"

"Annalee, we have Justin and a couple of other boys waiting in Principal Cormack's office, and we cannot allow them back in class today. We need to meet with you and Ned personally

A-S-A-P. We have called the other parents also. How soon can you both be here?"

"I'll speak to my supervisor right away and get ahold of Ned," Annalee said. "We'll be there as soon as we can."

♥ ♥ ♥

Ned and Annalee both pulled into the school parking lot about 11 AM. Ned's face looked like a thundercloud. "What's this about? What has he done now?" Clearly, he was angry.

She reached for his hand and said, "Honey, I have no idea what this is about, but whatever it is, we will get through it. We just need to stick together."

Ned pulled his hand from hers and shot her an icy stare. It was the first time Annalee could ever remember Ned withdrawing his hand from hers. She felt blame coming from him.

Against this difficult backdrop, they made their way to the principal's office. Justin was sitting with an aide in the principal's lobby. He was shuffling his feet. Annalee had never seen such a frightened look on his young face. She stepped over to him and said, "Son, we're going to have a meeting with Principal Cormack right now."

"Yeah, Mama, I know. I'm in really big trouble, huh?" He shook and nervously twitched his hands.

"I'm not sure what the trouble is, but we're going to talk to the principal right now to find out what happened. You wait here for us and we will see you soon." Justin's eyes filled with tears. Ned looked the other way. Annalee turned to the aide and asked, "Is it OK if Justin eats his lunch while he waits for us?"

The aide said that was fine and set up a portable table so Justin could start eating. She thanked the aide, who smiled sympathetically.

Kiara Adams walked in, along with Dr. Barry, the child psychologist.

Oh my, this must be serious! Annalee thought.

Principal Cormack opened his door and invited everyone in.

"Thanks for taking time out of your busy schedule, Dr. Barry," the principal said.

"I was able to take an early lunch, Mike. I'm glad you called me."

"Mr. and Mrs. Jackson, I'm very sorry you both had to take time off work. If this wasn't so important I would not have made the request."

"We want to be as supportive as possible, Mr. Cormack. Hi, Dr. Barry and Mrs. Adams," Annalee said.

"Hi, everyone," Ned said, but much more grimly. "Sorry for whatever happened with Justin again."

"Well, things happen with children sometimes," Cormack said gently. "I'm going to defer to Mrs. Adams to explain the entire situation."

The teacher looked ashen, and her eyes seemed red and swollen.

Drawing a breath, she began. "This will take a few minutes. This morning we were doing a science experiment that required using matches, so I had them sitting around my desk. Justin was right up close paying attention with a couple of his buddies. Considering all the previous issues with focusing and staying on task, it was great to see him paying attention to the science project. I thought we had discovered a new area of interest for him to learn, so I decided to let him contribute to the project by doing a small task. I needed a little bit of water in a plastic water pitcher. The water faucet is directly outside the classroom door, so I asked Justin if he would like to volunteer to get the water for me. He is such a friendly child, and he was enthusiastic to help. I turned my back for a few moments to get the water pitcher a few feet away.

"The other two boys asked if they could help with the door and faucet. Since the faucet is just outside, I didn't see any problem. They put on their coats, and I handed Justin the plastic pitcher, reminding him to come right back in. They stepped outside, and I got busy with the other children. In a few minutes, I realized the boys had been gone too long, so I called for an aide to watch my class and stepped outside. The boys were nowhere in sight. I went around the corner, smelled an odor of gas, and discovered the boys trying to strike matches against the large gas meter that connects the gas lines to the school.

"Justin admitted stealing the matches from my desk when I turned my back, then passing some to the other boys outside. Thank God there was no explosion. For those of you who don't know, that gas meter not only pipes the school, but also pipes gas to all the homes in this vicinity. If it would have exploded, the entire neighborhood could have gone up in flames."

Her shoulders shook; she seemed overcome with emotion. She then paused for a large breath. She had incredible stress on her face.

"I feel terrible about this, and take full responsibility," Adams said, continuing. "Justin has never stolen anything before to my knowledge, and I didn't realize the matches were within his reach. It was a mistake to entrust him with a task out of my sight. He is just not ready yet. Thank God this didn't end up becoming a tragedy, and I apologize to all of you." She was struggling to hold back tears.

Annalee stepped over and gave her a hug. Dr. Barry and Principal Cormack both assured her the incident wasn't her fault. Ned, looking numb, apologized for Justin.

Dr. Barry explained the behavior was consistent with the impulse diagnoses of his medical team and that he would inform Dr. Palmer, Justin's child psychiatrist. Ned looked at Annalee suspiciously. She had tried to avoid details to simplify matters at home but could tell Ned was not appreciative of not being in the loop on some of these things.

The principal said that he, Kiara Adams, and Dr. Barry would consult regarding school liability issues surrounding continuing to have Justin in attendance. If he remained at the school, they agreed, they would need a strict plan of action to keep him as carefully supervised as possible. Everyone reassured Kiara that she had done the best she could, and they did not want her bearing the guilt of the situation. Cormack kindly said he would be in touch with Ned and Annalee regarding the school's decision about Justin.

As Ned and Annalee walked into the house, storm clouds were definitely brewing—and these weren't the Montana kind. Amanda was still at school. Justin looked as if he wanted to disappear under the carpeting.

Ned and Annalee went to their bedroom to talk privately. Annalee was eight and a half months pregnant, so she sat. "That's it!" Ned exploded. "There's only one way to get through to him. He's getting a spanking!"

"The new medications need more time to take effect. Please give it more time!" Annalee pleaded. "There are some things that spankings will not correct—things he cannot help. Trauma on children has a devastating impact. We really need to balance discipline with love."

"I'm sick of hearing about love and discipline—those shrinks think they know it all!" Ned snarled. "Now tell me. What about all these diagnoses that psych talked about? Yeah, they told us about ADHD and his impulsive behavior, but what else is there?" Ned was thundering while standing over her.

"The neurology tests showed Complex PTSD and several other behavioral issues," Annalee quietly said.

"Because of Tina, right?"

Annalee didn't want Ned to get started on another rampage about Tina.

"There were things they were exposed to when they were with her, yes," Annalee said. "It's not Justin's fault. There were more issues than we realized. The original reports did not include everything."

With that, Ned seemed to hit another, disturbing gear.

"He's only been here a few weeks, and he's already driving me nuts! I can't even get enough sleep at night after his night-light situation!" He continued hovering over Annalee.

Annalee's mind quickly stirred to this dreadful thought: *Lord, have I done a terrible thing by bringing Justin and Amanda into Ned's hands?*

> *A gentle answer turns away wrath, but a harsh*
> *word stirs up anger (Proverbs 15:1, NIV).*

"It's time to start spankings. That's all there is to it! He almost burned the school down!"

"Ned, will you just agree to this much? Remember what we learned in parenting classes about a cooling-off period? Can you at least give yourself some time to cool off first before you take action?"

"All right. I guess you have a point there." Though still angry, he backed away from where Annalee was sitting.

Thank God, a reprieve.

She took the first chance she had to get away.

"I'm headed to the kitchen to start an early supper. Neither one of us had lunch."

"OK. I'm heading to the shower," Ned said.

"Well, maybe you'll feel better."

As Annalee started cooking, her mind began beating her up. The tears began again, but she knew she had to keep her head together. She didn't want the baby inside her feeling stress.

♥ ♥ ♥

After supper, in his room, Justin received his first spanking. It sounded like a couple of swats. When Ned emerged from Justin's room, he had tears in his eyes and headed straight to the bedroom. Annalee went in to speak with him. His demeanor was much milder than before.

"When I got in there, I felt bad for having to give Justin a spanking," he said quietly. "I went ahead because that's what I thought he needed, and I didn't know what else to do." He looked broken, remorseful.

"Afterward, did you give him a hug and tell him that you love him?" Annalee asked.

"Yes, I did. But I still feel terrible."

"Then I think that's our answer—corporal punishment is a bad idea. But I'm so glad you hugged Justin and told him you love him." She reached out to him. He laid his head on her shoulder, sobbing.

She hoped Ned would never spank again, because she had a feeling this could open a door they would come to regret.

When I was a child, I talked like a child, I thought like a child, I reasoned like a child. When I became a man, I put the ways of childhood behind me (1 Corinthians 13:11, NIV).

Fathers, do not provoke your children to anger by the way you treat them. Rather, bring them up with the discipline and instruction that comes from the Lord (Ephesians 6:4, NLT).

Twenty-Eight

Christmas, New Year,
and Easter Seasons

IN THE AFTERMATH it was determined that Justin was the ringleader of the incident and the other two boys had followed his lead. The school staff had several meetings with all involved parents. The final decision rested with Principal Cormack. He took into consideration Justin and Amanda's traumatic past and made a guarded decision to retain Justin at the school. Ned and Annalee were immensely grateful for this compassion.

All precautions were put in place for a heavily monitored program with constant adult supervision throughout the school day. Justin's child psychiatrist, Dr. Palmer, made some adjustments to his impulse-control medication. Through a bit of teaching, Justin became aware of what a gas explosion could do. Once he understood it could have destroyed the school, neighborhood, and deeply impacted lives, Justin seemed profoundly affected. He expressed the sincere regret of a seven-year-old. There were times when he would burst into tears. Annalee didn't want him to carry a continuing burden of guilt and shame. She realized at those key moments that Justin needed hugs, empathy, and reassurance that he was forgiven. For a time he displayed better control at remaining focused and calm, and he made much better efforts to suppress his childish curiosity at school, home, and church. The reduction of episodes also made life more manageable on the home front.

Annalee prepared for her mid-December maternity leave from work. On her last day, her colleagues gave her a baby shower; she was most grateful. So much had been accomplished through the fall. She was able to finish preparing little Josiah's nursery. She was physically tired, but the first Christmas season with Amanda and Justin more than made up for any fatigue. They made pumpkin pies, Christmas cookies, fudge, and loaves of banana bread. Amanda came up with the great idea of adding half yellow cake mix to the banana bread. It was the best banana bread ever! It became Amanda's own traditional family recipe loved by everyone.

One of the highlights of the season was Amanda and Justin's introduction to a festive family memory Luke had grown up with. The week before Christmas, they loaded up their sleds with tins of homemade goodies and Annalee's Christmas poem. Luke and Marie helped the children go from house to house presenting neighbors with their baked gifts and wishing them all a Merry Christmas.

Thankfully their Christmas baking and neighborly deliveries were finished early, because little Josiah made his entrance just a few snowy days later. Serious issues arose during his birth including a long, intense labor complicated by Annalee's age and petite size, but an excellent obstetrician specialist was called in from his family dinner to make sure 8 ½-pound Josiah arrived safely.

> *A woman giving birth to a child has pain because*
> *her time has come; but when her baby is born she*
> *forgets the anguish because of her joy that a child is born*
> *into the world (John 16:21, NIV).*

Following Josiah's birth, Annalee stayed a few extra days in the hospital for transfusions and recovery. Afterward, she chose to stay home with all the children, so she resigned her work position to be a full-time mother. She had always wanted more children and another baby, so this was her dream come true.

Josiah surprised everyone with his beautiful red hair and blue-green eyes. Luke, Marie, Amanda, and Justin were delighted to have a newborn baby brother to love. Everyone gave him an endearing name—Baby Bear—to join Sissy Bear and Brother Bear. Grandma Betsy was thrilled to have a new grandchild, and "Aunt Mercy" seemed always on the scene to cuddle the little one.

As Josiah grew week by week, his strong family resemblance became apparent. Ned seemed to settle down emotionally for a while after the baby was born. He worked more overtime to take care of Annalee and the family, but when he was home he spent much of his time snuggling with little Josiah.

> *Children are a gift from the LORD;*
> *they are a reward from him (Psalm 127:3, NLT).*

As winter transitioned into spring, the family routine moved forward. Annalee would load baby Josiah into his car seat to take the children to school and after-school appointments. Justin stayed under Dr. Palmer's care. Lots of prayer—and the help of medications—had a calming effect. Ned's overtime schedule worked out well because Annalee could handle the majority of issues while Ned was at work.

There were times Annalee felt Amanda didn't receive enough attention because of the time devoted to Justin and the baby. Amanda's favorite activity seemed to be going into town—outings were much more entertaining than being at home! As moms will do, Annalee's answer to Amanda's "boredom" was to assign a household task such as sweeping the floor or polishing the furniture—this made the words "I'm bored" much less common. Amanda's favorite home activity was helping with the baby. This seemed to reflect her loving nature. Amanda told Annalee that when she grew up she wanted to have twelve children and own a large hotel! They laughed together over this wonderful dream Amanda had for her future.

Easter came early that first spring with Josiah. Amanda loved helping in the kitchen, so, after church, Annalee invited her to help prepare her traditional Easter/Passover dinner of roasted lamb, homemade mint jelly (made with apples from their trees, flavored with sprigs of spearmint), roasted potatoes, peas, carrots, and peach cobbler. Along with the roasted lamb, the family read the Bible story about the Lamb of God "who takes away the sin of the world." Their first Easter together as a family was a special memory for Annalee.

❤ ❤ ❤

There were storm clouds, however, that seemed to be forming distantly on the horizon.

Annalee knew she had signed on to bring healing to Ned and his family, but in the midst of trying to create family memories she often found herself mediating different situations in an effort to keep the peace at home. When Ned was home, the atmosphere became increasingly tense. Those became challenging times. Her motherly instincts wanted to protect the children, but she also knew she should work to be supportive of her husband. She was also trying to protect baby Josiah from internalizing the surrounding stress. Justin's escapades could be difficult, but Annalee knew the compassionate leadership of an understanding father could make a world of difference to help their young son and bring peace to the household.

There were times Annalee was aware she was asking herself an important question: *I am trying to make peace, but is my own soul becoming wounded in the process?*

Annalee would often request Ned join her in the bedroom to discuss parenting as she nursed the baby. She tried to reason with him as his helpmate. Ned's view of parenting was a punitive one, while Annalee's view focused on reasoning with the children to help them comprehend what behaviors needed to be changed.

In time, Ned began to believe Annalee was against him rather than trying to assist him in developing a closer relationship with the children. To Annalee this was heartbreaking.

She reviewed with Ned what they had learned in their parenting classes, including that children can only retain a few minutes of clear, corrective instructions, not hours-long lectures. She shared a goal of helping the children understand the specific infraction they were being disciplined for.

These became very real questions for Annalee.

Were they up against an impossible battle?

What had PTSD really done to Ned?

Had she been blind to Ned's symptoms and past during their engagement and early marriage before the children arrived?

Had she been blind to the damage of his childhood, the military, and his former marriage?

A profound sense of guilt and shame began to pummel her mind. There were still more questions.

One day Annalee thought of an idea she hoped would help Ned understand the importance of becoming a more tender, gentler father.

Once again they had retreated to the bedroom. She wanted to show him honor by asking him to take the lead in praying for their family, which he did. Afterward, she decided to ask her critical question.

"Ned, I truly believe you love me and the children to the best of your ability. A wife is to be a helpmate, so let me be that to you. Remember the nightmares you had when you cried for the children to be back in your arms and in your life? You asked me for help, and I did everything humanly possible to help you win that battle. Don't you want to give them a happy home life now that they're with us?"

"Yes, of course I do," Ned said.

"OK. We also prayed that the children would be found long before their teens so we would have time to bring healing into their lives during their childhood. When our children become teenagers, do you want them to trust you for fatherly advice or be looking for a way of escape from home at about age 16 or 17?"

Ned looked horrified. "Of course I want them to trust me as their father."

"Then we need to improve communication now before it's too late. Relationships with teenagers are built on trust during childhood—not built on fear."

"I'm just trying to teach them to obey."

"What about counsel that any family leader needs? Do you want to talk to our pastor or your men's group?"

"Absolutely not!" Ned was quite curt. "Nobody else belongs in our private family business."

"But if you have no accountability to your men's group, or our pastor—not even God—how can our family be raised in peace? I need you to be a godly head of our home. The children and I are counting on you."

"The Bible has all the answers we need. I learned that in Bible college. I'm a Christian man!"

"Ned, if you don't want to consult anyone regarding what you call our private family business, how do we establish a peaceful, godly order in our home? Please understand. I'm not trying to undermine your position as head of the house. I want our family to have you as our leader with Christ as your leader. No person is an island. My concern is that we're drifting off on our own without any leadership accountability."

"I don't need some church telling me how to be a leader to my family." Clearly, Ned was annoyed and not hearing what Annalee was trying to convey.

"Ned, when we met you were attending Bible college to become a pastor, a church leader."

"Well, now I'm working full-time to support you and the family, remember?"

"Yes, and I appreciate your hard work, Ned. But we still need God's Word about family leadership." She reached for a Bible.

"Sure. You know I believe the Bible. Go ahead."

"OK. Here is a verse on a father's leadership. Maybe we can pray about it together." Annalee read out loud from Ephesians 6:4. (She was holding an Amplified Bible and read some commentary notes as well.)

"Fathers, do not provoke your children to anger—do not exasperate them to the point of resentment with demands that are trivial or unreasonable or humiliating or abusive; nor by showing favoritism or indifference to any of them— but bring them up—tenderly, with lovingkindness—in the discipline and instruction of the Lord."

Ned developed a somber look on his face, a look of repentance.

"This says we need to change things before it's too late," Annalee said. "The children will be teenagers before we know it. When that time comes, do you want them to trust their heavenly Father with their decisions?"

"You know I do, Annalee. I love our children."

"Then they need to know you love them by the way you treat them!" Annalee seemed to be nearly begging, though tenderly, at this point. "There's only one way for them to see a representation of their heavenly Father. It is through you— their earthly father. You are His representative in the children's eyes. Christian school and Sunday school can only do so much. Peace and order must rule and reign in our home."

"I'm doing the best I can. It's stressful around here." Now Ned seemed to be complaining as much as anything.

"Raising children can be stressful, but they're just children. And Ned, they're already afraid of you."

"Are you kidding me?"

"No. I wish I was. Have you seen the looks in their eyes? Ned, they talk to me about their fears of you."

Ned hung his head.

"I love you, but things have to change around here. You don't let me speak when you're on a rampage when I'm trying to encourage you to calm down. You become angry with me, which makes everything worse. I feel like I have no choice but to be quiet so things don't escalate and become worse for all of us. Now we have a precious baby to protect too. Do you want our children's faith to stand when they grow older and life gets tougher?"

"You know I do."

"Then what kind of memories do we want to leave them? What kind of *legacy*?" Annalee was pleading.

"I want them to have a legacy that our family is a family of honor."

"Then we have to do something about it now. It will take them a lot longer to turn back to God if they grow up feeling condemned. How can they believe in a God who loves them when they're accused of being demoniacs just because they make innocent, childish mistakes?"

Annalee decided to share another verse, from Colossians 3:21. This one she said from memory, from the New International Version.

> *"Fathers, do not embitter your children,*
> *or they will become discouraged."*

Suddenly, Ned began to cry. "I don't want that. I love you and the children. You're a good wife and mother."

"But Ned, I don't feel like a good mother. I actually feel like a terrible mother for being unable to stop volatile situations when our children are suffering. They are not demoniacs—they're just children who make normal mistakes!"

Ned looked down. "You're not a terrible mother. I need to be a better father and a better husband."

"And you can be! If our children experience your godly leadership as their earthly father, your example will enable them to trust their heavenly Father when they reach the age of accountability and begin to make their own decisions. His guidance will help spare them from destructive decisions to fulfill His plans for them."

"That's a good point. I never thought of it like that—as my example. Honey, I'm so sorry."

Annalee felt a sense of instant relief. "Thanks for being willing to listen. It takes a big man to step up and say he is sorry and admit he needs to change. It takes courage to admit our faults and be teachable. You've already won half the battle! You're a good man. I'm so proud of you! I want to do my part to make things better also. Together we can do this!"

"For I know the plans I have for you," declares the LORD, "plans to prosper you and not to harm you, plans to give you hope and a future" (Jeremiah 29:11, NIV).

Josiah had just finished nursing, and even he seemed more relaxed. They held each other with the baby between them, then went out to the living room and gathered the children in a family embrace. Ned picked up his guitar and led the family in a round of the old country song "Let the Circle Be Unbroken."

Joy reigned in their home that evening.

In late May, Ned suggested they take the children on their first trip to the zoo. They saw a family of Panda bear cubs with their mama Panda from China—a sight they never forgot.

Luke and Marie adopted an adorable puppy they named Tidbit who became the mascot of the property. He was an uplifting little encourager to everyone. The spring season brought its majestic beauty as the presence of the Prince of Peace settled in their home. Ned resumed his men's meetings, the children began to blossom in school and as growing children, and they sang their Sunday school songs around the house. Annalee joined the church choir and sang solos occasionally, and the family had a special ceremony in which little Josiah was officially dedicated to the Lord by their pastor.

Hope was renewed in Annalee's heart, the heart of a mother.

Twenty-Nine

IN LATE SPRING, Ned and Annalee hired a local attorney to prepare the necessary documents for stepparent adoption. Ned wanted Annalee to adopt Amanda and Justin, and she wanted the same—with all her heart. After the attorney put the initial work together, Ned and Annalee came to his office to sign the petition for stepparent adoption. Annalee felt a huge sense of relief that she would have equal legal parental authority to protect the children. After the signing, the attorney arranged an appointment with the judge to meet the family; the judge specifically requested that Amanda and Justin be present also. The judge felt including the children in the court process would be a wonderful family memory and educational for them as well.

On adoption day Josiah stayed with Grandma Betsy. Amanda and Justin accompanied their parents to meet the judge in his chambers, joined by Mr. Morris, their family attorney. The family dressed up for this important day. After all, they were meeting a real judge! Justin dressed up like his dad, wearing his church suit with a little tie. Amanda wore one of her prettiest dresses. Like many little girls, she usually resisted the tedious process of waiting for her mother to curl her hair, but that day, with Annalee's pleading, she allowed it without resisting. She even tolerated a ribbon in her hair to match her dress. Annalee wore one of her best dresses. The parents explained that the children should address the judge as "Your Honor" out of respect. They practiced a little on the way to the court building, and both children giggled, promising they would remember.

Judge Parker was a kind, older gentleman of large stature. He first asked Ned's permission to grant his wife the honor of adopting the children. Ned affirmed his support, explaining her role in their lives and commitment to raise them to adulthood. The judge, of course, asked Annalee to confirm her desire and decision to adopt the children. Last, the judge turned to the children, beginning with eight-year-old Amanda. He spoke gently to them.

"Amanda," he said, "would you like Annalee to become your mother?"

"Yes, I would, Your Honor," she said sincerely.

"Do you like her, and is she a good mother to you?" the judge asked.

"Oh yes, I love her! And I want her to be my mom!" She had a little giggle of girlish embarrassment. The judge smiled hugely, enjoying the children.

"Thank you, young lady," he said. He turned to Justin, who had remained focused if only a bit preoccupied with looking around at Judge Parker's massive desk and oversized bookcases. Justin looked a bit overwhelmed at meeting someone of such high distinction.

"Now, Justin," the judge said. The little boy instantly came to attention as if preparing for a military salute. "Young man, I would like to know if you would like Annalee to become your mother."

"Oh yes, I do sir—I mean, uh, Your Honor," Justin said. The judge and family attorney exchanged warm smiles, and it was evident both were enjoying this moment. Annalee was sure this was one of the most pleasant duties a judge could administer in his profession.

"Justin, do you like her, and do you think she is a good mother to you?"

"Yes, I do love her, and I want her to be my mama forever!"

"Well then, congratulations to your entire family," Judge Parker said. "Attorney Morris is present to witness that I approve this petition for adoption." With a flourish, he signed the document, hit the gavel, and came around his desk to shake the hand of each family member. Amanda and Justin were excited to shake the hand of a real judge! After the handshake they wrapped their little arms around both parents for a group hug.

Annalee's heart felt like it would burst with joy.

❤ ❤ ❤

Several days later the home phone rang. It was Mr. Morris calling; he had a concerned voice.

"Mrs. Jackson, I need to schedule an important meeting in my office with you and your husband."

"Yes, sir," Annalee said. "Is something wrong?"

"Yes, we have a complication with the adoption. But I prefer to discuss it in person."

Annalee's heart sank.

"I'll get my appointment book."

❤ ❤ ❤

Later that week Annalee and Ned met at the attorney's office.

"I have disappointing news," Mr. Morris began. "As you know, we have the petition signed by the judge, but we have a complication. Tina, the children's biological mother, refuses to sign a voluntary Relinquishment of Parental Rights and Consent for Adoption form. Both documents must be signed by her to finalize the stepparent adoption."

At the mention of Tina and yet another issue with his former wife, Ned looked as if he could explode with anger.

"Mr. Morris, with all due respect, I don't understand," Annalee said. "Tina, the children's bio-mom, is not only a convicted felon but also legally declared unfit according to court documents. And she is indigent. Without any income, how can she legally defend her position against our petition?"

"You are correct; Tina is indigent. However, her mother recently came into a very large sum of money from a life insurance policy—over one million dollars. Her mother is financially prepared to hire a powerful legal defense team to overturn your petition on behalf of Tina. Regardless of Tina's unfit history, money talks."

"Sir," Annalee said, "as you know, we have a valid Order to Show Cause issued by the Oregon court awarding full custody to Ned until both children are the age of majority, and that's confirmed under Montana jurisdiction as well. Doesn't that long-term OSC override any legal defense Tina's mother could try to launch?"

"Here's the problem: Regardless of the OSC, in order to finalize your stepparent adoption, we are required by law to obtain a certain order: an Involuntary Relinquishment and Involuntary Consent to Adopt because of Tina's unwillingness to sign. But Tina's mother has the bank account to launch a very expensive legal battle, against which we cannot compete." The attorney paused and looked down.

"By the way, I consulted with Judge Parker and he agrees this is where we are," he said. "He sees no viable solution to this."

"I can't believe this is happening!" Ned said. He looked as if in shock.

"So . . . since Tina's side has deep pockets, we're at a standstill, correct?" Annalee asked.

"Correct. I recall you telling me that you had to sacrifice to come up with the thousand dollars needed for me to prepare and file the adoption petition. Sadly, I'm thinking that the reality likely is that you don't have the same deep pockets to engage in extensive litigation to fight this." He paused again. "Not only that, but what if their expensive legal team overturns the OSC you now have in place on a ruse? Do you want an honest piece of advice on this matter?"

"Yes," Ned said. "Please tell us. What do we do?"

"There's an old saying: let sleeping dogs lie. Possession is nine-tenths of the law—you have already won custody of the children, Ned. Since you both are raising them, my advice is this: do not pursue the adoption petition any further. I would simply let it drop. The children already know and trust Annalee as their mother, and she has the authority to care for them in every other way—medical, dental, educational decisions, raising them as her own. Tina has abandoned her parental relationship, and the children know who loves and cares for them. That's what matters."

"So this means we can't finish the adoption?" Ned asked.

The attorney took a deep breath as though what he was about to say was critical. "Not unless you have a million dollars. Furthermore, Ned, you've just finished an exhausting major legal battle that has taken a heavy toll on both of you. It took Annalee's entire salary over a year to pay off both attorneys. You have two young children and a new baby to raise. Not to mention . . . " Once more, he paused. "If you press this any further, Tina and her mother may even pursue a vendetta and come out here to try to kidnap the children again."

"Oh no!" Annalee said. "We would do anything to protect them from ending up in that situation ever again!"

"Then just take care of them and let them grow up with you. Sounds to me like you've slayed enough dragons this past year." Mr. Morris rose to shake their hands. "My advice?" He repeated the phrase. "Let sleeping dogs lie."

"Thank you for trying your best and explaining everything," Annalee said.

"Thank you, sir," Ned said as he shook the attorney's hand.

They had faced another legal giant. But this was one, it seemed, they couldn't conquer.

The loss of the stepparent adoption was a bitter blow to both Annalee and Ned. In just under two years of marriage they had shared more trials than many couples endure in a lifetime. Ned was trying, even in the aftermath of the disappointment of the failed stepparent adoption. Annalee embraced the times when Ned went the extra mile to be kind and patient, and those times seemed to be increasing. He continued working a great deal of overtime driving his truck to take care of the family. They set aside funds for a few family outings planned during the summer months.

Frequently Annalee heard the words "I love you" or "You are a Proverbs 31 wife and mother." There were times Ned would wrap the children in his arms with their baby brother and tell them, "Daddy loves you all so much." He would use other times to teach guitar to Justin. Those moments were golden.

Ned also loved to cook, and he would often tell Annalee, "Take a break from the kitchen, honey. I'll do the cooking tonight." Ned could whip up an amazing meal in thirty minutes—much faster than Annalee. She appreciated those breaks from the kitchen because it gave her extra time to spend with the children and cuddle the baby. Josiah was always hungry and growing fast. He was a healthy, beautiful baby and already showing signs of being quite intelligent. Sometimes Amanda would join Annalee and Josiah in the bedroom and ask questions about baby brother's feeding habits. Annalee would explain lactation and how children and babies are gifts from God. Amanda had a sensitive spirit and loved to learn about motherhood. Annalee treasured those precious moments with her young daughter.

She also valued her moments with Justin to talk about the things that interested him—dinosaurs, Legos, animals, and science. He was a typical little boy with a curious mind and creative interests. Justin loved to sing songs and also enjoyed writing poems! Annalee would write down his ideas for him. Her background was in music, art, and creative writing, so this was a great fit.

In early June, Ned suggested the family visit a dinosaur museum because Justin loved dinosaurs so much. Justin was enthralled seeing the massive reconstructed dinosaur bones. Another time, a local mall held a robotic dinosaur exhibit with a giant T-Rex that moved and roared. They all went to see it along with Marie, Luke, and Mercy. The entire family loved that incredible robotic T-Rex!

Those memories brought renewed hope, healing, and restoration to the children.

The family was fragile, but that made Annalee love them all the more.

♥ ♥ ♥

One evening Ned said he needed to talk to Annalee after supper, so they found a spot on the sofa.

"Remember the last few weeks I told you about my work truck?" Ned asked.

"Yes, you said it was having some problems."

"Well, I checked it out several times at the company shop. The shop mechanic tested it after work yesterday. We both agree there seems to be something wrong with the steering, but the diagnostics at the shop haven't confirmed it. We're gonna test it again tomorrow."

"What's the age of the truck?"

"That old beast is sixteen years old with lots of wear and tear. It doesn't even have a padded headliner—it's all metal inside! In an accident, that would really do a number on the poor shmuck behind the wheel. The seat belt is kind of frayed, and it's so old it's even snapped open a few times on the road. When that happens, I pull over and resnap it. So now I'm looking around the shop for a newer seat belt to install in that old truck."

"That's dangerous for a seat belt to come undone!"

"I know. Today I talked to Frank, one of the owners of the company, and told him the truck is not roadworthy. I asked him for a safer truck to drive. Would you believe it? He says if I want to keep my job, that's the only truck he's willing for me to drive."

"I remember Frank, Ralph, and Otis from the Christmas party last year. So they have nothing else available?"

"Oh, they have newer delivery trucks on the lot. But they refuse to assign me a better one to drive."

"Oh my. Do you want me to update your resume so you can apply at other trucking companies?"

"That would be great. I'll quit as soon as I'm hired at a new job. Right now, I need to stay put because we can't afford a gap with no income."

"I understand. I'll update your resume ASAP."

"Thanks, honey." He gave her a big hug.

The LORD executes righteousness And justice for all who are oppressed (Psalms 103:6, NKJV).

Cast all your care upon Him, for He cares for you (1 Peter 5:7, NKJV).

Come to me and I will give you rest—all of you who work so hard beneath a heavy yoke. Wear my yoke—for it fits perfectly—and let me teach you; for I am gentle and humble, and you shall find rest for your souls; for I give you only light burdens." — Jesus (Matthew 11:28, TLB)

Thirty

Tuesday, June 14: Brain Trauma

THE CHILDREN were on summer break, and they were spending one morning building a Lego project together. Baby Josiah was now five and a half months and contentedly sitting in his bouncer seat cooing and watching Mama clean up the kitchen from breakfast. She was laughing, smiling, talking to him, and coaxing him to say "Ma-ma."

All in all, it seemed pretty close to a perfect morning.

About 9:15, the telephone rang.

"Hello. May I please speak with Mrs. Jackson?"

"Yes, this is she."

"Mrs. Jackson, are you sitting down?" Suddenly, Annalee felt weak. She sat down next to the baby.

"Yes. I am now."

"I'm a registered nurse calling from Glacier Regional Medical Center. Your husband Ned was involved in a truck accident this morning and flown in by Life Flight helicopter. He is being transferred from our ER for admission to our neuroscience ICU unit." Annalee fought back tears and felt her voice weaken.

"Neuroscience unit? Nurse, is my husband being transferred there because of a brain injury?"

"I'm sorry, Mrs. Jackson, but I can't release your husband's medical details by phone. He is currently undergoing evaluation by our chief neurologist. His physicians will have more information when you arrive."

Years before, Annalee had spent many long hours with her small son Lance in the neuroscience unit at Children's Hospital during his short life. Her mind went into overdrive, asking—and answering—questions.

Life Flight helicopter?

That's serious.

Neurologist and neuroscience unit?

Brain trauma.

And then this question, for which there was no easy answer.

Am I destined to deal with brain traumas with my loved ones?

Glacier Regional Medical Center was a Level II Trauma Center for the entire region within 30 minutes of their home. She was grateful Ned had been flown there.

"Thank you for calling. I'm on my way," Annalee said.

Before she left the house she called the women's ministry leader at their church and requested that Ned be put on the prayer chain.

Yea, though I walk through the valley of the shadow of death, I will fear no evil; for You are with me; Your rod and Your staff, they comfort me (Psalm 23:4, NKJV).

After hurriedly packing a lunch and dropping the children off at Mercy's house, Annalee and baby Josiah quickly headed for the hospital. On arriving, she was directed to wait in the Neuroscience Department lobby. As she gave her name at the nurse's station, a nurse told her that she was emotional and said, "Mrs. Jackson, please have a seat. I'll be right with you." The nurse came around the counter. "Hi, little fella," she greeted the baby. Josiah grinned back at her.

"I'm Nancy, a registered nurse. You've been told about your husband's accident, right?"

"Yes, but I know very little," Annalee said. "I'm concerned because ER told me he arrived by helicopter and that he was transferred here for admission to the Neuroscience Unit."

"That's correct. He was transported by our Life Flight helicopter with a trauma team for the best care en route from the scene of the accident. They informed us it was a multiple rollover crash,[16] and Mr. Jackson is being evaluated for a head injury."

Annalee began softly crying.

"I promise you: your husband is in good hands, Mrs. Jackson." The nurse reached over and patted her on the shoulder. "He's under the care of our best brain trauma specialists, and the next few days are the most critical ones. We are a state-of-the-art facility, and he has been admitted to our Neuroscience Unit so our neurology team can keep him under observation post-accident while he undergoes a thorough diagnostic assessment." She paused. "His physician will be out shortly to visit with you and answer any questions you may have." She paused again. "May I get you something, or some formula for your baby?"

"That's so kind of you, but no. My baby is still nursing, and I brought everything else we needed from home. Thank you, Nancy."

"My pleasure. I'm letting his doctors know you're here. Please let me know if you need anything."

Annalee and the baby had waited only a short time when a distinguished-looking physician appeared and pulled up a chair.

"Mrs. Jackson?"

"Yes, doctor."

He extended his hand to Annalee and smiled warmly at the baby.

"I'm Dr. Todd, the chief of neurology here at the hospital. I am in charge of your husband's care. As you know, Ned is still undergoing a number of tests to determine the extent of his injuries."

"Dr. Todd, what do you know so far?"

"Based on his symptoms, he appears to have sustained a moderate-level traumatic brain injury.[17] We won't have a definitive diagnosis until the results of the CT scan are completed. We've also placed him under consistent EEG monitoring because he has had two grand mal seizures today from which he spontaneously recovered. He is also having periodic vomiting. I'm consulting with neurosurgeon Doctor Baldwin."

"Oh no! Does my husband need neurosurgery?" Annalee asked.

"Probably not. Doctor Baldwin's consult is precautionary, due to your husband's bilateral black eyes—also known as raccoon eyes. He's ordered an MRI and additional tests to determine the integrity of his skull to confirm the absence of any fractures or cranial pressure that may need to be relieved. We'll know more later."

"Understood. Is he conscious?"

"He was unconscious at the scene of the accident. The in-flight trauma team said he awakened aboard the helicopter after the first grand mal seizure. He opened his eyes, then fell to sleep. Since arriving here he is vacillating between semi-conscious and sleep states. He moans and mumbles but does not articulate words."

"When can I see him, Doctor?"

"He's still undergoing Doctor Baldwin's assessment, but we will arrange for you to see him ASAP."

"Thank you, Doctor." They shook hands and he left. She headed to the restroom to nurse Josiah and pray.

We are hard-pressed on every side, yet not crushed; we are perplexed, but not in despair; persecuted, but not forsaken; struck down, but not destroyed—
(2 Corinthians 4:8, 9, NKJV).

It was a long wait that day.

Two more hours passed. While Annalee waited, she wrote down some questions for doctors and calls that should be made.

From the hospital courtesy phone she called Mercy with an update to relay to family. She then checked the phone book to call the local Montana Highway Patrol non-emergency number. After reaching the MHP office, she introduced herself and requested to speak with one of the first responders. She was connected with Officer Anderson, who identified himself as one of the first on Ned's accident scene.

"Officer Anderson, my husband, Ned Jackson, was the truck accident victim at the scene you investigated this morning." She provided him Ned's identification, date of birth, truck description, and truck license plate, along with her ID.

After a few more facts were exchanged, she said, "I need your assistance to determine what occurred at the scene today."

"I'm sorry to hear about your husband's condition," Anderson said. "A local farmer spotted the crashed truck and called us from his house. Our unit headed to the scene ASAP. We found the truck upside down in a cornfield. We don't know what caused the truck to lose control and leave the road, but based on the distance we measured to its location, the truck evidently rolled multiple times. We found your husband trapped inside, unconscious, crumpled against the metal truck top. The seat belt had snapped, so it was evident he was unrestrained during the rollover impact. His head and face had sustained multiple contusions and bilateral black eyes. The windshield, side windows, and rear window were all shattered, so your husband was hit by projectiles from shattered glass. The truck is totaled, crushed on every side. We immediately called Life Flight and requested a trauma team for transport. He was extracted by Jaws of Life and loaded onto the helicopter."

"Officer Anderson, did my husband regain consciousness before the helicopter arrived?"

"Not before arrival. But he opened his eyes a few minutes during extraction and transfer to the gurney."

"Do you know the length of time he was unconscious before MHP arrived?"

"Unfortunately not, because there were no witnesses to the crash, and it was a single-vehicle accident in a rural area. I can tell you this much: from the time the farmer called us to the time of our arrival was twenty minutes. Plus the ETA of the helicopter and trauma team took an additional twenty-five minutes."

"That's helpful. After my husband was removed from the vehicle, what towing company was called?"

"We needed a large-platform towing rig, so we called Speedy Towing. They're nearby in Alpine View."

"Do you know where Speedy Towing took the truck?"

"Yes. They said they were taking it to Security Salvage and Storage, also located in Alpine View. They said the truck will be held there until the trucking company's insurance adjuster examines it."

"OK. Last of all, how soon will the MHP sheriff's report be ready for pickup?"

"It will be ready in five to seven business days."

"Good. I'll pick it up then. Thank you for all your information and helping my husband, officer."

"Glad to be of service, and I hope your husband recovers soon."

Once she hung up, Annalee thought: *Who else do I call? We both need legal protection immediately.*

She was up against Frank, Ralph, and Otis—Ned's wealthy trucking company owners, clearly liable for refusing to assign him a safe truck. Ned was brain-injured and she needed the best possible defense for him. She picked up the phone and called someone she knew in town, an assertive accident attorney. She explained Ned's accident, injuries, and the company's refusal to issue him a roadworthy truck. She also told him what she knew about the faulty condition of the truck—especially the steering and seat belt—and asked him to arrange a thorough third-party examination, ASAP, of the truck's mechanical condition and the cause of accident. She also requested the attorney implement an immediate chain of custody to protect the truck's whereabouts 24/7. This would avoid having the truck dispatched to salvage for crushing; that would constitute a disappearance of evidence. She gave all details on where the truck was being held.

They committed to a verbal contractual agreement, and Annalee scheduled to stop by his office that week to sign a contingency retainer on Ned's behalf. The attorney assured her he would get to work immediately and handle all communications. After hanging up, she breathed a sigh of relief knowing she would be spared the ordeal of having to answer probing questions from the trucking company's insurance adjusters.

With an attorney on their side, Annalee could concentrate on Ned.

Josiah fell asleep in his stroller moments before Dr. Todd appeared again.

"Mrs. Jackson, your husband's CT scan is complete. Based on impact, it appears he sustained a moderate-level traumatic brain injury, also known as a TBI. Thankfully, his skull remained intact during the accident, so there are no skull fractures. This type of brain injury is called a closed head injury. I've just spoken with the neurosurgeon, Doctor Baldwin. The MRI and other tests completed so far negate any evidence of fluid pressure on his brain, and they show no fractures in his neck. He doesn't appear to require any surgical intervention."

"Thank God!" Annalee said.

"Indeed," Dr. Todd said. He glanced at Josiah. "Do you expect your baby to remain asleep for a while?"

"Yes, he just fell asleep and should remain sound asleep for about another hour or so."

"In that case, I'll make an exception for the sleeping baby. Your husband is in an individual ICU room. He is very confused, but I know you want to see him, and I believe it will do him good if he's aware you are there."

"Thank you."

She followed Dr. Todd down the hall.

They paused outside Ned's room. The ICU nurse glanced questioningly at the sleeping baby, then up at Dr. Todd. He spoke to her and authorized permission for the visit as long as the baby remained quiet. The nurse smiled as they passed.

Annalee was unprepared for what she saw, but she had learned to remain calm during her years of taking care of Lance. Ned lay stabilized in a large neck collar with his head elevated. Multiple cranial electrodes protruded from his head in every conceivable angle leading to several monitors at the head of his bed. Ned's hands were in restraints attached to the bedrails to prevent him from accidentally pulling out electrodes. He was receiving oxygen via nasal cannula tubes and had heart and blood pressure monitors. His head and face revealed the multiple contusions and bilateral black eyes, plus a knot that swelled from his frontal lobe.

Ned's ICU nurse entered the room to check his vitals and IV. His face, neck, shoulders, and arms were laced with bleeding cuts of various sizes oozing small particles of blood. None, though, appeared large enough to require stitches. The nurse began swabbing the cuts with antiseptic. She used surgical tweezers to remove small particulates of transparent, shiny objects extending from his skin.

"Nurse, are those cuts from broken glass?"

"Yes they are." She continued working as she talked. "The transport team reported the windshield shattered during impact, so he was sprayed with shards of broken glass."

"That confirms what the Montana Highway Patrol saw at the scene," Annalee quietly said.

"We've removed many of them so far, but the tiniest under-surface shards are continuing to create little cuts," the nurse said. "Some are working their way to the surface of the skin and protruding. Most are tiny, like splinters. We're tweezing them out and cleansing the abrasions."

"Does he have other areas like this where shards sprayed into his skin?"

"Yes, the velocity of the flying glass penetrated his clothing. So he has multiple sites in his chest and back as well. It is much like a severely skinned knee during childhood, with pieces of asphalt, but over a widespread surface."

"Oh, that must hurt!"

"Yes it does, according to patients who've verbally explained to us how it feels." She continued tweezing and cleaning the cut areas.

While Annalee stayed back from the bed with the stroller to avoid being in the nurse's way, Ned's eyes wandered aimlessly as he moaned in pain. She wondered if he knew she was in the room.

"Is my husband conscious yet?" she asked.

"He is conscious, but still quite drowsy. Part of that drowsiness is an aftereffect from the two grand mal seizures he had today. The moaning indicates he's aware of the pain in his head and is trying to acclimate to his surroundings."

"This is heartbreaking."

"Yes, it is. I'm so sorry your husband has been brain-injured," the nurse said compassionately.

"Thank you so much."

"Would you like to move near the bed in your husband's line of sight? Maybe he will respond to you."

Annalee and the baby moved in the direction of Ned's wandering eyes. "Hi, honey. We love you."

Ned's eyes continued wandering, and then tears began streaming down his cheeks.

Just then, Josiah woke up. Annalee lifted him from his stroller and held him up for Ned to see. In spite of the bruises, the baby recognized his daddy and gave him a grin and a coo.

Dr. Todd patted the baby gently on the back and said, "If there's anything that can bring a smile to life, it's a baby. This moment just made my day!"

Ned was still moaning in confusion. Annalee bent and tenderly kissed him on the cheek.

She turned to the doctor. "Doctor Todd, thanks for taking such good care of my husband. I'm going to have to get this little guy back home to his brother and sister. We will see you tomorrow."

"Sounds good. Meanwhile, till then, we'll do everything we can to take good care of Ned."

As Annalee prepared to step from Ned's room with the baby, she was dismayed to encounter the three owners of the company: Frank, Ralph, and Otis. She nodded politely. All three looked uncomfortable as they passed Annalee upon entering the room—especially Frank, who had refused to assign a better truck for Ned to drive. As they walked in and caught their first glimpse of Ned, the horrified looks on their faces were unmistakable. Annalee had worked for enough attorneys and corporate executives to catch the glances exchanged between all three: this couldn't spell good things for their company.

Annalee stopped and spoke quietly with Ned's ICU nurse. "Would you please keep an eye on those three gentlemen who just entered Ned's room and make sure they don't stay very long? They're the owners of the trucking company, and I don't want them to disturb my husband."

"Of course, Mrs. Jackson," the nurse said with a cautious glance in their direction.

She immediately stepped into Ned's room, and Annalee and the baby headed home.

❤ ❤ ❤

Call upon Me in the day of trouble; I will deliver you, and you shall glorify Me (Psalm 50:15, NKJV).

You shall not be afraid of the terror by night,
Nor of the arrow that flies by day,
Nor of the pestilence that walks in darkness,
Nor of the destruction that lays waste at noonday
(Psalm 91:5, 6, NKJV).

Let us not become weary in doing good,
for at the proper time we will reap a harvest
if we do not give up (Galatians 6:9, NIV).

Thirty-One

THAT EVENING Annalee had a meeting with all the adults in the family to discuss details on Ned's accident and the seriousness of his injuries. Amanda and Justin were told that Daddy was in the hospital, needed to stay for a while to get better, and had lots of good doctors taking care of him. Mercy and Grandma Betsy worked out a summer program of care for the children; the baby would remain with Annalee.

The next morning Annalee was up early to pack lunches and get the children ready for Mercy's house.

"Mama, can't we go with you to the hospital to see Daddy?" Amanda and Justin pleaded.

"Daddy has to sleep a lot right now, but you kids will see him soon." Given Ned's physical appearance, Annalee wanted to protect them from the shock of seeing their dad just yet, so she redirected their attention.

"Hey, guess what? Today, you're going to have a playday at Aunt Mercy's!" The children quickly got excited. She tucked her soft briefcase into the baby's diaper bag. She had five business stops en route to the hospital. These included the Workman's Compensation office to pick up an application for

Ned's family income payments; another stop to get his medical payments form from the same office; to the Disability Office to pick up an application for Ned (both temporary and permanent, depending on prognosis); the auto insurance office to apply for bi-monthly accident income payments; and to the accident attorney's office to sign her retainer.

At the hospital, nurse Nancy greeted her. "Good morning, Mrs. Jackson. The doctors are examining Ned. I'll let them know you're waiting."

"Thank you," Annalee said. "Did he have a good night?"

"I believe he did," Nancy said with a smile.

"That's great. I'll be in the restroom for a few minutes, Nancy. The baby is hungry."

The two women admired little Josiah for a couple of minutes. "Where did he get his beautiful red hair—and those turquoise eyes!" Nancy said.

Annalee described how the other children looked with their chestnut hair and stunning blue eyes. She reached into her purse to show Nancy a family portrait.

After finishing with Josiah in the restroom, Annalee took a seat in the lobby. In between entertaining the baby, she began filling out the paperwork necessary to keep the family income activated. She did some rough calculations and discovered that the combined accident and disability income from the different agencies would be about three hundred dollars per month more than Ned's income with overtime. She felt greatly relieved.

About an hour went by, and Dr. Todd rounded the corner. "Hey there, little buddy!" he greeted the baby. Josiah grinned back.

"Good morning, doctor."

"Good morning, Mrs. Jackson. I have some encouraging news. As you know, Ned was unconscious yesterday for quite a while post-accident. Considering that length of time, he has surprised us with the apparent level of consciousness he's already regained. Ned is in acute phase of recovery, so we are still evaluating his situation. TBI patients need a lot of sleep to recover from a head injury because the brain is the slowest organ of the body to heal. Depending on progress, he'll remain in Neuro ICU for the next three to five days then transfer to a regular room on the neuroscience floor as we continue assessing his needs and progress."

"Thank you, Doctor Todd. It sounds encouraging. Anything else I should know?"

"Yes. As his neuro team, we are taking this one day at a time, and his progress will determine his release date from this hospital. When Ned is released to home, he will need to transition to daily outpatient treatment at a rehabilitation center. Doctor Baldwin and I are discussing options. This is a bit premature, but given your family responsibilities, we wanted to make you aware so you can prepare for his future needs."

"Doctor, how often will Ned need to attend the outpatient rehab center, and for how long?"

"Most TBI patients require a rehab schedule of five days per week, six hours per day, for about one year post-accident. The clinic will schedule according to your family's needs."

"Wow. A huge investment of time."

"Yes, but rehab is very effective and necessary. Ned will regain abilities like talking, walking, and compensatory skills for brain functions compromised in the accident. One more thing. Doctor Baldwin and I initially assessed his injury as a moderate-level TBI based on his length of unconsciousness and the severity of the multiple rollover impact to his cranium. However, your husband has surprised us with several behaviors which are atypical for the acute stage, so we are collaborating with several other neurophysician colleagues."

"So my husband's injury may not be as severe as you first thought?"

"We hope that is the case, but it's still premature," Dr. Todd said. "We're redoing tests with our colleagues in the hope of a more promising prognosis. Afterward, we may reevaluate Ned between mild and moderate-level TBI."

"Thanks for the update and preparing me in advance for what lies ahead," Annalee said. "I'll begin making long-term arrangements for the family to accommodate Ned's rehab schedule. By the way, no more seizures?"

"None since yesterday. We're encouraged and glad to be of service, Mrs. Jackson. I'm getting ready to visit with Ned right now. Would you like to follow?"

"Yes, thank you!" She quickly tucked away her paperwork. "What about the baby?"

"This little guy seems to be pretty happy and quiet, and it will do Ned some good to see both of you." The doctor headed down some hallways and into Ned's room.

"Ned, look who is here to see you!"

Annalee lifted the baby and stepped directly in front of Ned. His eyes wandered, blinked, then stared at Annalee and Josiah. The baby wiggled and cooed while looking at his daddy.

Ned tried to make a sound, but it came out, instead, like a moan.

"Is he in pain?" Annalee asked.

"Yes. Horrific headaches account for most of his discomfort. In the acute stage after head trauma, we have to be careful what we prescribe for pain, but we're trying to make him as comfortable as we can."

"Thank you for everything you are doing to help him, doctor." She stepped over and kissed Ned's cheek, trying to avoid the bruised areas of his face. "I love you, honey. We all love you." His eyes tried to look in her direction.

A minute or two later, Dr. Todd quietly asked, "Did you notice Ned's eyes staring at you and the baby, then trying to look your direction when you kissed him? That is called tracking. We don't usually observe tracking until at least several weeks post-accident. That is one of the hopeful symptoms we're paying attention to."

"Thanks for pointing that out. I'll be watching for that. Doctor, I have some business to attend to, but I'll stay in touch. You have my home phone number, and the home phones of my family members."

"Yes. I'll stay in touch," he said.

"Bye, honey." She blew Ned a kiss.

Annalee stopped at the hospital cafeteria and finished the paperwork for the various agencies, then dropped them off one by one along with copies of hospital documents as proof of Ned's injuries.

Within a couple of weeks, Ned was approved and the checks began coming in to keep the family going. All of Ned's medical expenses were covered by the trucking company's Workman's Comp medical insurance.

The summer routine moved on. With the extra disability finances every month, Annalee was able to reimburse Mercy and her mother Betsy for their help with childcare.

Every day Annalee and the baby visited Ned. His responsiveness continued to improve. Ned was now in his own room on the Neuroscience Unit, and his physicians continued his retesting. The electrodes were disconnected, and Ned's hands were taken from the restraints.

Two Weeks Post-Accident

About two weeks into the ordeal, Annalee held Josiah in front of Ned. His eyes focused on the baby, and the edges of his lips tried to curl into a smile as his hands attempted to reach for the baby. It appeared he was attempting to reach to Annalee as well, so she stepped closer and took one of his hands in hers. A few tears rolled down his cheeks as his fingers tried to curl around hers. The ICU nurse was in the room as this happened.

"This is an excellent sign, Mrs. Jackson," she said. "He not only knows you're here, his emotions are connecting with you. His eyes are looking toward you, and his fingers are responding to his brain's command. I'm going to let Doctor Todd and Doctor Baldwin know. They will be so pleased!"

Annalee stayed with Ned as long as she could. He continued to demonstrate awareness of her presence. A while later, Dr. Todd entered the room.

"I hear our patient is improving!" He turned to Ned. "Hello, Ned. I'm Doctor Todd. You're in the hospital." Ned's eyes slowly shifted to the sound of Dr. Todd's voice.

"Will you do me a favor?" He raised one finger in front of Ned's eyes. "Can you see my finger?"

Ned's eyes sluggishly attempted to focus on the doctor's finger. "Good job!

"Ned, let's see if you can follow my finger with your eyes." The doctor moved his finger from right to left. Ned's eyes very gradually moved with the finger. The doctor smiled broadly.

"I think we're making progress!"

The doctor continued testing Ned's eye movements, then asked Ned some basic questions.

"Do you remember taking a ride in a helicopter?"

Ned's mouth tried to move. "Good for you. You're trying to talk to me. I just want you to nod yes or no."

Ned very slowly nodded his head.

Dr. Todd reached for Ned's hand and said, "Do you remember driving your truck? Squeeze my fingers two times for yes and one time for no."

Ned squeezed the doctor's hand twice. The doctor smiled and turned briefly to Annalee. "We have memory."

Annalee smiled back. This truly was a good sign.

Ned started to moan. "Are you in pain?" the doctor asked. Ned nodded and moaned again. "Ned, we'll try to make you more comfortable. You have a head injury, so we have to be very careful what we can give you for pain. We'll see what we can do."

Three Weeks Post-Accident

The hospital was decorated for the Fourth of July, and some patriotic music was being played across the overhead. Annalee was dressed in her typical attire for the season, wearing red, white, and blue.

Dr. Todd entered while Annalee and the baby were visiting and asked, "Ned, do you know what month this is?"

Ned tried to hold up four fingers, then started to cry. "I'm sorry," Dr. Todd said. "Something wrong with the month?"

Suddenly, realization came to Annalee.

"It's OK, honey! Doctor, it's our anniversary. He remembered we can't celebrate."

Ned nodded.

"Oh my goodness!" Dr. Todd said. "I had no idea. But do you know what this means? Ned's memory is increasing!"

Suddenly the moment didn't seem so sad after all.

Annalee kissed Ned on the cheek. His facial bruises were improving a great deal, and he didn't have those raccoon eyes anymore.

"Doctor, may I ask you a question?" Annalee asked him privately a few minutes later.

After the doctor nodded yes, she lowered her voice even more. "Would it be OK if I bring our other children to celebrate our second anniversary here in Ned's room? They haven't seen their father since the accident."

"Of course," he laughed. "That's a great idea!"

She gave Ned a quick kiss and said, "Honey, the baby and I will be back soon."

He looked confused.

"I promise—you'll be glad. I won't be long."

She stopped at the hospital courtesy phone to call Mercy and asked her to get the children ready in patriotic colors to visit their dad at the hospital. She invited Mercy, Betsy, Luke, and Marie. Then she hurried out to order a patriotic cake with the words Happy Anniversary and added some festive balloons as well. Josiah had a great time with those, so she bought extra.

She and the baby dashed home, picked up the family, then stopped at the bakery to pick up the cake and some ice cream.

Amanda and Justin were thrilled to help celebrate Daddy and Mama's anniversary. On the way, she explained the protocol for being quiet in hospitals and told them their daddy's face was a little bruised up from the accident and that he had some tubes connected but not to worry—he was OK. She warned them to be very gentle with their father, not to hug him too hard. They promised to be careful.

The family entered Ned's room carrying a party. "Happy anniversary!" said the children as they came bouncing in. The nursing assistants had kindly set up a table with a red tablecloth in the corner, so they unloaded the cake and ice cream and hung balloons around the room. It was a festive atmosphere! Ned's face displayed the first recognizable smile Annalee had seen since the accident; he even appeared to have a little twinkle in his eyes. Dr. Todd and the nurses were invited in for cake and ice cream.

Annalee introduced Justin and Amanda to Dr. Todd and explained he was the man taking good care of their father. They each politely shook his hand and said, "Thank you, Mister Doctor, for taking such good care of our daddy and helping him get better." The nurses were greatly enjoying this event.

Dr. Todd grinned ear to ear. "You're very welcome." He chuckled and said to Annalee, "You have an adorable family."

Everyone thanked the doctor and nurses while the children chattered on. "Would ya like some cake and ice cream, Mister Doctor?" Justin asked.

"Why sure!" He pulled up a chair. As he glanced over at Ned's face, he said, "I think this party is just what the doctor ordered!" Ned slowly turned toward the doctor and curled the corners of his mouth into a smile.

Baby Josiah was grinning at everyone and enjoying the cake with the rest of them—it was all over his face, his red, white, and blue outfit, and his stroller. He was a sight to behold.

A bit later, Annalee scooped up the baby to head out to clean him up and nurse him. As she stood holding this delightful messy bundle, she glanced over and saw Ned's mouth curled in a funny-looking smile. He had focused from across the room and was amused at the mess his baby had made with the cake.

What a precious moment!

She realized Ned had just turned another corner in his recovery. He could enjoy life and smile.

Four Weeks Post-Accident

When Annalee arrived one morning, Dr. Todd met her in the room. "We're going to try something new," he said. "Ned is trying to make sounds."

"That's great!" She stood by Ned's bed and looked into his eyes to encourage him.

"Ned, can you say your wife's name?" Ned tried to move his lips. Suddenly a sound emerged.

"A-a—"

Annalee knew this also meant great progress. She turned away to hide her tears of joy. Ned was going to regain his speech. "Good job, Ned!" the doctor said. "How about one more time? Can you say your wife's name?"

"A-a-n—"

"Awesome!" the doctor said. As if on cue, little Josiah giggled, and Ned curled his lips into a small smile.

Annalee stepped over and kissed Ned lightly on the cheek. "Great job, honey!" Ned tried to curl his lips again, realizing he had done something well.

Doctor Todd then had a big announcement.

"I believe Ned will be ready to be released from the hospital within two weeks. You and little fella here are definitely improving his progress! Considering the impact he sustained, this is amazing!"

"That's great news!" Annalee replied.

He turned to Ned. "Ned, your mouth and lips are responding to your brain. You'll be talking again before you know it!" Ned's lips tried to curl once more.

Over the next two weeks Dr. Todd assigned an occupational therapist to assist with adaptive physical therapy and a speech therapist to work with Ned's language skills. Annalee began attending classes at the hospital to learn how to assist Ned after his return home.

Doctors Todd and Baldwin had a meeting with her to discuss Ned's rehabilitation program. After his discharge from the hospital he would be transferred to outpatient therapy at Glacier Neuroscience Rehabilitation Clinic under the care of neuropsychiatrist Dr. Brad Nelson, founder and director of that center.

Give your burdens to the LORD, and he will take care of
you. He will not permit the godly to slip and fall
(Psalms 55:22, NLT).

Commit everything you do to the LORD. Trust him, and
he will help you. He will make your innocence radiate like

the dawn, and the justice of your cause will shine like the noonday sun (Psalms 37:5, 6, NLT).

Don't be afraid, for I am with you. Don't be discouraged, for I am your God. I will strengthen you and help you. I will hold you up with my victorious right hand (Isaiah 41:10, NLT).

"So anyone who becomes as humble as this little child is the greatest in the Kingdom of Heaven."
—Jesus (Matthew 18:4, NLT)

Thirty-Two

Pivotal Moment

ANNALEE SAT across the desk from neuropsychiatrist Nelson. Ned was to be released from the hospital to return home in a few days.

She rocked Josiah in his new cushioned reclining stroller Grandma Betsy had purchased to keep him comfortable during the long hours they would be spending at the clinic. He was a happy baby, easy to manage, cooing and playing with his attached baby toys.

"Mrs. Jackson, I arranged our meeting this morning to have a serious discussion with you," Dr. Nelson said. "As you probably know, the national divorce statistics are approximately 50 percent—a very unfortunate statistic."

Annalee could only quickly wonder: *Why is Dr. Nelson raising this issue?*

"The purpose of my meeting with you is to discuss the impact of Ned's post-injury life versus his pre-injury life, and what that will look like with his life going forward." He paused. "I don't know if you are aware of this, but when one spouse has a brain injury, the divorce statistics jump to the ninety-plus percentile."

"Oh my!" Annalee said. "Why?"

Dr. Nelson shifted in his seat. "Let me put it like this: your husband's brain has been radically altered. Life presents normal day-to-day trials, such as conflict resolution, parenting, or relational issues—even household chores or just fixing the bathroom sink. The average person negotiates a way to problem-solve life issues.

"However, those same challenges feel like impossible hurdles to a brain-injured patient. Those irritations result in a wide range of unpredictable emotional responses. Rage, for example." He paused briefly and shifted once more.

"To put it bluntly, Mrs. Jackson: if your husband had a short fuse pre-accident, he will have *no* fuse post-accident. Most spouses of brain-injured patients comprise the ninety-plus percent who leave the marriage because they are unable to cope with the emotional outbursts and multitude of other behavioral and physical aftereffects suffered by a spouse with brain trauma.

"So, Mrs. Jackson, I need one answer from you. How committed are you to this marriage?"

"Dr. Nelson, I only have one choice: First of all, I am the mother of three young children who need me at home—not only our baby here, but two young children ages seven and eight. In addition, the accident was not Ned's fault. I can't abandon him when he needs me more than ever. So I'm in it for the long haul."

"Well, that's what I needed to know," Dr. Nelson said. "Since you've told me you are in this for the long haul, I'm immediately ordering therapy sessions for you and your children. It will be completely funded by the insurance covering the accident. This means I'm putting you all into full-time therapy to learn how to manage living with a brain-injured husband. There are many new things you'll need to learn, so every day that you bring Ned to the neuroscience clinic for his rehab, you'll attend therapy at the same time."

Annalee could only suddenly reflect. *So this is what life will be like when Ned comes home to the family.* She felt a bit nauseous. It must have shown on her face.

"Are you all right, Mrs. Jackson?"

"Uh, yes," Annalee said. "It's a lot to take in, but I'll be OK. Thanks for explaining some things I didn't realize. Ned has seemed to be so peaceful at the hospital. I realize it is a different atmosphere from home life. So, Dr. Nelson, I have two questions: First, why would Ned's behavior change from what it has been in the hospital neuroscience unit these last four weeks?"

"Because he will not be helpless anymore," Dr. Nelson said. "He has been in acute care at the hospital, unable to speak or ambulate. We are teaching him to speak and walk again. While it is positive for a person to be as self-sufficient as possible, Ned will encounter the frustration of brain deficits he has never known before. That's why we often see a difference between the behavior at the acute stage in the hospital and the recovery stage after the patient returns home and begins rehab."

"Oh, I see. My second question is this: Are these emotional outbursts you've just described usually temporary or long-range?"

Dr. Nelson's face took on a look of strain. "Mrs. Jackson, the brain is the slowest organ in the body to heal. It is a *long* process. With a mild-moderate brain injury, we usually see improvement over a period of years, but it is basically a lifelong process. It can also be complicated by any prior life issues the patient has experienced. It would be so much easier if a TBI patient could have amnesia regarding painful memories, but unfortunately those are typically the intact long-term memories. The patient may dwell and ruminate on those memories and project those memories onto their family. That's where our plan for you and your children comes in."

"What do you mean?"

"Our team considers each patient's individual family dynamics. In your case, the baby is so young he will only grow up knowing your husband's behavior post-accident, which means that as he grows up, he will have the most understanding of him relationally because post-accident is the only way he will know and remember his father.

"However, your grown children and your seven- and eight-year-old will remember the difference, so our clinic will include your grown children in an adult therapy group, and your young children will attend a children's group. In these groups our therapists teach them ways to adapt to living with a brain-injured parent and ways to respond that will hopefully help diffuse reactive situations."

"Doctor, I have a concern," Annalee said. "My seven- and eight-year-old have recently been rescued from a prior trauma situation themselves from which they are still recovering. They are still in therapy for that. How do we prevent them from being retraumatized by their dad's situation?"

"I understand. I will meet with my children's therapist who can coordinate with their other therapists to take those issues into consideration. Her goal will be to train your children how to live with a brain-injured parent. You will be trained as a mother and spouse to diffuse situations that may arise."

"It sounds complicated," Annalee said.

"I would be the first to tell you this will not be easy, but my team and I are dedicated to doing everything we can to help all of you," Dr. Nelson said gently. "While you and your family are undergoing therapy, Ned will be receiving a variety of modalities for brain injury recovery—patterning to regain walking and gait, speech therapy for aphasia, biofeedback, brain massage, clinical therapy for PTSD, compensation methods for his brain to learn new pathways to replace neurons which were damaged in the accident, and more. It is very comprehensive. Since he has a family he'll be living with, our therapists will be heavily focused on teaching your husband non-aggressive outlets for episodes of brain frustration, and appropriate social interaction with the family in an effort to minimize episodes of aggression, rage, outbursts, things of that nature."

Annalee felt a bit nauseous and realized she needed to hold herself together. She reached for her stomach.

She knew she had a lot to learn, but she was committed to doing so.

♥ ♥ ♥

After Ned's return home, he was still in a wheelchair when he and Annalee were given the complete tour of the treatment facility of the Glacier Neuroscience rehab clinic. It was an amazing, comprehensive outpatient brain injury treatment facility that would become their second home for the next year. The clinic was a sight to behold—unlike anything either of them had seen. It had an extensive array of state-of-the-art equipment and incredibly knowledgeable neurological specialists trained in every facet of brain injury convalescence.

Ned writhed with brain-pounding headaches and occasionally thrashed with seizures as he battled to regain some semblance of life before the accident. When the horrendous headaches were at their worst, Ned sometimes seemed to want to give up. Annalee's heart went out to him as she realized he was suffering nearly constantly. His occupational therapists worked to ease the headaches. Annalee was taught that the sleep and wake cycles were known as circadian rhythms, and that she could help encourage Ned by assisting him with regular schedules to help him restore normal rest cycles. The patterns of rest would help relieve cranial pressures.

Annalee's relationship with the Lord deepened as He met her in the painful places of helping her husband recover. She found the journey a paradox. The physical care was difficult, but Ned's gratitude and patience more than compensated for it. While it was heart-wrenching walking with him through this journey, Ned's early months of recuperation were also his greatest moments of victory as a husband and father. His vulnerability and physical weakness revealed a depth of appreciation his family treasured.

Ned was becoming a new person!

With this news, strengthen those who have tired hands, and encourage those who have weak knees. Say to those with fearful hearts, "Be strong, and do not fear, for your God is coming to destroy your enemies. He is coming to save you" (Isaiah 35:3, 4, NLT).

"Do not be afraid, for I have ransomed you.
I have called you by name; you are mine.
When you go through deep waters, I will be with you.

*And through the rivers of difficulty, you will not drown.
When you walk through the fire of oppression, you will not
be burned up; the flames will not consume you
(Isaiah 43:1, 2, NLT).*

Thirty-Three

Returning Home

NED'S SIX weeks in the hospital had been difficult ones, but they were weeks filled with learning. Ned and Annalee said goodbye to Dr. Todd and the wonderful neuroscience team. Ned was still in a wheelchair, but the occupational therapists had started his patterning exercises with a walker. With outpatient rehabilitation, he was expected to transition to a full-time walker soon.

The entire family, including Mercy, met several times to create an advance plan to accommodate Ned's homecoming. All the adults explained to the children "the new normal" after Dad returned home.

The entire family, and Mercy, helped transport Ned home. Annalee was so proud of the children's efforts. Their willingness to help with new daily routines was amazing. Even Justin's focus seemed more intentional as he recognized the need for concentrating on caregiving for his father and the baby.

Between the wheelchair and baby's stroller, Mercy's assistance with daily transport to the clinic was a godsend for the family's therapy classes. During the children's remaining month of summer, their therapy schedule was Monday to Friday from 9 AM to 3 PM with a break for lunch in the cafeteria. Amanda and Justin's therapy classes included children's support groups with frequent breaks on the rehab playground. They made friends with other children their ages whose parents were also clinic patients. Luke and Marie attended therapy classes after work. Annalee and the baby made the rounds to her therapy sessions and support groups for adult family members.

With thirty hours a week in rehab, Ned quickly progressed from wheelchair to walker—and he also wore a big smile on his face. Smiles were not natural for Ned. Hours of daily speech therapy started to overcome aphasia, and he began to enunciate syllables that later became words.

At first, Ned's renewed ability to communicate seemed to infuse new joy in his personality. He interacted with his family in a loving, happy way. Though in broken speech, he often expressed a new enjoyment of home life with the family and gratitude for everything they were doing to help him. In spite of horrific head pain, Ned was a new person. In fact, Annalee realized, his overall demeanor was well advanced versus what it had been in May when the family visited the zoo and dinosaur exhibits.

Ned was becoming the father and husband the family had never known. He was a joy to have around! Annalee found her spirit drawing close to him again.

Her mind began to doubt Dr. Nelson's foreboding comments regarding anticipated post-accident rage. That daunting question—"How committed are you to this marriage?"—no longer concerned her.

Ned must be an exception to Dr. Nelson's rule, Annalee found herself thinking.

She saw the emergence of the true man God created Ned to be. She thanked the Lord every day for a transformed husband and father. Even if she needed to be his caregiver for life, this beautiful soul, and the tranquility in their home, was worth every effort. The man she had known during their engagement and earlier days of marriage seemed to have returned. Of course, Annalee felt immense empathy for his suffering, but she rejoiced in the peace that emanated from his soul—a serenity that somehow seemed to accompany his vulnerability.

She also sensed relaxation in the children, who no longer retreated to their rooms. The home quickly transformed into a place of emotional security that overcame the physical caregiving responsibilities. Justin and Amanda played board games with their daddy, and this also provided brain therapy for Ned! Justin brought out his Legos and dinosaur kits and spent time building with him. All of this was good for Justin's development as well.

❤ ❤ ❤

The children returned to school in the fall, so their rehab therapy was reduced to twice a week after school. By that time Ned was full-time on his walker, so Annalee could handle the daily rounds herself.

This became a routine for the next year. Josiah's stroller and diaper bag remained packed, and every morning Annalee dropped the children off at school, headed to rehab for six hours, picked up the children, and returned home.

That fall Justin never got into trouble at school. Mrs. Adams and Mr. Cormack were amazed! By September Ned was speaking in very short or partial sentences. After he started to regain his ability to speak, Annalee took in his sincere, faltering syllables as he struggled to articulate words such as "I can't remem . . . your name, but . . . I love you." Other times he remembered, and lovingly said, "A-a-n-a- . . . " The absolute joy of their peaceful home life was worth every bit of sacrifice.

So let's not get tired of doing what is good.
At just the right time we will reap a harvest
of blessing if we don't give up (Galatians 6:9, NLT).

The man who returned home from the hospital was so much different from the father they had known before, even in the best of times. Annalee was amazed how quickly the children learned to trust their "new father." She watched with joy as Ned sat on the sofa, smiled, and beckoned the children to him. Amanda and Justin willingly snuggled into his embrace to watch family movies together while Annalee fixed supper.

Thanksgiving

Ned continued to surprise the rehab specialists with his progress. That fall Amanda turned nine and Justin eight. Along with their dad's medical progress, the children showed improvement in school and at home.

Ned's language skills continued to improve, and he became more adept with his walker. Ned's rehab team decided he should continue using the walker through the winter to avoid a fall on snow or ice.

Thanksgiving that year was like no other. It was a wonderful atmosphere. School and rehab were closed for Thanksgiving week, so Annalee and the children bought a large pumpkin and baked it, then made eight homemade pumpkin pies using their family recipe. They also made several loaves of Amanda's now-loved banana bread recipe using half yellow cake mix. As the entire family, including Mercy, gathered in the kitchen preparing the turkey and fixings, Ned sat at the kitchen table smiling at everyone with the baby in the highchair next to him. Justin even wanted to be part of helping in the kitchen, so the ladies kept him busy assigning him tasks; he loved being part of the action.

Ned's language was improving every week. "You kids are d-o-o-ing so good!" he said, complimenting the children on their baking. He asked to try their various recipes.

The family had so much to be thankful for that Thanksgiving. Annalee's heart was overjoyed with gratitude. Their home was a sanctuary of happiness and security.

Christmas, New Year

Once the school and rehab clinic closed for Christmas, Annalee and the children got busy making their homemade pies, fudge, banana bread, and cookies. The week before Christmas, the children were excited to load their sleds for the annual family tradition of sharing their baked goods and Christmas poem with neighbors. Marie and Luke supervised as they made the rounds.

Ned sat at the kitchen table cheering everyone on. Josiah clapped his little hands along with his daddy.

The family celebrated the Savior's birth along with Josiah's first birthday. Ned clapped his hands and sang Happy Birthday to Josiah along with everyone else.

That Christmas was an amazing memory, one they would never forget.

♥ ♥ ♥

With the new year the school and rehab clinic resumed their activities. It was a bit of a challenge to navigate Ned's walker through the snow, so Annalee parked the Suburban as close to the house as she could. One morning in February it was snowing when it was time to leave the house. The children and baby were already loaded in the vehicle. Annalee stepped back into the house to help Ned as she always did. As they stepped across the threshold, she was about to close the door behind them. Ned accidentally stumbled with his walker, but he didn't fall.

"Honey, are you OK? Let me help you," Annalee said.

Ned had managed to make it off the threshold, but he was just standing there. She reached out to stabilize him.

"I don't . . . need . . . your help! I . . . can . . . do . . . this my-self!" Ned yelled, followed by a word of profanity Annalee had not heard from him in almost a year. He glared at her with a look of frustration and anger.

She reached behind Ned and closed the door, feeling in shock. There were two porch stairs ahead. She walked a few feet ahead of him and turned to be ready to help him when he realized he could not descend by himself. Ned continued struggling to slide the walker through the snow as he stood at the edge of the stairs. He looked Annalee's way and snarled, "G-e-t . . . me . . . down from here."

She reached over and helped him down the stairs the same way she had the previous six months. After getting down the stairs, he pushed ahead of her toward the Suburban. She opened the vehicle door for him, wondering what to do next. Ned snapped at her. "So . . . aren't you gonna . . . help . . . me up?"

"I didn't know if I should," Annalee said.

"You know _____ well I can't climb up . . . here by my–self!" he yelled.

The children heard most of this, and they looked frozen in unbelief. She silently helped Ned into the seat, then put his walker in the back. Instead of the usual chatter and singing inside the vehicle, there was silence all the way to school. Even Josiah had a confused look on his face as if unsure how to act. The children reached over to comfort the little guy. Ned appeared oblivious to the way his behavior had affected his family.

It was a long ride into town.

Annalee avoided Ned that day at the rehab clinic because she didn't know how to react to him. She purposely took her lunch break with the baby separately. For months she had been telling her therapist about the incredible positive chang-es her family was experiencing at home, the renewed trust, and the children's enjoyment of their father. Her therapist had remained cautiously optimistic, encouraging Annalee that she hoped the atmosphere would remain this way.

Annalee couldn't hold back tears when she spoke to her therapist about the incident that day. Her therapist was com-passionate and shared that she hoped Ned's emotions would once again settle down.

"Don't blame yourself, Annalee," she said. "I can't begin to tell you the number of clients who have experienced simi-lar episodes months after their spouse's accidents, after their families had learned to trust again. We will stand with you to believe for the best. This is very confusing for your children, so I'll be sure to discuss the situation with your children's ther-apists also."

After 3 PM, Annalee reluctantly met up with Ned. His occupational therapist had heard about the situation because he offered to walk out with them and assist Ned into the Suburban and load his walker.

On the way to the children's school, Ned was silent.

For the first time since the accident, Annalee felt awkward around him.

When they picked up the children, the first thing Amanda and Justin did was look at their father's face. It looked like a thundercloud, so the children were extremely subdued the entire way home. Annalee tried to make conversation with them, asking about their school day and if they had homework. They replied that their day was fine and they had no homework. It was obvious they were trying to avoid conversation. Annalee turned on some relaxing music. Ned looked annoyed.

After they were in the house, Ned sat on the sofa. The children came into the kitchen and asked Annalee if she needed help. She whispered that she could handle supper and gave them permission to go play; they headed straight to their bedrooms. Meanwhile, Ned remained on the sofa and looked around as if he wondered why the children weren't coming to sit by him.

When supper was ready, Annalee went down the hall and called the children for supper. Ned stayed on the sofa, so Annalee walked over and asked if he would like to join the family. He just glared. Annalee asked if he would prefer a TV tray table in front of him to eat his supper. He continued staring at her, so she knew there had to be a disconnect. The children had washed their hands and gathered around the table while looking curiously at their dad. Annalee served the children, then served Ned a plate on a TV tray.

After supper the three of them cleared the table and did dishes. The children still wanted to stay clear of their father, so Annalee gathered his dinner plate and drink.

Annalee attempted to carry on with the evening as normal. She sent the children to take their showers and put on their pajamas for bed. She gave Josiah his bath and put him to bed. When Amanda and Justin were ready for bed, Annalee approached them.

"Why don't we go in and say goodnight to Daddy?" she asked.

The children looked hesitant. "I'll go with you," she said.

All three went to the sofa to say goodnight to Ned.

"So ya don't wanna . . . watch a movie with your old dad to . . . night?" he said. The children looked confused.

"Honey, it's bedtime now. They wanted to say goodnight to you."

"Oh," Ned said sadly. "Well, goo . . . night." Amanda and Justin reluctantly gave him hugs. He reached out and patted them on the back, and for this they seemed grateful.

The atmosphere in the home was now radically different from what it had been in the early days after Ned's accident. Annalee prayed the earlier atmosphere would return.

She accompanied the children to their rooms and asked them to sit together on Justin's bed.

"I have two Scripture verses to give all of us hope," she said. "You ready?"

"Yes!" They snuggled up as Mom read the Bible verses, the first from Psalm 56:3, the second from Psalm 91:11 (New King James Version).

Whenever I am afraid, I will trust in You (Psalms 56:3).

For He shall give His angels charge over you,
To keep you in all your ways (Psalm 91:11).

"So when we're afraid, we can put our trust in Jesus," Annalee said. "He will never leave us, right?"

"Right!" they said.

"And who does he send to protect us? The ones with the big wings?"

"The angels!"

Annalee was always astounded at the faith of young children.

"That's right. Always remember that, OK? Let's pray."

The children seemed much more peaceful as they entered their prayer time.

"Remember, I love you guys *this* much!" She stretched her arms out as wide as she could.

"Love you too, Mama."

As Annalee left the room, her mind swirled with thoughts of Dr. Nelson's earlier warning:

"If he had a short fuse before, he will have no fuse after..." Her faith tried to reject those thoughts.

Maybe Ned will recover emotionally again. Lord, is that possible?

♥ ♥ ♥

Over the next few weeks, Ned's behavior continued to decline. He became progressively more frustrated with ordinary tasks that had become difficult. Once the family heard things being banged around in the garage. The noises were so loud that Annalee had to step out to look. She thought maybe Ned had taken a fall. It turned out Ned had tried to hang up a small ladder, but he couldn't find the correct bracket. After looking for the bracket for quite a while, he became so aggravated he began to throw things around in sheer frustration. The bracket was laying on a shelf, so Annalee handed it to him. He snatched it out of her hand without a word. She thought about how discouraging it must be to have a brain injury, especially a frontal lobe injury that impacts the ability to analyze and make decisions.

Another day, Ned suddenly decided he was able to cook the way he used to. He pulled a frozen pizza from the freezer and put it in the oven while Annalee was cleaning at the other end of the house. In about thirty minutes she smelled an odor of smoke and went running into the kitchen. The blackened pizza was smoking in the oven, which had been set at 500 degrees. Ned came in from the garage yelling about the smoke. He glared at Annalee, who was removing the burned pizza from the oven.

"Well, I was hungry," Ned said. "I didn't know it was going to burn up." Annalee quietly dealt with the mess and didn't respond.

Annalee reported the incidents to the rehab clinic therapists to see if there were any treatments that could help Ned with short-term memory loss. They discussed the situations with Dr. Nelson, who prescribed additional treatment modalities in an effort to strengthen Ned's decision-making and memory skills. He also prescribed an anti-anxiety medication to help Ned relax around the family at home, but Ned refused to take any medications because he thought his doctors' intentions were to harm him.

A few weeks later Ned told the therapists he thought Annalee was conspiring with the doctors to harm him. He was beginning to resist and distrust all the physicians in charge of his care. He had been attending the clinic for many months. Not only was he tired of attending, he had become suspicious of the medical team, so he insisted Annalee expedite the accident settlement with the lawyer as quickly as possible so he could discontinue rehab and therapy sessions. Annalee knew the rehab clinic was a lifeline for Ned, but she couldn't force him to continue attending. The rehab clinic suggested Annalee find a private psychologist or psychiatrist that Ned could trust after the settlement was final.

Dr. Nelson's clinic had taught Ned to regain the ability to walk and talk, but he tragically used those abilities to bring pain to those who loved him. In the aftermath of the brain injury, Ned's neuropsychiatrist's warnings became alarmingly clear. How could Annalee forget that day sitting across the desk from Dr. Nelson as he posed his cautious question regarding a brain-injured spouse with a temper? As Nelson had predicted was likely to be the case, Ned's actions and words became progressively more toxic as time went on.

Annalee arranged for the attorney to complete the accident settlement.

She and the children learned to avoid Ned as much as possible because they didn't know any other way to keep peace. During difficult moments Annalee found herself alone in the bathroom crying out to God for strength, praying for all the children, and seeking His direction for their future lives.

In time Annalee would learn that God never wastes the sufferings we experience. He can use them to enable us to comfort others.

In the difficult years that followed, she sometimes encountered others on similar journeys with brain-injured family members to whom she was able to reach out with hope, encouragement, and comfort.

He comforts us in all our troubles so that we can comfort others. When they are troubled, we will be able to give them the same comfort God has given us
(2 Corinthians 1:4, NLT).

Jesus, Annalee's Prince of Peace, became the life preserver to whom she clung in the middle of a raging ocean in the terrifying years ahead.

Thirty-Four

ALTHOUGH DR. NELSON and the rehab team wanted to work longer with Ned, suspicion had overtaken his mind and he demanded to end his work with the clinic. Rehab, though, would continue until his accident settlement was finalized. As he insisted, Annalee requested the accident attorney finalize his settlement. The family finished the remaining weeks at the clinic. Annalee made another appointment with Dr. Nelson and prepared a list of questions.

The family had spent a year learning how to accommodate, and help in every way they could, Ned. Now Annalee felt she needed to focus on helping her suffering family. Ned's behavior was affecting everyone—even the baby. She could tell by the look on his small face when Ned would yell.

During his earlier post-accident stage, Ned had been vulnerable, loving, and appreciative, but as he regained his abilities and strength, he became progressively more insensitive, demanding, and even hostile.

Annalee began to wonder: *Is this the same pattern for all brain-injured patients?*

During the course of the preceding year, she had met other TBI patients who didn't appear to fit the behavior Ned was showing. She became acquainted with other families at adult caregiver support groups. Many brain-injured loved ones had made exceptional progress and yet behaved in a loving manner to their families. Annalee paid close attention to these patients and their families' relational interactions. She compared these situations to Ned's mood at the clinic. He sometimes glared at others waiting in the lobby as well as those in his family. More and more, people began avoiding him.

Was there any way to help Ned?

Maybe Annalee would know more after her next visit with Dr. Nelson.

Another Pivotal Moment

Annalee again sat across the desk from Dr. Nelson as she rocked Josiah in his stroller.

"Mrs. Jackson, it's good to see you again. I'm sorry to hear that your husband has decided to terminate his treatment here. He is in need of emotional rehabilitation. We can provide that if he is willing."

"I wish he was willing, Doctor," Annalee said. "Ned has made amazing progress here, and I thank you for all your support to him and our family. May I ask some questions?"

"Of course."

"A year ago at our first meeting, you warned me that if my husband had a short fuse pre-accident, he would have no fuse post-accident."

"Correct. I based that on his history. In some TBI patients, we see behaviors known as impulsive anger."

"My husband is very angry, but he was a different person for seven months." Annalee explained to Dr. Nelson the vast personality difference post-accident and the sudden personality decline after his speech and walking abilities returned. She shared her observation of other patients who seemed loving and happy, asked about the differences between patients, and shared the painful disappointment in her own family.

"Based on your training and experience," she asked, "why is there such disparity between patients, and do you believe there is a chance that Ned will return to his kind self in the future?"

Annalee was not someone to easily give up on hope.

"I wish I could offer a promising answer to this dilemma," the doctor said. "Before Ned began treatment here, I requested and reviewed his military records and discovered his pre-existing PTSD, along with his prior VA psych evals in which he disclosed assault and betrayal issues in his first marriage and the loss of his military officer career."

"So that negative history relates to his present behavior?"

"Yes. He can remember events 20 *years* ago easier than 20 *minutes* ago." The doctor took a breath. "Here's an example: his short-term memory loss was the cause of the pizza-burning incident. Other brain-injury patients with positive long-term life experiences are able to return to the positive. Unfortunately, Ned has reverted back to his long-term negative past. That's why I initially warned you about the prognosis regarding possible rage outbursts."

"So, without a miracle, Ned won't regain being the same kind person he was during early recovery?"

"Very unlikely. Let me explain. In Ned's particular case, he was unconscious for a lengthy period of time at the scene. During his multiple rollover accident, his head was severely assaulted from numerous directions by steel and metal, resulting in sustained injuries to the frontal lobe area of his brain along with several other regions. From our assessment, Ned's brain has shown adverse impact in four out of five major ways, but the two most disabling are cognitive function and mood regulation. With these types of brain injuries, delayed decreases in function can begin to manifest over time. They are gradual, but they are now starting to become apparent to Ned. He has recovered enough to realize that his life has dramatically changed—he has lost his occupation and academic skills. These disappointments have led to relational breakdowns."

"Even though there were no relational breakdowns earlier?" Annalee asked. "In fact, the family was closer than ever."

"Ned was not aware of what he had lost in the early months of his recovery. He was disoriented, helpless, and vulnerable, so he was focused on survival mode in the here and now. He was grateful for the day-by-day, functional support he received from the hospital, and then from his family."

Dr. Nelson glanced at Ned's file. "So now Ned has reached MMI: maximum medical improvement. He has regained the basic abilities of walking and talking, but as he tries to resume more complex life tasks—like hanging up a ladder—his short-term memory gets in the way of things like trying to remember the location of the bracket to hang up the ladder. Things just don't make sense the way they used to because he doesn't comprehend the same way. That is very frustrating for him. It is caused by cognitive impairment, especially the damage to his frontal lobe. This is why I strongly recommend emotional rehab to help him through this."

"So is that why he became angry when I saw the bracket and handed it to him? It reminded him of his inability to remember where it was, so he resented me for finding it?"

"Precisely. But it wasn't your fault. You were just trying to help. That's where relational breakdowns come into effect."

"Wow. That makes life complicated. I will make every effort to persuade Ned to remain here in rehab. But I must be honest, Doctor Nelson. Ned refuses to take any of his medications for anxiety and paranoia because he is unreasonably suspicious regarding the intentions of the clinic, his medical team—even me."

"One of his therapists advised me of that. I'm so sorry to hear of his mistrust, because that will make his life and recovery much more difficult for him, and especially for you and the family."

"What we can expect? Any suggestions?"

"He will have good days and bad days depending on how he feels. As for suggestions, if he is unwilling to continue here, I strongly recommend finding him a good psychologist or psychiatrist that he can trust. Perhaps the VA can assist."

"OK. I'm working on his VA benefits also to help him with compensation," Annalee said.

"That's good, because according to the medical records I've reviewed over the past year, Ned will probably never be employable again due to his relational difficulties, short-term memory loss, and cognitive deficiencies."

"I thought so," Annalee said quietly. "I have a couple more questions. First, is it possible to distinguish between Ned's brain impairment and his behavior choices?"

"Based on Ned's individual case and progress, I believe he's more aware of his behavior than we realize, but perhaps he's not yet fully aware of how those behaviors are damaging his family. Having said that, Ned is capable of choice, and only he can choose to be more cooperative and trusting of his care providers and loved ones so he can improve his behaviors with time and recovery. That is why emotional rehab is vital for him to improve his relational skills."

Annalee paused, then dove in with her second question. "Do you think it is premature to hold him accountable for his behaviors? Especially since he is making decisions regarding the clinic and attorney?"

"That is something only you can decide," Dr. Nelson said. "Some situations are simple while others are more complex. I strongly recommend that you continue in therapy for yourself to help you recognize certain behavior patterns that reveal greater accountability related to TBI impulsive anger episodes.

"To simplify matters, my advice is this: make every effort to keep things on an even keel at home. Due to your husband's anticipated unemployability, he will probably be around the home for the rest of his life. Try to manage schedules, the children, and all their appointments apart from Ned. By all means, avoid any conflict with him if at all possible. And in your spare time, find him a psychologist or psychiatrist he is willing to trust."

Annalee knew this was a great deal to take in. She thanked the doctor for his time and patience.

If it is possible, as far as it depends on you,
live at peace with everyone (Romans 12:18, NIV).

After the accident settlement was completed, Ned had no interest in continuing at the rehab clinic, so the family ended its routines there. As Dr. Nelson said, Annalee found it best to avoid conflict. She handled all meetings at the school because it made life less complicated.

She grieved the loss of marital friendship and the companionship she and Ned once shared. She offered to drive Ned to veterans' meetings so he could have some fellowship. He began to attend those meetings again fairly regularly, and she knew this was good for him. At times Ned returned home upset; he had the impression that another veteran had offended him. But Annalee was glad he had somewhere to go to fellowship with other men. Church attendance also became sporadic for the same reasons. Annalee and the children attended church from time to time, and Josiah went to Sunday school for periods of time. Amanda and Justin were able to occasionally attend youth groups and a few events at a local Christian summer camp. Annalee was grateful for the wonderful youth ministers who reached out to them.

Ned never returned for emotional therapy. Annalee searched to find a therapist he could trust. After several months she was grateful to find Dr. Jennings. He was a psychologist who specialized in working with veterans with PTSD and brain injuries. Fortunately, Jennings and Ned hit it off immediately. Within the first few months Ned trusted him and began to share his thoughts and feelings. Annalee was grateful Ned had a professional he could confide in.

Dr. Jennings was Ned's therapist from then on. When things became explosive at home, Jennings would call and help diffuse situations by talking with Ned. By then Annalee was confident Ned knew what he was saying and doing. She felt the stinging guilt of the impact of the outbursts on the children. The battleground led to marital devastation and the inability to rescue her children from the daily onslaught of violent abuse. Annalee lived with shame and remorse.

She was left to ponder questions from one end of the spectrum to the other.

I love Ned, and I always will. But where are the answers to bring peace to our household?

How could I have been so blind as to return Amanda and Justin into the arms of an angry father?

Why did I allow the ties that blinded me to Ned to bring suffering to my innocent family?

How could I have used my legal skills to bring these precious children into a situation from which I now cannot rescue them?

Absent a legal stepparent adoption, she had no authority to rescue Amanda and Justin. But if it had been possible, she would have secured an administrative position and a separate apartment with the children near Ned to give the children a refuge—a peaceful residence from which they could have chosen to spend time with their dad during days he was calm. Ned was not in his right mind, so he would have filed charges against her if she made that move, and that could have led to Amanda and Justin being returned to foster care. Legally Annalee could only rescue Josiah, but there was no way she could leave his brother and sister behind. They had become part of her and always would be.

♥ ♥ ♥

Cycles

About two years after Ned's accident, patterns emerged that Annalee didn't understand, but she remembered Dr. Nelson's warnings that she would begin to recognize patterns that would relate to Ned's ability to be accountable for his actions. He had called it TBI impulsive anger.

This involved a span of time where she and the family walked on eggshells as some sort of invisible tension filled the air. Ned would become progressively more upset during this phase. Then something would happen that would set him off, and an unpredictable explosion would occur. Everyone would be crying and upset. There were times Ned would express he was sorry and tell Annalee it would never happen again. Annalee had no idea what cycles of abuse were. Once these patterns began, they repeated themselves.

When the explosion phase struck, hours of raging profanity filled the airways; at times, furniture was broken and things were hurled against walls. Once that phase was over, Ned would quiet down; sometimes it ended with an apologetic period in which Ned was remorseful and asked forgiveness. Annalee would forgive him.

After an explosion happened, the "honeymoon phase" would then repeat itself.

Annalee had been swept off her feet, then emotionally flung to the floor.

It was extremely difficult to understand whether these behaviors were related to the brain injury, PTSD, or Ned's own decisions.

Ned never exploded in front of Mercy or Grandma Betsy, his veteran friends who came to visit, or their church friends. All Annalee knew was that when everyone else went home, their home felt like a war zone.

The Lord was always Annalee's refuge. He was the Prince of Peace she so deeply needed. In the volatile years that continued, the raging ocean increasingly became tidal waves.

As the cycles continued, Annalee cautiously tried to anticipate the brief times of respite that represented the breaks between the tidal waves behind closed doors. She believed these breaks might be similar to something she had read about: a mysterious tranquility of serene air space during hurricanes and tornadoes known as the eye of the storm. She and the children looked forward to any relief from the storms.

As the years moved painfully forward, the brokenness had a devastating impact. As her marriage to Ned spiraled into violence, ferocious anger crushed her spirit with destructive words that shattered the day-to-day world of the family. As Christmas seasons came and went, the music "Peace on earth, goodwill toward men" brought comfort to Annalee and the children in ways she could never have described to anyone. Only the Lord understood the depth of her family's deep heart pain. Life was relentlessly difficult.

God would never leave her, and He would never forsake her children. No matter how life appeared, she knew her Father was always faithful to comfort her. She tried to convey that same comfort to the children as they grew. They continued in their faith, and she prayed they would continue turning to God for their strength. Sometimes after Ned went to sleep at night, Amanda and Justin approached Annalee to pour out their feelings as they shared their pain. Their heart-to-heart talks would sometimes go way past midnight.

Secrecy and isolation made their world smaller as domestic violence took its toll.

The LORD is close to the brokenhearted and saves those
who are crushed in spirit (Psalm 34:18, NIV).

As Amanda and Justin became adolescents, teenage mistakes resulted in "discipline" involving long monologues interspersed with intense profanity. The children sat like stone statues staring down at their laps or out at the pine trees. Annalee realized that after the first ten minutes they were not retaining any of the lectures but were obviously trying to project their minds into a less painful place—anywhere but in the presence of these long sessions of emotional pain. By junior high age, Justin became more brokenhearted. He had become "the scapegoat" in Ned's perspective of blame. After one particularly horrific day when Josiah was eight, he asked his mother privately, "Mama, when I get to be a teenager, is Dad going to treat me the way he treats Justin and Luke?" She embraced him and reassured him that would not happen because "Dad will get better."

Josiah didn't know this, of course, but she later hid in the bathroom and cried her eyes out.

Had she lied to him?

So do not fear, for I am with you; do not be dismayed, for
I am your God. I will strengthen you and help you; I will
uphold you with my righteous right hand
(Isaiah 41:10, NIV).

A 'Lesson' on Submission

One evening Ned told Annalee to have a seat. It wasn't a request. The children scattered. He had been angry about something that day and thought that she had not shown enough support. He didn't call her names, but the things he said were hurtful. He said, "Wives are supposed to submit to their husbands. Can't you even remember that? You are not submissive enough. You don't follow my lead."

If she dared offer any advice, he said, "If you were a submissive wife, you would stand up for the way I do things," or "We wouldn't have problems if you would agree with how I talk to the kids." Or, "You're not with me, you're against me." She longed for the days when he used to say she was a Proverbs 31 wife.

"I'm on your side, Ned, but children shouldn't be cursed at," Annalee said, trying to reason. "They should never hear that kind of language. If you want to find a way to help the children understand in a few minutes—not a few hours—I'll be glad to tell them what you want them to know in a few minutes."

"Don't you dare try to take my authority away from me, woman! I'm the boss of this house, and I have the final say—not you. You got that? It's all your fault they don't listen to me. They know you don't agree with me. When I'm making a point with them, you just sit there like a bump on a log."

Another day, Ned said, "Sit down. I have something to say. In case you don't know it, I know everything you think before you even think it. You need to learn to think the way I think because my thoughts are higher than your thoughts and my ways are higher than your ways."

Annalee couldn't believe her ears. She said, "Ned, those are the words in the book of Isaiah that God says about Himself and the way He thinks. We human beings cannot claim to have the thoughts of God."

"For my thoughts are not your thoughts,
neither are your ways my ways," declares the LORD.
"As the heavens are higher than the earth,
so are my ways higher than your ways
and my thoughts than your thoughts"
(Isaiah 55:8, 9, NIV).

"You think you can outsmart me, woman? I know the Word of God."

She began looking into her lap the way the children did, and then she did what she always did to escape. She excused herself to the bathroom to go pray to her heavenly Father. He was always there for her.

And I am convinced that nothing can ever separate us
from God's love. Neither death nor life, neither angels nor
demons, neither our fears for today nor our worries about
tomorrow— not even the powers of hell can separate us
from God's love (Romans 8:38, NLT).

The LORD is my rock, my fortress, and my savior; my God
is my rock, in whom I find protection. He is my shield, the
power that saves me, and my place of safety
(Psalm 18:2, NLT).

Nocturnal Utterances

In the middle of the night, Annalee stirred awake to hear angry words being spoken by Ned. She laid in terror, opening her eyes just a crack to see his shadow sitting up, glaring toward her as he snarled words about her. The words accused her of being unfaithful, of stealing money from their bank account, of planning harm against him, and included profane name-calling he would never use during their waking hours. In between the words were sounds like growling, like the utterances of an animal. What was going on? Was Ned in some kind of brain-injured trauma state?

These nocturnal utterances continued several times a week for the next twelve to thirteen years. After the first few episodes Annalee grabbed her pillow and quietly headed to sleep on the floor of their walk-in closet, where she slept for years so she would have the uninterrupted sleep and energy to care for Ned and the family when morning came. When Josiah was a teenager, she finally had the courage to tell a pastoral couple who were counseling them at church.

Ned was furious, but it never happened again.

As teenagers, Amanda and Justin found ways to be gone from the home as much as they could. Annalee understood. They stayed with friends as much as possible because they were looking for peace wherever possible. Annalee was grateful that they returned for visits at Christmas, birthdays, and for special events. Josiah was growing quickly and became involved with the praise and worship team at the youth group on Wednesday nights. He was gifted at guitar and vocals. He was popular and had a number of activities going that kept him busy. In spite of the enormous suffering at home, he made good grades and was a son to be proud of.

Josiah's good grades prepared him to plan for college education with an IT programming major.

He gives His beloved sleep (Psalm 127:2, NKJV).

Hope deferred makes the heart sick, but a longing fulfilled is a tree of life (Proverbs 13:12, NIV).

O LORD, rescue me . . . Protect me from those who are violent (Psalm 140:1, NLT).

Thirty-Five

NED WAS NEVER able to return to work.

The home atmosphere became a dangerous minefield through which every family member cautiously navigated to avoid triggering the expected explosions. No one escaped becoming a casualty on this war front. When Ned's fury erupted, Annalee and the children became the targets. Violent verbal assaults took an enormous toll. Annalee concealed details from her 70-year-old mother, Grandma Betsy, and even from her friend Mercy, who clearly discerned that there was more happening behind the scenes. Without her finalized stepparent adoption, Annalee feared that reporting their home life would return Amanda and Justin to foster care, or worse: back to Tina.

Dr. Nelson's rehab team had trained Ned to regain his abilities to speak and become fully ambulatory. Annalee became his administrator, caregiver, and assistant. He was still handsome and physically vigorous. Though his brain trauma was not visible, daily support was needed—scheduling and transportation to medical appointments, assistance with independence, damage repairs, time-consuming searches for lost items. He tried to assist by collecting the mail. In winter, if Annalee didn't reach the mailbox before him, she had to search through snow for lost bills dropped along the path to the house.

During Josiah's childhood Annalee needed a hysterectomy; she was grateful Mercy was able to visit during her recovery. Paranoia escalated the various offenses as Ned uprooted his family from fellowship, their church family, and supportive friendships. Contact with Mel and Monica in Oregon faded into the past as isolation hung over the Jackson home like a storm cloud.

By far the most intense and agonizing heartbreak was a very personal one. Ned had been an athlete his entire life and had a robust and muscular frame. He later became convinced Annalee was his enemy, so after his physical strength returned, she was punished in the most vulnerable moments within the most private place: their bedroom. He called it romance, she called it agony. (Just not aloud.) She was confused with her marital responsibility. She dreamed of the most sacred union of love between a husband and wife. That shared place was intended to preserve the sanctity of true intimacy, the utmost expression of married love. How had it become a place of twisted aggression followed by two to four days of painful recovery and shedding of blood?

Sometimes Ned apologized, but at other times he acted annoyed, as if Annalee was somehow being "wimpy." She tried to remind him of their conversations before their wedding when she had carefully explained her medical history and need for TLC in their future private life. Not only was she petite, she had suffered extensive internal damage from the surgical misuse of forceps during Lance's birth resulting in her baby's brain injury and multiple subsequent miscarriages. Annalee shared details in advance to give Ned the option to change his mind. He reassured Annalee that her heart was what he valued most, along with her desire to help him rescue the children. He insisted that he loved her so much he only wanted to be tender and considerate.

After the private assaults began in the post-accident years, she repeatedly tried to explain to Ned that daytime kindness warms a woman's heart. She told him she was trying to fulfill her part as his wife but needed his gentleness to prepare her to welcome his love in return.

His response, however, was one of the few Bible verses he remembered.

"'The marriage bed is undefiled.' What I do is fine with God," Ned would say. And, "You should just obey your husband."

For Annalee, these dreaded moments represented anything but love; they were just attempts to avoid pain.

Years later, Ned finally admitted to Annalee that the bedroom was his way of punishing her in private.

It took many years for Annalee to open up to a Christian therapist who recognized "marital sexual assault" and explained that what she was enduring was not God's definition of married love or a wife's "duty."

As the children grew, their response patterns emerged exactly as the neuropsychiatrist expected. Amanda and Justin grew sadly distant from their father as they entered their teen years. Though Annalee and her children continued to share a close bond, she understood why they lost confidence in her ability to protect them. Gentleness was a weakness as she became lost in this family maze. She privately grieved the inability to legally rescue Amanda and Justin; they were as indelibly imprinted on her heart as if she had given them birth.

❤ ❤ ❤

Ned's life became an enigma—from outrage to vivid imagination to hero. He had an amazingly creative mind. He dreamed big and wanted to feel successful again. His work ethic returned along with his strength. He thought of remarkable business ventures, including an exceptional marketing idea for the military. Ned hearkened back to his active duty years and thought of unique strategies to provide products for use on military bases. As he shared his insights with Annalee, she agreed to join him on the projects.

On his good days he was her cheerleader with uplifting words such as, "Honey, do you realize we have created a multimillion-dollar marketing plan?" Or, "We can do this!" or "We are the J-Team!"

Developing Ned's concepts into a massive military marketing project became a therapeutic way for Annalee to refocus her hopes of achieving financial stability for their family. For three years, with Ned's ideas and encouragement, she researched government commerce, collaborated with the military and corporate world, and met with military procurement officers to secure government contracts. Their enterprise became an LLC. Their contract attorney launched their company as a liaison between military bases and corporate production facilities. As Ned's helpmate, Annalee invested untold hours of administration, research, and appointments that nearly landed a major government contract with multiple military bases.

One week before their multimillion-dollar contract was scheduled for signatures, their LLC was cut out of a three-way contract by an underbid offered direct to the military by their wealthy corporate production partners. It was a massive economic loss to the family. Annalee cried for three days and wanted to give up, but she knew she needed to forgive the businessmen and release this heartbreak to the Lord.

Following this blow, she refocused her attention on activating Ned's VA benefits.

Commit everything you do to the LORD. Trust him, and he will help you. He will make your innocence radiate like the dawn, and the justice of your cause will shine like the noonday sun. Be still in the presence of the LORD, and wait patiently for him to act. Don't worry about evil people who prosper or fret about their wicked schemes (Psalm 37:5-7, NLT).

One summer, Ned became a hero by saving a man's life. He and Annalee were in town stalled in traffic when they spotted a man trapped in his crashed car. Smoke was rising from under the hood and sparks began erupting within the car. Emergency vehicles had not yet made it to the scene. Ned didn't think twice. He raced over, putting himself in harm's way. With lightning speed, he lifted the man out of the vehicle seconds before flames engulfed it. The man immediately hugged Ned. The paramedics and police also commended Ned for his courage. A gathering crowd cheered. Annalee shared how proud she was of his bravery, affirming to him that this was a perfect example of the true man he was inside.

After the three-year entrepreneurial venture, Annalee promised Ned she would resume petitioning his appeals until his Veterans Association disability benefits reached 100 percent. Annalee credited Ned's psychologist, Dr. Jennings, for his intervention and support. His training, expertise, and influence secured Ned's military records, providing details critical to successive appeals to finalize 100 percent approval. His ability to maintain Ned's trust enabled him to provide ongoing psychological support and friendship to Ned. Dr. Jennings also prayed for everyone, providing faithful professional support critically needed by the family.

After ten years the united efforts of Dr. Jennings, Veteran's Service officers, and Annalee's administrative appeals finally paid off.

During the summers, on Ned's good days, he sometimes let the family take a break to enjoy the crystal blue rivers and magnificence of Glacier National Park. On those days the family would pack a picnic lunch, Ned and the boys loaded fishing poles, and the family headed out in the Suburban for a day of fun and adventure. Montana is known for its spectacular beauty as well as its brutal winters. Though the sunny days and growing seasons are short, the locals can always count on July and August for their long-awaited sunshine. The local newspaper posted articles so people could prepare for the big day when the enormous accumulations of snow and ice were finally cleared to allow for a large event held every year in mid-June. It was held on a breathtaking mountainous highway that attracted more than a million visitors every summer. The 50-mile trek ascended to the summit of Glacier National Park and its visitor center and picnic area. (To prepare for the huge influx of tourists, massive plows would begin the job of the colossal snow removal needed in late spring to clear the remainder of the highway's winter blizzard remains.) The incredible journey en route is an experience like no other: gigantic, muscular white mountain goats stand precariously on the edges of spectacular icy cliffs with icicles hanging below their hooves. Enormous wildlife such as moose, grizzly bear, antelope, and mountain lions roam the mountainsides eating huckleberries and fishing in the cold rivers. At times Amanda and Justin, then teenagers, along with Luke and Marie, dove into the rivers on the hot summer days, guiding young Josiah along on a raft beside them. They were definitely mountain kids.

Occasionally the family also went camping and fishing. Ned seemed more relaxed in the scenic outdoors. Sometimes the family went huckleberry picking in the Montana mountains—the fruit is great for jams and ice cream toppings. These were fun times and built wonderful memories.

But behind closed doors the bittersweet years moved slowly forward. Ned could be kind and apologetic, then transition to demanding unquestioned "obedience and submission" so frightening that his family felt like prisoners of war. Amanda and Justin endured these adolescent years with determination in astounding ways. Josiah became a different type of casualty: an innocent observer. In childhood his young, caring heart and innocent eyes suffered as a helpless witness to the war zone. (Statistically, young males like him are the most likely to become the one in seven men who will go on to live in an abusive adult relationship.)

A major medical emergency arose with Ned during Amanda and Justin's teen years. One day he climbed atop a 16-foot ladder to fix something high in the garage, and this ended in a devastating fall that crushed Ned's ankle and foot. As the ambulance rushed him to the hospital, intense prayer support began. Miraculously, a renowned Montana orthopedic surgeon was on duty. After X-rays the surgeon told Annalee that Ned's foot required amputation; his ankle bones were nothing more than "mush." Ned's refusal to sign amputation consent led to the surgeon operating for seven hours to install twenty-eight pieces of hardware, creating a sort of "bionic" foot and ankle.

Ned's recovery was nothing short of a miracle, and the family was grateful to God and the surgeon. His ankle and foot recovered in record time, and he walked amazingly well from then on.

But after recovery, Ned started believing that the surgeon had installed a homing device in his ankle, and he insisted he was under "GPS tracking surveillance." He felt compelled to continually escape people, places, and situations.

A terrifying episode occurred on family property when Luke was 30 and Justin 18. Ned went ballistic in the presence of the entire family because they didn't complete some field chores to his satisfaction. Mayhem escalated as he slugged Justin with his fists. The family called 911 immediately. Ned then choked Luke until he began passing out. The family's hysterical screams caused him to release Luke just in time.

Police transported Ned to a mandatory thirty-day inpatient psychiatric assessment at the VA hospital. Along with PTSD and brain injury, he was diagnosed with schizophrenia and psychosis and placed on anti-depressants, anti-anxiety, and other medications for stabilization. The family hoped his

VA psych team and Dr. Jennings could assist Ned to become calmer on a more long-term basis. Josiah, still quite young, was traumatized with fear. He had more questions for Annalee, for which there were few clear answers.

Annalee wondered: *Will Ned be stable after returning from the VA Hospital?*

Peace lasted about three months.

Amanda and Justin reached adulthood. They talked about hopes, dreams, and more promising futures, and felt the best way for that to happen was to leave home at young ages. They both married young and started families when Josiah was in the very last stages of finishing grade school. Their early responsibilities postponed their schedules to attend college, so they both began employment. As Josiah grew older, his response pattern was radically different from the other children. As Dr. Nelson had predicted, since he was a baby when the truck accident occurred, his inability to remember his father's personality pre-accident resulted in a unique perspective. Ned continued to display many honorable characteristics, including participating with veterans' community efforts and Christmas fundraising events for families. Josiah was able to see beyond the minefield at home and form an amazing allegiance and friendship with his dad. Josiah's viewpoint reminded Annalee of night goggles, the visual aids used by the military to see and navigate through dangerous territory after dark. His natural creative talents transitioned into performance and perfectionism. From his earliest childhood memories as an innocent witness, he grew in his desire to help his family. Forgiving herself for the sufferings of all her children was overwhelming, but Annalee's greatest heartbreak was the mistakes she made in parenting Josiah after his siblings left home. She recalled she should have had more in-depth communication with him to understand his feelings during his teens, especially considering how hard he worked to maintain his excellent GPA. She later understood more of his viewpoint. He suffered much more than she realized. Her remorse was crushing.

The impact of living for years in survival mode created a painful path for the family, so Annalee moved forward by focusing on the children's future financial security. Ned's disability and military retirement pensions established his 100 percent benefit payment for life. In addition, they also provided full-ride college educations up to age 26 for Amanda, Justin, and Josiah as Ned's dependents under the GI Bill. After all the children had been through, the least Annalee could do was to make every effort to provide them the best possible education to begin their adult lives with a new beginning and hope.

"For I know the plans I have for you," declares the LORD, "plans to prosper you and not to harm you, plans to give you hope and a future. (Jeremiah 29:11, NIV).

Ned remained a well-respected member of his veterans' group and a well-liked member of a men's ministry at an area church—until a terrible incident happened one night. He thought another man had given him a disrespectful look. Without warning, Ned leaped over multiple chairs and lunged toward the man using military assault tactics. Several men restrained him. As he left he became so enraged he smashed the church door from its hinges, shattering the framework.

Needless to say, the family never returned to that church. The pastor's wife called Annalee to comfort her, extend their forgiveness to Ned, and offer continued prayers for the family.

Systematically Dismantled

Annalee felt much like that church door: totally dismantled. Even shattered.

As she succumbed to verbal and psychological brokenness, she knew she had to survive for the sake of her family. Once Josiah was raised, she would take care of herself. What she didn't realize was that she had already been systematically dismantled. She needed help quickly. She and Josiah found another church.

> *The LORD is my helper; I will not fear.*
> *What can man do to me? (Hebrews 13:6, NKJV).*

♥ ♥ ♥

Josiah was, of course, now the last child living at home.

He made friends easily and was musically gifted. He played guitar for the midweek teen praise and worship service at a church the family had started attending a few months earlier. One evening after supper Ned dropped Josiah off at youth group. After returning home, Ned went into a rampage, cursing and stomping back and forth across the living room. Nothing made sense. Annalee went into survival mode, struggling to recall what could possibly have gone wrong. She was unable to remember anything she or Josiah had said or done to account for Ned's abrupt explosion. She found herself too exhausted to diffuse the situation. Her main concern was to avoid Josiah coming home to an explosion, so she decided to head to bed early. If she was out of the way, she reasoned, maybe Ned would cool off. She told him she hoped he would feel better and said goodnight.

Annalee had not yet told her children that recent cardiac tests had revealed she had a heart blockage. More tests were needed, but the symptoms included frightening episodes of severe chest wall pain and panic attacks. They always intensified during Ned's verbal outrages and mimicked the symptoms of a heart attack, so she never knew if she needed to call 911.

Shortly after she climbed into bed, Ned burst into the bedroom, flipped on the light, and cursed loudly as he towered over her by the bed.

As his rage became more intense, severe chest pains worsened. As Annalee struggled to breathe, she cowered in a fetal position. She pleaded with him to calm down. He roared, "Calm down? You blew it again and won't even admit it!"

"Ned, I can't read your mind. I know I make many mistakes, but please tell me what I did so I can apologize and try to set things right with you." She was trying to reason with him; she desperately wanted him to finish venting his rage before Josiah returned home.

Ned only mocked. "Apologize, huh? You think you're sooo perfect and pretend you don't even understand. Nobody could be that stupid!" His eyes narrowed and looked black with hate.

"I'm not perfect. I just don't know what's wrong."

"I don't need to tell you what you already know," he further mocked, expletives filling the air.

Annalee could only think: *What can I do to calm him down so Josiah won't suffer?*

"Would you please take just thirty seconds and explain what you're upset about?"

"You're acting like a prissy little princess who doesn't even know what she does wrong. How could you be so stubborn and stupid to act like you don't know?"

"Ned, I really don't. If I said something to offend you, please help me understand and I'll ask your forgiveness." This was met with only more vague, ranting accusations mixed with obscenities. Annalee didn't want to call 911, but she began wondering if he was going to finish her off once and for all.

Annalee had recently consulted a therapist who was extremely worried about her and warned that Ned's verbal assaults were way beyond his control—that Annalee could become a fatality. She couldn't imagine his temper leading to homicide. The therapist encouraged her to plan a safe exit to a friend's home or domestic violence shelter before she became another newspaper statistic. Annalee couldn't deny the terrifying episodes at home including the ongoing private marital assaults.

Josiah was a young teenager; Annalee knew only that she had to remain alive to finish raising him. Would it help if she went into a shelter or recovery home? She also had her grown children to think of. She felt selfish but also was beginning to believe she could lose her life if she did not regain her emotional and cardiac health.

She was grateful when Ned finished his rage and had calmed himself by the time Josiah returned home.

That night she made a decision.

How could she seek refuge? Conflict resolution was impossible in their home.

The next day she contacted her therapist about the previous evening. Her therapist was gravely concerned for both her and

Josiah's safety. Annalee insisted that Ned had always expressed such love for Josiah that she couldn't believe her son would be endangered living with his dad.

She had no separate income. A long-distance elderly widow friend invited Annalee and Josiah to stay with her. Since she had never been to a shelter, she accepted the invitation. She invited Josiah to go with her, but he insisted he wanted to stay with his dad. She was unable to persuade him. Annalee felt caught between staying for his sake and being too emotionally broken to remain in the home herself. She truly thought Josiah would not stay if he was afraid and was so loved by his dad that he would not be harmed.

Years later she found out she was mistaken. Another regret. Could she ever forgive herself?

Amazingly, Ned allowed her to take the family van. She stayed with her elderly friend from a women's ministry and remained separated from him for five weeks. She was amazed at how much stronger she felt. Annalee took phone calls from Ned in which he professed his undying love for her, but she had no idea what Josiah was going through. She missed Josiah terribly and, after five weeks, thought she was strong enough to reconcile with Ned, trusting that life would be improved.

She was wrong.

Why hadn't she left after Amanda and Justin grew up?

After spending a lifetime preparing a financial future for Ned and trying to prepare a way for the children, she had failed to protect herself. The dedicated mission of caring for Ned resulted in years of being out of the job market. She was growing older, had no income to sustain herself, and felt reluctant to burden her friend Mercy without the ability to contribute any income.

How could she have overlooked her own needs?

She later discovered the reason: Rescuers do that. Those who are overly empathetic and devoted to a fault make this mistake. Those who fail to spot the red flags end up in this place.

♥ ♥ ♥

As she had always done, Annalee thought focusing on the bright side would solve everything. She understood the hearts of each of her children as they forged ahead in life. Ned expressed pride in their grown children as they married and began their families. He was wonderful to their grandchildren— little Lani, Cheyenne, Jeremiah, Allen, Ashley, and Nathan, who were dearly loved by their grandfather and never saw his harsh side. Years later, Opal, Ivy, and Destiny were welcomed. She reflected how different life could have been if their grown children had experienced this same kindness from Ned. As Amanda and Justin began their careers, Luke and Marie enjoyed farming and raising animals. Josiah's talents with technology led to a computer science major in college. He developed a lifelong passion to use his technology education and expertise to assist his family to promote their careers.

♥ ♥ ♥

Every devoted mother rejoices with her children in their victories and cries with them in their struggles as they endeavor to overcome the challenges they inevitably face. Beyond all the pain, Annalee's love for her amazing grown children uplifted her spirit. As a mother, she was so proud of them! She admired their determination to be victorious over their past and prepare for their future to overcome against all odds.

After Amanda grew up, she once said to Annalee, "Mom, adulting is hard!" Amanda's husband even bought her a T-shirt with the phrase. Annalee chuckled and told her daughter she couldn't agree more.

As they hugged, Annalee beamed with joy, so grateful for the maternal bond she shared with her adult children. In spite of her many mistakes, God had been faithful. He had led them to become responsible, productive adults, parenting with love, raising the grandchildren she and Ned were so proud of.

After Josiah began college, Ned and Annalee were invited to participate in fundraising musical concerts for veterans returning from deployment. Ned had a beautiful baritone voice. Together they formed a band, Country Jamboree, featuring Ned on lead vocals and acoustic guitar; Annalee on her violin, singing harmony; their good friend Jason, a talented lead guitarist; and another friend, Gwen, on bass guitar. They all enjoyed the benefit concerts and jam sessions with local veteran musicians. These events were reminiscent of community orchestra concerts Annalee enjoyed with her violin during her teens years. Ned honored her in public for her contributions to these events that were important to him. He never exposed rage in the presence of their band or other musician friends. They were creating positive memories. Annalee was studying "the love chapter," 1 Corinthians 13. This verse (v. 5 was particularly important: "Love keeps no record of wrongs." Tentative trust began slow restoration in her heart.

The renewal of his musical side encouraged periodic gentleness in Ned—always in public and more often at home. Music was calming, even therapeutic, to his soul. Ned and Annalee enjoyed writing music together and performing it for their community. It even rekindled moments of tenderness between them.

The eternal optimist within Annalee sensed hope on the horizon as gradual renewal of affection began to reawaken. She pondered a new question: *Could these be the seeds of a promising future for their older years?*

♥ ♥ ♥

Love is patient, love is kind. It does not envy, it does not boast, it is not proud. It does not dishonor others, it is not self-seeking, it is not easily angered, it keeps no record of wrongs. Love does not delight in evil but rejoices with the truth. It always protects, always trusts, always hopes, always perseveres. Love never fails
(1 Corinthians 13:4-8, NIV).

Now faith is the substance of things hoped for, the evidence of things not seen (Hebrews 11:1, NKJV).

Thirty-Six

ANNALEE RARELY had nightmares, but something far more traumatic awaited her: night terrors.

Ned's previous nocturnal battles ended after about twelve years following confrontational ministry by Christian counselors involved in their lives. The previous episodes were disturbing, but they paled in comparison to what started three years later during Josiah's early college years. Suddenly a confusing reverse pattern emerged. It was even more frightening during the initial phase because Ned nearly convinced Annalee she had lost her mind.

One evening began with a lovely banquet dinner followed by a musical fundraising benefit concert for veterans returning from deployment. Annalee and Ned had composed a new original gospel country song, one of several she had registered with the Library of Congress. Ned hugged her all evening for rushing to complete the song, typing out new lyrics and chords, printing them out in advance, and scheduling the band's rehearsal practices in time to perform for the concert. After the group premiered the new song, they were thrilled with the rousing applause from the audience. One of their fellow musicians, a wealthy investor, surprised them with an offer to rent a recording studio for their band to create a professional CD to introduce their music to a celebrity country singer. The late night ended with an exciting discussion of musical plans all the way home.

Both Annalee and Ned hit the bed and quickly fell asleep.

Annalee's pleasant dream was rudely awakened by . . . a punch in the ribs at about 2 AM. This was a completely new shock.

"You must be having a bad night," Ned growled.

"What?" she mumbled. "Why . . . are you . . . waking me up?"

"You were cursing me in your sleep," he snarled. "You're having a nightmare about me!"

"I was . . . having a . . . nice dream," she stammered, still half asleep.

"No you weren't!" Ned snapped, hurling another shove into her ribs. He had large, strong hands. The impact hurt.

"I don't . . . remember . . . any bad dreams. Let's go back to sleep."

"You gotta stop swearing at me!"

"Swearing?" Annalee muttered. "You know I don't swear."

Nothing was making sense.

"You were cursing me in your sleep." Ned continued making snarling sounds.

"Sorry you're under attack," she murmured.

Disturbed, she rolled over and finally fell back to sleep.

The next morning Ned said nothing. He pleasantly served Annalee coffee with fruit and pastries as he shared new song ideas and upcoming studio plans. She chose not to bring up the middle of the night incident, hoping it was an isolated event. She tried to enjoy the morning and interact with Ned about the music. The incident was even more confusing because she and her family knew she didn't use foul language.

Several nights later, around 2 AM, Annalee felt herself being punched in the ribs again.

"You're having another bad night," Ned roared in the darkness.

"I . . . don't . . . remember anything, Ned," she slurred in her sleep. *A nightmare?*

"Don't lie to me! You were cursing me again in your nightmares! I know you remember!" he hissed.

She grabbed her pillow and headed to the walk-in closet. "Don't you dare leave me alone!" he growled.

"I don't know what else to do," she muffled sleepily. "I'm going to the closet so we can both sleep."

Ned fell silent.

The following morning Ned's countenance was stormy.

"You had a really bad night," he said, scowling. "You kept saying wicked things about me."

"I don't remember any nightmares, Ned. But I have an idea. Why don't we put the tape recorder on my nightstand with a blank tape and record whatever you need me to hear?"

He flew into a rage. "Don't you dare record it!"

"Why not? If you believe I'm saying something, I want to hear it. I'm trying to help you!"

"Read my lips: I don't want anything recorded! You hear me?!"

Now Annalee had to wonder: *Had she been married to Ned for so long that she was now tormented in her sleep? . . . Had she finally lost her mind?*

Annalee didn't think she used foul language at night, but the unknown was terrible. She had to know for sure. She remembered a mouth device prescribed by her dentist to prevent grinding her teeth at night. He said doing so was stress-related, but she never confided in her dentist the hard details in her life. She tested the device in front of the mirror and verified it was impossible to speak through. After the light was out, she placed it in her mouth but didn't tell Ned.

Once again, about 2 AM, Annalee was sound asleep when she felt her ribs being punched. By now they were starting to feel sore.

"Knock it off! Stop cursing me about your evil plans!" Ned yelled. "You're seeing your ex!"

Annalee started to answer, then awakened enough to realize the device was still in her mouth, so she removed it while the light was out.

"Sorry you're having a bad night. I'll let you go back to sleep now," she mumbled. She grabbed her pillow and headed to the walk-in closet. She said a silent prayer of thanks, knowing that, with the dental device, she could not possibly have said anything like what Ned imagined.

She wasn't going crazy after all.

The next morning Ned awoke without mentioning anything from overnight. She was trying to evaluate what might be going on with him so she asked, "Ned, did you take your prescriptions I gave you before bed?"

"No, I threw them away," he said. "I stopped taking that stuff a while back. The VA wants to kill me with those meds, and I think you're in on it. You try to give them to me every night." Annalee was realizing Ned had made the choice to discontinue his psychiatric medications.

After well more than two decades together, tragically, Ned still considered her his enemy.

He was running on pure torment, paranoia, and adrenalin. Now, however, she understood.

She decided to try to communicate as clearly as she could and attempt to reason with Ned.

"Ned, the VA is not trying to kill you, and neither am I. Do you really think I would ever want to do such a thing? I'm your caregiver, and your doctors rely on me to give you your medicines every night."

"Fess up! You want me out of the way because you're seeing your ex-husband, aren't you?"

"What? Of course not, Ned. I would never betray our marriage. Neither would you. We both know that. Besides, do you actually think I would want anything to do with a man who is a child or teen predator? It makes me sick to even imagine being near a man like that!"

Ned even told Luke and Marie he thought Annalee was seeing her former husband. They didn't believe it. (Two years later, when Annalee filed for her Social Security benefits, the office mentioned that her former husband had been deceased many years prior to the time Ned accused her.)

Annalee went back and forth between sleeping in the bed and on the closet floor, but she wasn't young anymore. It was much more comfortable sleeping in bed.

A few nights later, Ned punched her in the ribs once more, seething, "Stop cursing me!"

When she didn't awaken immediately, he tapped the touch-tronic lamp before she could awaken enough to remove the dental device. When he saw the device in her mouth, he leapt from bed in a rage.

"You think you can fool me?" he screamed. "You can still curse me with that thing in your mouth!"

All of this was becoming completely exhausting. Since the dental device had not persuaded Ned, the next day she went to the garage and found a roll of silver duct tape and a pair of scissors and placed them in her nightstand drawer.

After the lights went off that evening, Annalee was ready. She had cut two wide bands of duct tape, each about eight inches long. She placed the strips tightly over her mouth to eliminate all doubt that any words could escape her lips.

Once more, sometime around 2 AM, Annalee felt the punch against her ribs.

"You're having another bad night. Stop cursing at me! You're making plans with your ex-husband!"

Annalee was barely awake, but she knew it was impossible to have said anything that could be heard. She replied with certainty that she had not spoken in her sleep.

"You're having more nightmares about me!" Ned yelled nonetheless. "There's another man in your life —it's him. Your ex-husband! Admit it!" She peeled off the duct tape in the dark and tucked it away.

"Ned," she murmured, "I never said . . . anything. Please . . . let's go back to sleep."

He continued to grumble in anger before drifting off to sleep.

The next morning Ned served Annalee coffee and pastries with a smile and kiss. Annalee knew this was insane. She felt like she was being gaslighted, but she was grateful for a peaceful morning.

Through all this, Ned was desiring that Annalee write more songs. She loved the music, but her creativity for songwriting was impeded by the horrific nights. She knew there was a definite disconnect happening in Ned's mind. She continued writing music, but she had increasing difficulty completing new songs focusing on rhyme and meter, not to mention writing her own vocals and violin for performances. Of course, none of their veterans musician friends knew anything of their private life. And Ned wanted to move forward with their studio plans.

Two more nights passed without any incident, and then her ribs were punched in the middle of the night once more. Annalee had her mouth tightly covered with duct tape. She didn't awaken immediately, so he punched her again.

"You're doin' it again, woman! Swearing at me and talking about your ex!" He then tapped the touch-tronic lamp and saw the two strips of silver duct tape over her mouth and across her cheeks—all the way back to her ears. He sprung from bed in a rage. It was obvious Annalee couldn't have spoken, but he was so tormented he couldn't admit it.

That night the crazed frenzy went on for hours as he towered over her, lashing out obscenities and false accusations. The terrifying episode was exhausting. She recoiled into a fetal position trembling in fear, wondering if *this* was finally the end.

"Don't you *ever* put that stuff on your mouth again! You hear me?"

"Ned, I wanted to prove to you and even to myself that I could not be saying anything against you."

"You think this proves it, huh? I know what I heard."

A question quite clearly went through her mind: *What wife actually believes she has to go to such lengths to prove her devotion and love to her husband after decades?*

She realized the answer might well be: A woman whose heart has been crushed, whose emotions have been systematically dismantled, who thinks she has no other options. Annalee still had no income of her own, and Ned made it clear he would withhold all financial resources if she left him, including cancelling his portion of their life insurance policies. After years of devotion to him, she felt abandoned . . . like an orphan.

The thoughts going through her mind were relentless: *This must be the classic definition of insanity—repeating the same thing over and over again, but expecting different results.*

She realized her spiritual discernment had been blurred by the "ties that blind."

The musical concerts continued to bring a bit of joy and some pleasant memories. They provided moments of peace between her and Ned. When he was focused on music, he calmed down. It reminded her of the stories in the Bible in which the young David would play his harp and the tormented mind of King Saul would temporarily become peaceful.

These nocturnal patterns with Ned continued about three to four times a week for the next two years. It reached the point that Ned would flick on the light at about 2 AM to see if Annalee had duct tape over her mouth. She always did, sleeping with duct tape over her mouth from then on. Regardless of his reactions after seeing this, she had no choice. Annalee continued to retreat into the closet or the restroom—her private prayer closet when life was exploding in their home.

Her mother, Grandma Betsy, was almost ninety and had been placed on hospice for congestive heart failure. Annalee was trying to preserve her emotional strength and get enough sleep to look after her mother, meet with her medical team, and spend all possible remaining time with her she could.

"I will not leave you as orphans;
I will come to you." —Jesus (John 14:18, NIV)

The LORD is close to the brokenhearted; he rescues those
whose spirits are crushed (Psalm 34:18, NLT).

Thirty-Seven

THE FOLLOWING spring Ned helped a friend spray his ranch with a chemical weed killer. By summer he began complaining of severe abdominal pain. He went to the VA hospital several times and was told he had irritable bowel syndrome and sent home with stomach medication to relieve gas symptoms.

Ned was willing to take the stomach medication. Annalee tried multiple times to persuade him to get checked out at their local hospital by a few excellent doctors she knew, but he refused. One afternoon the week before Thanksgiving, she found him curled in a fetal position moaning in pain. She pleaded with Ned to let her take him to the ER.

"Yes, honey, please take me. I'm in agony," he said. They immediately headed straight to the hospital.

The ER physician was a kind, compassionate man who immediately ordered an abdominal CT scan with dye contrast. After the scan, Ned was brought back to ER. In about 90 minutes, the doctor returned with a grieved look on his face. He pulled up a seat next to Ned's bed.

"I have some bad news for the two of you," he said, tears in his eyes. "Ned, you have a mass on your pancreas the size of a peach, and your liver looks like swiss cheese."

No physician had ever cried in their presence before.

Ned and Annalee looked at each other in shock.

"We need to schedule a liver biopsy as soon as possible," the doctor said. "I'm admitting you to the hospital immediately and calling in the consultation of an oncologist."

The doctor paused. "I have a question for you, Ned. Have you come in contact with any chemical sprays, like weed killers, in the last six months?"

At first Ned answered with a no.

Annalee thought about it, however, and said, "Remember when you sprayed your friend's ranch last April, seven months ago?"

"Oh yes. You're right," Ned said.

The doctor was convinced the weed killer was the culprit.

Ned became angry at the VA hospital for not diagnosing the condition sooner, but the physician explained, "A pancreatic mass is one of the most difficult types to diagnose early. It is usually too large by the time we can observe it on a CT scan. I'm so sorry."

The next few days were a blur of tests and the completion of the biopsy.

Ned was diagnosed with pancreatic cancer that had metastasized.

The oncologist said the size of the mass was too large and aggressive to treat with chemotherapy. Since Ned's diagnosis was terminal, he was immediately admitted to hospice with the prognosis of only a few months to live. Annalee ordered multiple cancer remedies and called churches around the country and national Christian prayer lines for Ned. He also called his ranch friend to warn him of the risk on his property and to protect his friend's family.

Annalee and Ned called their children one by one, and Annalee notified Mercy, who was extremely sympathetic. Grandma Betsy sobbed when she was told in person with her own hospice nurse present.

For a few days Ned continued in anger and resentment at the diagnosis, his ex-wife Tina, the VA doctors, Annalee, even anger against his dad and the world in general.

With both Ned and Grandma Betsy on hospice at the same time, Luke and Marie were a godsend, helping with the caregiving day and night. Annalee was so grateful for their devoted assistance.

Becoming an Overcomer

On a morning just before Thanksgiving, Ned awakened and stepped from the bedroom. He knelt in front of Annalee as she sat on the sofa. He was weeping uncontrollably, his head in her lap.

"Honey, I know I am dying and I'm terrified to meet Jesus. This morning as I woke up, He showed me something. He opened my spiritual eyes. He revealed to me what I've put you and the children through all these years, and that I must repent and ask your forgiveness. You were a faithful wife to me, but I was so tormented and treated you and the children horribly.

"Can you ever forgive me?" He sobbed. Her heart broke for him.

"Honey, you are already forgiven. I forgave you every time it happened. I just wanted it to stop." Annalee cried with him while wrapping her arms around his neck.

"I need to be sure. I'm going to see Jesus soon, and I can't face Him like this. I'm so undone! I need to call all of our kids and ask them to forgive me too. Will you please pray for me?"

"Of course I will," she said. She reached for their prayer oil. "Ned, before we pray, are you also willing to forgive Tina, the VA, your dad, and everyone else who has ever hurt you? We all want you totally set free of all the torment."

"Yes, yes. I want to forgive everyone, and I want everyone to forgive me," he cried.

Annalee anointed Ned with the oil as he wept before her. It was her honor to lead her husband before the Throne of Grace that day in a prayer of repentance and forgiveness, releasing everyone who had ever harmed him.

Ned called each of their children and tearfully asked their forgiveness. Each assured him they loved and forgave him. What grace they gave their earthly father! Annalee knew they still faced much healing in their journeys, but they exchanged the greatest Thanksgiving gifts that year with this release and forgiveness.

Ned only lived a few more weeks, but from that day on he was truly a new man. He was never tormented day or night again. His countenance became serene. He expressed sincere kindness and gratitude. Although he suffered physically, he was at peace as he awaited his appointment to meet the King of Kings.

In January, Ned went home to Heaven at the local hospice house. He passed peacefully with a smile on his face. Annalee wept quietly as she held his hand and embraced the presence of his serene expression.

Grandma Betsy followed him seven weeks later.

Annalee's greatest comfort was the absolute certainty that Ned made it safely home to his heavenly Father—he was forever free of torment, his eternal soul secure in the presence of God forever. She knew that someday they would meet again. She trusted in a future family reunion—unlike one they had ever known—a day in which she and her children would be reunited with him as he was always meant to be—the loving man she and her children knew on earth for the first few months after the accident. Looking forward to that beautiful future reunion gave her hope for all eternity with this promise:

~ Love Never Fails ~

Godly sorrow brings repentance that leads to salvation …
(2 Corinthians 7:10, NIV)

Mercy triumphs over judgment (James 2:13, NKJV).

For I consider that the sufferings of this present time are
not worthy to be compared with the glory which shall be
revealed in us (Romans 8:18, NKJV).

* God's Promise to Ned *

"As a mother comforts her son, so will I comfort you…"
(Isaiah 66:13, Berean Study Bible).

—

Crisis Hotlines: A-Z

In an abuse situation or living environment and need help? Here are resources that can provide critical aid:

ASAP - DOMESTIC VIOLENCE HOTLINE (USA) – 800-799-SAFE (7233) or TTY – 800-787-3224
CRISIS intervention website: www.TheHotline.org

CHILD Protection and CUSTODY Legal Help – 800-527-3223
Website: www.rcdvcpc.org/ – Information for legal assistance and help with advocacy

CHILDHELP Child Abuse Hotline – 800-4-A-CHILD – or 800-422-4453
Website: www.Childhelp.org

CUSTODY and Legal Protection Issues – 800-527-3223
Website: www.rcdvcpc.org/ – Information and resources for legal advocacy

DATING Abuse Hotline – 866-331-9474
Website: https://youth.gov/youth-topics/
teen-dating-violence/resources

Human Trafficking Center – 24/7 Hotline – 888-373-7888

MEN – Help for Abused Men – 800-799-SAFE (7233) or TTY Line – 800-787-3224
Website: www.helpguide.org/articles/abuse/help-for-abused-men.htm

SEXUAL Assault Hotline – 800-656-4673

SHELTERS for Women and children –
Website: www.DomesticShelters.org
Approximately 3,000 women's shelters are available in USA, Canada, Puerto Rico, and Virgin Islands. Support offered includes shelter, advocates, and legal services (free or low-cost).

SUICIDE Prevention Hotline – 800-273-TALK (8255)

VICTIM Witness and Victim Assistance – 800-TRY-NOVA (879-6682)
Website: www.TryNOVA.org – Agencies providing victim services, criminal justice assistance, and mental health assistance

Human Trafficking – It Only Takes 42 Hours Or Less
Sadly, children and teens raised in homes with domestic violence often seek escape from the trauma at home. Running away places them in critical danger on the streets. USA statistics suggest that approximately 50 percent of young girls and 30 percent of young boys will encounter a human trafficker within 42 hours on the streets. Predators lurk in public places frequented by teens and children, observing their behavior and sensing their loneliness and emotional pain. Like

a bullseye, predators target the vulnerability and naiveté of this endangered group. They need education on the dangers of social media, meeting strangers, and assistance with safe living resources.

Shared Hope International produces resources for teens, pre-teens, and older children. Every teen and parent should view the film Chosen, a 20-minute DVD available at https://sharedhope.org/. Chosen is an important piece of work. This eye-opening PG-rated video exposes well-documented, actual trafficking cases.

Webinars and printed safety guides educate grade school children to protect them from online predators eager to meet them. Visit https://sharedhope.org/what-we-do/prevent/awareness/internetsafety/

The SOAP Project (Save Our Adolescents from Prostitution) SOAP is a rescue project developed by Theresa Flores, a courageous Christian overcomer in Ohio
https://www.soapproject.org/
614-407-4749
PO Box 645, Worthington, OH 43085

Human Trafficking
800-THE-LOST or 800-843-5678
Website: www.SharedHope.org

Human Trafficking / Human Slavery
Website: www.EndSlaveryNow.org
Founded by Jerome Elam, victorious overcomer of human trafficking from ages 5-12
Website: www.TheNewAbolitionists.com

Truckers Against Trafficking
Website: TruckersAgainstTrafficking.org
888-373-7888
Truckers who contact authorities when girls are prostituted at truck stops by traffickers. Goal: To help rescue girls and women and bring traffickers to justice. Missing girls have been found!

"We must invade the darkness of the online world where the predators are communicating with our kids. With the strong support of caring friends like you, Shared Hope is doing just that." – Linda Smith

Cycles of Abuse and How They Work

Understand Unhealthy, Destructive Relationships

Power and Control Wheel: Cycles of Abuse
https://www.mayoclinic.org/healthy-lifestyle/adult-health/in-depth/domestic-violence/art-20048397

Phase 1 – Tension / Buildup
Symptoms: Partner and family walk on "eggshells" in fear of what may happen next. Partner may be gaslighted (told he or she is forgetful, "going crazy," unstable, etc.). Family is kept emotionally off balance, unsure of when the rage will occur.

Phase 2 – Explosion
Symptoms: Perpetrator "explodes" with rage in numerous unpredictable ways. These may include physical, verbal, sexual assault, spiritual abuse, isolation, financial punishment, child custody retaliation, legal retaliation, rage against partner, children, pets, withholding of phones, and threats of homicide or self-harm to prevent disclosure to authorities, family, or friends.

Phase 3 – Remorse / Apologies / "Honeymoon period"
Symptoms: Having spent his or her rage, perpetrator winds down with apologies, tears, remorse, gifts, may attend to physical wounds of victim, promises the behavior will never happen again. Perpetrator's goal is to retain power and control. Victim loves perpetrator and wants to believe that life will improve. If authorities have been called, he or she often recants any charges against the perpetrator in false hope.

Phase 3 may last for a few days before the Phase 1 tension buildup process begins again. This is a repeat cycle. Statistically, most victims will leave a minimum of seven times before final separation. The exit is the most dangerous time frame, because perpetrator realizes he or she has lost control once and for all.

Understand Healthy Relationship Patterns

Respect Wheel, Healthy Relationships:
https://www.futureswithoutviolence.org/wp-content/uploads/RESPECT-Wheel.pdf

Author's Testimony and Endorsement
For My Life® Program at www.BeInHealth.com:

Personal testimony:

In 2018, Darlene Leonard attended an internationally re-nowned program in Thomaston, Georgia, called the For My Life® Program. At the time, she suffered with heart and lung issues as well as PTSD.

Beginning in 1977, she enjoyed more than 30 years of great cardiac health. In 2015, cardiac symptoms resulted in a referral to a cardiologist who discovered two holes in the ventricles of her heart. They were causing her severe fatigue and labored breathing. During her five-day For My Life® Program, Darlene learned principles she had never understood before.

Heart condition:

She was afflicted with fear as she tried to recover from major life issues. She overcame fear by applying Scriptural principles she learned at For My Life®. These were the verses that helped her understand the daily battles on earth that can lead to fear, and a powerful verse to help her overcome it.

"Men's hearts failing them from fear and the expectation of those things which are coming on the earth, for the powers of the heavens will be shaken" (Luke 21:26, NKJV).

"For God hath not given us the spirit of fear; but of power, and of love, and of a sound mind" (2 Timothy 1:7, KJV).

After attending For My Life®, Darlene returned to her cardiologist for follow-up. He was surprised to discover her new EKG was absolutely normal, so he decided to prescribe a 72-hour EKG halter for her to wear along with an episode journal to monitor her heart. After she returned the EKG halter monitor, the cardiologist reviewed her results and discovered her heart had functioned perfectly for 72 hours. The cardiologist then decided to schedule a cardiac nuclear stress test to confirm the exact performance of her heart. Amazingly, the nuclear stress test revealed that the two holes in her heart had completely disappeared! Since 2018 her heart has remained in perfect function since her first For My Life® Program.

Moderate-Level Asthma:

In 2016, Darlene began suffering effects of moderate-level asthma and was later diagnosed by her pulmonologist. She took daily medications and carried an inhaler in her purse for asthma attacks. While attending For My Life® she realized she was struggling with rejection and abandonment after the loss of several family members and close friends. Although it is never the fault of a loved one who passes on, the grief she experienced after the losses caused her to feel the emotions of rejection and abandonment. By the grace of God, Darlene overcame rejection and abandonment. Since returning from her 2018 For My Life® Program, the asthma is also entirely gone, and she no longer needs any asthma medications or in-haler! Praise God!

"Don't abandon me, neither forsake me,
God of my salvation" (Psalm 27:9, NAS).

"The LORD is close to the brokenhearted; he rescues those
whose spirits are crushed" (Psalm 34:18, NLT).

"We are no longer orphans, but have been adopted into His kingdom as His children" (John 14:18; Romans 8:16).

Restoration Resource – Healing from Abuse and Illness

Website: www.BeInHealth.com ; www.YouTube.com – Log onto the BeInHealth channel for free classes and video testimonies

BeInHealth Campus Location
4178 Crest Highway
Thomaston, Georgia 30286
706–646–2074
Founder: Dr. Henry W. Wright, Ph.D.

The late Dr. Henry W. Wright and his wife, Pastor Donna Wright, have dedicated their lives to serving others and training the next generation to carry on the mission of BeInHealth. This wonderful team of caring people hosts a world-renowned five-day retreat at their Thomaston, Georgia campus. The retreat teaches attendees biblical principles to overcome life's challenging issues. Their mission has birthed a legendary conference, the For My Life® Program. This amazing five-day program has drawn more than 40,000 attendees from all over the world in the last three decades.

The BeInHealth Team imparts the teaching legacy of its Founder, Dr. Henry W. Wright.

The For My Life® Program retreat is available at the Thomaston Campus. (As of Fall 2020, check current Covid-19 regulations for in-person gatherings.)

At the Thomaston campus, attendees are taught to be overcomers. They are given cutting-edge information and outstanding, informative classes.

Virtual Option: For My Life® Online Program
https://www.beinhealth.com/for-my-life-2-2/
The same outstanding program is taught via online classes at your convenience.

The author highly recommends Dr. Henry W. Wright's flagship book, *A More Excellent Way*, a national bestseller (Whitaker House; first printing, 1999). It is a phenomenal biblical resource.

Author Notes

The following are various notes from my research as I compiled this book. This material, I felt, didn't classically fit as specific Endnotes, but is important material which might benefit the reader.

From Chapter 5, on how destructive relationships may develop and lead to marriage during stage 1 of a romance. It is critical for couples to allow time to reveal godly character and maturity in both individuals.

• Common temptations for Christian couples that may account for divorce:

Christian couples sometimes enter marriage too quickly for several reasons. Phase 1 is a particularly vulnerable time (aka the "falling in love" or "infatuation" stage). A rapid engagement period may lack necessary time, in part due to the desire for fulfillment of post-marriage biblical intimacy. It may also include premature planning of mutual life goals without sufficient prayer confirmation and godly counsel. It is critical to allow necessary time to evaluate the potential mate's character development to observe day-to-day responses to the normal challenges of life.

• Phase 2 is a necessary component for preparation to a successful marriage; this consists of the "bonding" commitment.

• Phase 3 can and should last a lifetime with a healthy relationship and true godly marriage commitment.

Secularists or non-Christians may describe this as follows: "Happily ever after in a 'perfect world.'"

From Chapter 9, various:

• Regarding delayed brain syndrome: around the early 1980s "delayed brain syndrome" became a medical term explained by pediatric neurologists to define a neurological congenital anomaly resulting in the failure of the myelin sheath to properly form around the brain stem and nerves in utero. The condition resulted in significant early childhood and adolescent LD (learning disabilities). The educational protocol required an annual IEP (individualized education program) and placement into a non-mainstream segregated self-contained classroom with personalized attention by teachers who had a specialized LD teaching credential certification.

• M.E.N.D.: Mommies Enduring Neonatal Death. Miscarriage, loss, and infant stillbirth support. Website: www.mend.org/infant-loss-organizations

• Regarding naming lost babies, miscarriage loss, and trying for children after miscarriage:
Dr. David Jeremiah. What About the Children? Website: https://sermons.love/david-jeremiah/4446-david-jeremiah-what-about-the-children.html
Jenny Schroedel. Book: *Naming the Child: Hope-Filled Reflections on Miscarriage, Stillbirth, and Infant Death* (2009) www.amazon.com/Naming-Child-Hope-Filled-Reflections-Miscarriage/dp/1557255857

Miscarriage Association: "Common Feelings After Miscarriage." Visit:
www.miscarriageassociation.org.uk/your-feelings/common-feelings/
Mayo Clinic. "Getting Pregnant After Miscarriage." Visit:
www.mayoclinic.org/healthy-lifestyle/getting-pregnant/in-depth/pregnancy-after-miscarriage/art-20044134

From Chapter 25, regarding the ministry foster parents like Mel and Monica provide to children like Amanda and Justin:
• Please visit Compassion International: https://www.compassion.com/poverty/what-the-bible-says-about-children.htm
It is a tremendous blessing to love, serve, and protect the most vulnerable in this world and share God's love with them. He is the greatest Protector of all.

"God executes justice for the fatherless and the widow, and loves the sojourner, giving him food and clothing"
(Deuteronomy 10:18).

From Chapter 26, regarding the various conditions Justin was living under:
• Attention deficit hyperactivity disorder (ADHD) is a condition which is characterized by inattention, hyperactivity, and impulsivity. ADHD is most commonly diagnosed in young people. An estimated 8.8% of children aged 4-17 have ADHD. While ADHD is usually diagnosed in childhood, it does not only affect children. An estimated 4.4% of adults aged 18-44 have ADHD. With treatment, people with ADHD can be successful in school and work and lead productive

lives. Researchers are using new tools such as brain imaging to better understand the condition and to find more effective ways to treat and prevent ADHD.

• Toxic Relationships:
Is passive-aggression an individual's default behavior?
www.psychologytoday.com/intl/blog/
the-time-cure/201310/toxic-relationships-part-ii?amp

"Although passive-aggressive behavior can be a feature of various mental health conditions, it isn't considered a distinct mental illness. However, passive-aggressive behavior can interfere with relationships and cause difficulties on the job." — Mayo Clinic Psychiatrist Daniel K. Hall-Flavin, M.D.

• Complex Post-Traumatic Stress Disorder (CPTSD): young children can develop this, but the symptoms are different from those of adults. (This recent recognition by the medical field is a major step forward; research is ongoing.) Young children lack the ability to convey some aspects of their experience. It is essential that a child be assessed by a professional who is skilled in the developmental responses to stressful events. A pediatrician or child mental health clinician can be a good start. CPTSD can occur at any age and is directly associated with exposure to trauma. Adults and children who have CPTSD represent a relatively small portion of those who have been exposed to trauma.

From Chapter 32, regarding how home life would be different with Ned post-brain injury. More can be learned here:
• Brainline: "All About Brain Injury and PTSD: What Effect Will Moderate or Severe TBI Have on a Person's Life?"
www.brainline.org/article/what-impact-will-moderate-or-severe-tbi-have-persons-life

From Chapter 34, various:

• Annalee discusses in the early days that Ned showed vulnerability and kindness as his early rehabilitation was beginning. For more on the power of vulnerability, see:

TED Talk: The Power of Vulnerability,
Dr. Brené Brown: www.ted.com/talks/
brene_brown_the_power_of_vulnerability?language=en

• Dr. Nelson discussed with Annalee Ned losing areas of function in four of the five areas of his brain.

Learn more at: Psychology Today, Dr. Robert J. Hedaya, MD, DLFAPA, ABPN, CFM / Health Matters / Trauma

"Traumatic Brain Injury After-Effects Show Up In Adults," October 25, 2019

Five major ways that TBI can affects patients:
1. Cognitive function (memory, math, reading, language, organization, speech, recognition of faces/objects/orientation)
2. Mood regulation (rage, depression, anxiety)
3. Energy and alertness (dysregulated sleep, trouble with attention)
4. Ability to filter environmental stimuli
5. Sensory and motor functions and coordination

• On the cycles of abuse and control:

Power and Control Cycles of Abuse: cycles of tension, explosion, and remorse ("honeymoon") can be found at:

www.mayoclinic.org/healthy-lifestyle/adult-health/in-depth/domestic-violence/art-20048397

The Power and Control Wheel: www.ncdsv.org/images/PowerControlwheelNOSHADING.pdf

Endnotes

1. What happens to the brain when people fall in love?
Source Credit: Dr. Trisha Stratford – UTS, Sydney, Australia
University of Technology Sydney UTS · School of Medical
and Molecular Biosciences
Source Credit: INSIGHT TV, Australia / Program: Can Love
Really Conquer All? February 9, 2016 / Advance video to:
12:25 min.
www.youtube.com/watch?v=tX20WxHFIkc

2. Scientists identify three phases when people fall in love:
• Phase 1: Lust
When brain scientists look at the brain of someone in love,
it's exactly like a brain high on heroin. Totally addicted. Same
chemicals. People in Phase 1 produce an adrenaline-like
love-drug cocktail called PEA. PEA floods the system of the
"in love" person with dopamine and endogenous opioids.
The person is attracted to the other person and there is a
reward at the end of it, so they just keep going.

The problem with dopamine: It stops people from being
able to make critical decisions.

"Love is blind" in the sense that, in this phase, they only
see the good in the other person.

Primal networks of the brain kick in, including meeting, developing a relationship, and mating.

• Phase 2: Bonding
When the dopamine neurotransmitters and love-drug chemicals begin to settle down, people begin a bonding phase.

• Phase 3: Nurturing / Long-Term Love
This phase begins after about 18 months.

3. Epilepsy Foundation
https://www.epilepsy.com/living-epilepsy ; and Mayo Clinic, Epilepsy
www.mayoclinic.org/diseases-conditions/epilepsy/symptoms-causes/syc-20350093

4. Ian D. Duncan and Abigail B. Radcliff. Inherited and acquired disorders of myelin: The underlying myelin pathology; Sept. 2016
www.ncbi.nlm.nih.gov/pmc/articles/PMC5010953/ ; and Hypnagogic Hypersynchrony [HH]
www.ncbi.nlm.nih.gov/pubmed/12717648

5. HSP – Highly Sensitive People
Elaine N. Aron, Ph.D. *The Highly Sensitive Person: How To Thrive When The World Overwhelms You* (1997)
https://hsperson.com/
www.youtube.com/watch?v=FQLBnUBKggY

6. TEDxIHEParis. Elena Herdieckerhoff. The Gentle Power of Highly Sensitive People (June 2016) www.youtube.com/watch?v=pi4JOlMSWjo

7. "Therefore, to him who knows to do good and does not do it, to him it is sin" (James 4:17, NKJV).

8. "If you keep quiet at a time like this, deliverance and relief for the Jews will arise from some other place, but you and your relatives will die. Who knows if perhaps you were made queen for just such a time as this?" (Esther 4:14, NLT)

9. Dr. Gary Chapman. *The Five Love Languages* (1992); www.5lovelanguages.com/5-love-languages/

10. Pinebluff is a fictional name for an Oregon mountain town.

11. ADHD is Attention Deficit-Hyperactivity Disorder. www.mayoclinic.org/diseases-conditions/adhd/symptoms-causes/syc-20350889. ADHD is classified as a neurological disorder. ADHD: Attention-Deficit/Hyperactivity Disorder www.mayoclinic.org/diseases-conditions/adult-adhd/symptoms-causes/syc-20350878

Adult attention-deficit/hyperactivity disorder (ADHD) is a mental health disorder that includes a combination of persistent problems such as difficulty paying attention, hyperactivity, and impulsive behavior. Adult ADHD can lead to unstable relationships, poor work or school performance, low self-esteem, and other problems.

12. IEP: Individualized Education Plan. These are implemented in public schools in the US. A customized program is based on collaboration between the school Special Education Department, the school psychologist, the student's family physician or physician specialist, and the parent(s) to accom-

modate a student in need of special educational services. An IEP is done annually or biannually based on individual needs and progress.

13. "Yet who knows whether you have come to the kingdom for such a time as this?" (Esther 4:14, NKJV)

14. Glacier Vista is a fictional name for a Montana town.

15. Here are further terms and resources for the conditions listed in this chapter that Justin suffered from.
• NAMI – National Association on Mental Illness: www.nami.org/About-Mental-Illness/Mental-Health-Conditions/ADHD

• NOS (nonspecific psychosis)

• Trauma – A traumatic event such as a death, war, or sexual assault can trigger a psychotic episode. The type of trauma, and a person's age, affects whether a traumatic event will result in psychosis.

• Treatment through Coordinated Specialty Care. CSC uses a team of health professionals and specialists who work with a person to create a personal treatment plan. www.nami.org/About-Mental-Illness/Mental-Health-Conditions/Psychosis

• Passive Resistance Evaluation – www.expertsupervisor.com/article?ID=pub_eTip_012005

• "What is Passive Aggressive Behavior?" www.webmd.com/mental-health/passive-aggressive-behavior-overview#1 ; www.verywellmind.com/what-is-passive-aggressive-behavior-2795481

• CPTSD – Complex Post-Traumatic Stress Disorder:

www.nami.org/About-Mental-Illness/
Mental-Health-Conditions/Posttraumatic-Stress-Disorder

16. TBI is short for traumatic brain injury. National statistics estimate between 50 and 70 percent of TBI accidents are the result of a motor vehicle crash. Source: American Association of Neurological Surgeons; Assessment and Treatment.
Definition: Closed head injury (non-penetrating brain injury).
www.aans.org/en/Patients/Neurosurgical-
Conditions-and-Treatments/
Traumatic-Brain-Injury
Prevalence: About 1.7 million cases of TBI occur in the U.S. every year. Approximately 5.3 million people in the U.S. live with a disability caused by TBI.

17. Moderate-level TBI: 10 symptoms of moderate or severe traumatic brain injury (TBI) can be found at:
www.theraspecs.com/blog/
symptoms-moderate-severe-traumatic-brain-injury-tbi/
Additional information: Mayo Clinic: Moderate Level TBI.
Overview, symptoms, physical, cognitive, mental:
www.mayoclinic.org/diseases-conditions/
traumatic-brain-injury/symptoms-causes/syc-20378557

18. From Chapter 35: Proverbs 24:16: The Matthew Henry Commentary on this verse: "The sincere soul falls as a traveler may do, by stumbling at some stone in his path; but gets up, and goes on his way with more care and speed. This is rather to be understood of falls into affliction than falls into actual sin."